A Nip of
MURDER

Also by Carol Miller

Murder and Moonshine

A Nip of
MURDER

CAROL MILLER

MINOTAUR BOOKS

A THOMAS DUNNE BOOK

NEW YORK

A THOMAS DUNNE BOOK FOR MINOTAUR BOOKS.
An imprint of St. Martin's Publishing Group.

A NIP OF MURDER. Copyright © 2014 by Carol Miller. All rights reserved. Printed in the United States of America. For information, address St. Martin's Press, 175 Fifth Avenue, New York, N.Y. 10010.

www.thomasdunnebooks.com
www.minotaurbooks.com

Designed by Omar Chapa

Library of Congress Cataloging-in-Publication Data

Miller, Carol, 1972–
    A nip of murder : a moonshine mystery / Carol Miller.—
First edition.
        p. cm.—(Moonshine mystery series ; 2)
    "A Thomas Dunne book."
    ISBN 978-1-250-01927-1 (hardcover)
    ISBN 978-1-250-01928-8 (e-book)
    1. Waitresses—Fiction.   2. Virginia, Southwest—Fiction.
I. Title.
    PS3613.I53277N56 2014
    813'.6—dc23
                                                    2014027068

Minotaur books may be purchased for educational, business, or promotional use. For information on bulk purchases, please contact the Macmillan Corporate and Premium Sales Department at 1-800-221-7945, extension 5442, or write to specialmarkets@macmillan.com.

First Edition: December 2014

10 9 8 7 6 5 4 3 2 1

For Rudy and Anna

A Nip of
MURDER

CHAPTER

1

"I'm gonna need a red velvet cake, Daisy."

Daisy's only response was a slight nod. She was too busy hurriedly transferring a dozen gooey, swollen cinnamon buns that were dripping with white icing from a baking sheet to the decorative platter in the display case. The baking sheet hadn't cooled as much as she had expected, and she was holding it with a flimsy flour sack towel instead of the thick protective oven mitt that she usually used.

"Gosh, those sure smell good."

"They are good." Having deposited the last sticky soldier on the platter, Daisy spun around and dropped the baking sheet on the work table behind her with a clatter. She blew on her overly warm, overly pink palm. "Good and hot."

"Maybe I should get some of those too."

"How many would you like?" Turning back to the display case, she reached for a piece of waxed paper and a foldable bakery box. "I assume you want to take them with?"

"I . . . Well, I . . ."

The hesitation was long enough so that Daisy looked up at him with a touch of annoyance. "It's not a difficult question, Bobby. How many cinnamon buns do you want? And are you planning on eating any of them here?"

Bobby hesitated some more and shuffled his boots. It was typical behavior for him. Daisy had known Robert Balsam since they were together in kindergarten, and he had never been the sharpest tool in the shed. He was the last one to learn how to tie his own shoelaces. The only one to eat an entire box of crayons, repeatedly. And the first child in the history of the Pittsylvania County school system to have a sense of direction so bad that he managed to get himself lost while standing in the middle of the playground at recess, also repeatedly. Now at the supposedly mature age of twenty-seven, Bobby's favorite activities were pretty much the same as they had always been—drinking, shooting, and not thinking too hard. Daisy didn't ordinarily care how long it took him to reach a decision, but it was Saturday, and the bakery was especially busy that morning. She didn't have time for him to deliberate whether his indubitable hangover would be better cured by a couple of chocolate-glazed doughnuts or an apple turnover.

"Okay, Bobby." She set the box and waxed paper aside with a shrug. "I've got work to do. The frosting doesn't pipe itself. Give me a holler when you've made up your mind."

To her surprise, he replied almost immediately.

"Can you do red velvet cake, Daisy?"

"Of course I can do red velvet cake."

"Are you sure?"

She frowned at him. "Yes, I'm sure."

Bobby shuffled his boots again. "But the place is called Sweetie Pies. I thought you might only have pies."

Rolling her eyes, Daisy gestured toward the delectable contents of the large glass display case in front of him, followed by the plethora of cookies, brownies, muffins, and scones all bagged and tied with colorful ribbons and organized in neat rows on the shelves along the wall to his right. "Do you see only pies?"

"No—"

"We've been open for over a month now. You've been in here at least ten times since then. You've tried every type of cupcake I make. And now you're suddenly confused about pies and red velvet cake?" Daisy's frown deepened. "What's going on, Bobby?"

"It's about R—"

He was interrupted by the clank of the rusty bell that was strung up above the front door of the bakery. A gust of fresh autumn air accompanied Beulah inside.

"Hey there!" Daisy smiled warmly at her friend. "What brings you by? I thought you had lots of appointments scheduled for this morning."

"I did." Beulah made an effort to smooth down her tangled, twisted curls, but she had little success. Her flaming red mop was in a permanent state of unruliness. Today was especially bad. She looked like Medusa with a double heap of windblown snakes.

"Are you done already? Did the time go by that fast?" Daisy glanced at her watch.

"Oh, I'm done, but it's not because I've finished with all my appointments."

Beulah swung a sturdy leg over the first emerald

green stool in line at the counter and plopped herself down on it. Before becoming Sweetie Pies, the bakery had been a diner. The kind of good old-fashioned country establishment that took pride in serving first-rate baked beans, collard greens, and authentic chicken stew. The long white counter and vinyl-topped stools were vestiges that Daisy and her business partner, Brenda, had neither the money nor the inclination to remove. They had both been waitresses at the diner before its owner died, and they felt a strong sentimental attachment to it.

"I'm done," Beulah repeated. "Only I never got started. When I opened the door to the salon this morning, there was two feet of water on the floor."

"What! How did that happen?"

"I haven't a clue. I couldn't see a thing wrong. There wasn't any busted pipe or leaky hose. At least not that I could find. Nothin' was gushing out of nowhere. But there was clearly a problem—a big one—considering that I was wading around in a flood up to my knees. So I called Connor Woodley over at the hardware store. You remember him, don't you? He's the one who did all the plumbing and wiring for the salon originally. I was so happy when I got him on the phone. I was afraid that since it's Saturday and the middle of October, he might be out scouting hunting sites for when deer season opens next month. And I know Aunt Emily wouldn't want me getting anyone but Connor. She's particular in that way."

"She's particular in a lot of ways," Daisy said.

Beulah laughed in agreement. Aunt Emily wasn't actually their aunt, but they had known her for as long as they had known each other, which was nearly all their lives. Emily Tosh was the grand old proprietor of the grand old Tosh Inn. There wasn't much tourism in their little corner of rural southwestern Virginia, so the inn was inhabited mostly by local strays, who for one reason or another found themselves otherwise without a home. Both Daisy and Beulah lived at the inn, along with Daisy's sickly momma. Beulah's hair salon occupied a former potting shed on one edge of the property, making it necessary for her to consider Aunt Emily's views regarding any major repairs. Aunt Emily was always generous with her advice and opinions. Taken on the whole, a bit too generous, and more often than not, it wasn't so clear whether that advice tended to be brilliant or batty.

"Is Connor at the salon now?" Daisy asked Beulah.

"No, he can't come until the afternoon. He said he's alone at the store this morning. Duke went down to Tightsqueeze for a delivery, and Connor has to wait for him to get back. So of course I had to cancel all my appointments for the day. It's not like I can ask the ladies to slap on a bikini and swim up to a chair. Plus, it's impossible to do a shampoo or color when there's no pressure in the sink. Hopefully, it'll be a quick and easy fix, but," she grimaced, "somehow I doubt it. I have a bad feeling that this is going to be long and expensive."

Having recently completed her own renovations to the bakery, Daisy nodded with sympathy.

Beulah sighed. "Well, there's no point in worrying about it now. That's why I came here. You know my philosophy. Whatever else happens in this miserable life, there's still good news in the form of sugar and cinnamon. Please tell me you're not sold out of snickerdoodles."

"Never. I've always got my special secret stashes." Daisy reached down into the cabinet below the cash register.

"Shortbread for my momma. Lemon bars for Aunt Emily."
She pulled out a pink plastic box with a matching snap-
on lid. "And snickerdoodles for you."

With the enthusiasm of a parched desert camel suddenly unearthing a cool pool of water, Beulah grabbed the
box, yanked off its lid, and shoved a pair of cookies into
her mouth. Bobby eyed the box with interest, but Beulah
paid not the slightest attention to him. He might as well
have been a bucket of sand. The first two snickerdoodles
were swiftly followed by a third. As she chewed, Beulah
glanced around the bakery.

"Bless you and your secret stash, Daisy," she murmured
gratefully. "Without it, I might have had to resort to something with peanut butter in it. This place is packed tighter
than a jar of pickled onions today."

"Wonderful, isn't it?" Daisy beamed. "I can't complain. That's for sure. The whole week has been great.
Tons of work, of course, but great."

Beulah studied the pastry-eating, coffee-swilling
crowd more closely. "I don't recognize a single person in
here. Are they all from that meeting—or whatever it is—
going on in the mountains?"

"I think so. Lots of them seem to know each other.
And if you look in the parking lot, the cars are mostly
from out of state."

"How long is it supposed to continue for?"

"Another week. At least, that's what somebody told
me. And let me just say that another week with this kind
of business would be fantastic." Daisy dropped her voice
discreetly. "They all get breakfast in here every morning
and take along piles of snacks for the day. The shelves are
stocked full now, but by the time the group clears out
later, they'll be empty. I can barely keep up."

"What about Brenda?" Beulah selected another cookie from her box. "Shouldn't she be helping?"

"She's in the kitchen, and she is not just helping, she's a baking dynamo. I couldn't have asked for a better partner. I might be the one with the good family recipes and the finer touch for putting together the fancier stuff, but Brenda can mix and measure, scoop and proof like she just graduated with honors from cooking school. And she loves to clean, which is a real plus, considering that there is always a layer of flour dust on everything. It's much fussier cleaning now with the bakery than it was with the diner."

"I don't know about flour dust, but you'd probably have less cat hair flying around if you didn't let Blot wander at will."

"Blot?"

"Blot." Beulah pointed a crumb-covered finger toward her ankle.

Daisy leaned over the counter and saw Brenda's humongous black cat rubbing up against Beulah's sneakers, purring heartily for his share of the treats. Blot was equal parts spoiled and fat, precisely because he found himself so frequently rewarded for his friendliness. He was such a monstrous mass of shaggy fur when he sprawled out on the floor that he looked like a giant ink stain, hence his name.

"Oh, jeez. What are you doing here, Blot? Brenda knows she's not supposed to bring you to work." With a quick step, Daisy scooped up the offending kitty and carried him away from her customers as unobtrusively as possible. "You are a major health code violation, sweetheart." She pushed open the swinging door to the kitchen, set Blot down on the other side, and hastily shut the door again before he could slip back through.

"Isn't he just as much of a violation in there?" Beulah said, returning her attention to her snickerdoodles.

"Probably more—if we're being technical about it—because it's a food preparation area. But I don't really have a choice. I can't put him outside. He wouldn't last five minutes, even in the parking lot. Blot is a serious scaredy-cat. Everything puts him on edge and sends him scampering for the hills. Everything except for food, mind you. He's got the weirdest taste too. Last week Brenda offered him a stale piece of carrot cake, and he went crazy for it. It might as well have been a hunk of tuna wrapped in a sheet of bacon."

Bobby meekly cleared his throat. "About the red velvet cake, Daisy . . ."

For the first time since her arrival, Beulah turned toward him. She surveyed Bobby's appearance with a sharp hazel eye, then gave an amused snort. "Whenever I see you, Bobby, you're always wearing the same thing. You've been wearing the same thing since high school. A tired old T-shirt, shredded old jeans, and dirty old boots. It's been almost ten years now. Don't you think it's about time for an upgrade?"

He blinked at her. There was no anger or resentment in his expression. Bobby rarely exhibited such strong emotions. Aunt Emily often compared him to a hamster. Kind of cute. Generally harmless. Prone to making foolish choices. In the hamster's case, that meant running in never-ending circles on a plastic wheel. In Bobby's case, it meant playing with loaded firearms while guzzling corn whiskey.

"Laurel likes my jeans," he replied. "And my boots. She told me so just this morning."

"Who?" Beulah said.

"Laurel," he repeated.

Beulah squinted at Daisy. "Who's Laurel?"

"No idea. Never heard of her." Curious, she was about to ask Bobby for an explanation when Beulah announced, "Blot's back."

"He is?"

"Either my sneakers smell really good because I stepped in something icky coming over here, or he's awfully determined to get one of these cookies from me."

Breaking a snickerdoodle in half, Beulah handed a piece to Daisy as she trotted around the counter and scooped up the begging kitty a second time.

"Here you go." Daisy gave Blot the treat, then once again pushed him through the swinging door into the kitchen. "Now I hope you're happy and will stay where you're supposed to."

Beulah shifted her focus back to Bobby. "All right. I'll bite. Who's this Laurel? Should I know her? Have I met her?"

He shook his head. "Naw. I don't think so."

"So how do you know her? Where did you meet her?"

"I . . . She . . ." Bobby seemed uncertain how to answer.

"Oh, wait," Beulah said. "I forgot about that weaselly brother of yours. I should have guessed. She's his newest plaything, isn't she?"

Bobby started to respond, but Daisy didn't hear him. She felt a warm pressure against her leg, looked down, and found Blot wrapping his thick tail around her calf.

"Good Lord! How on earth do you keep getting out here?"

Exasperated, Daisy lifted the big bundle of fur and marched toward the kitchen. As much as she liked Blot, she couldn't take the risk that her fragile, fledgling business—the only means of financial support for her and her momma and Brenda—might get shut down because of him. Cats were not allowed in bakeries. There was no exception in the Virginia Department of Health regulations for extra-sweet, extra-fuzzy felines with burgeoning pastry addictions.

This time she didn't simply deposit Blot on the other side of the swinging door. She had to talk to Brenda, to insist that in the future Blot remain at home and that she figure out a way to keep him in the kitchen and out of sight from the customers—not to mention possible clandestine health inspectors—for the rest of the day. With the cat tucked under one arm like a lumpy sack of potatoes, Daisy shoved open the door with her elbow. She took no more than three steps into the kitchen and promptly halted. Blot dropped to the ground and immediately scurried back to Beulah.

"He's out here again, Daisy," she called.

Daisy didn't reply.

Beulah rose from her stool. "Blot's made another dash in search of treats. Should I bring him to you?"

She still didn't reply.

"Daisy?" Leaving behind the cat but not the cookies, Beulah headed toward the kitchen. "Do you need any help? I'd be happy to do something if you want an extra hand."

Bobby shuffled after her, mumbling incoherently about red velvet cake. Beulah snapped at him in irritation, "Quit blathering, Bobby."

"I need a red velvet cake."

"So buy one. Nobody's saying you can't."

"But Daisy's gonna have to—"

He didn't finish the sentence. Both his tongue and his boots stopped moving the instant he passed through the swinging door behind Beulah. The box in her hand fell to the floor. Bits of broken snickerdoodles went flying around the room, but she didn't pick them up. Neither did Bobby or Daisy. The three were frozen in speechless surprise.

Brenda stood in front of the oversize refrigerator. Although it was wide open, she made no attempt to close it. She didn't move a muscle, not even to adjust the apron that was hanging off one shoulder. The tortoiseshell clip that normally kept her black hair high up on her head in a tight bun sagged at her neck, clasping only a few graying strands. Brenda's face was as white as the smashed eggshells that were dripping from the shelves behind her. It was in sharp contrast to her hands. She had perpetually cracked and peeling hands, but today the worn skin wasn't visible. Instead it was covered with blood. A thick coat of vivid scarlet blood, dripping just like the eggs, oozing down Brenda's fingers and over her palms, spreading along her wrists to her arms. It came from the chef's knife that she was holding. The stainless steel blade looked as though it had been dipped into a pot of crimson paint. A matching crimson puddle was slowly growing around the man lying motionless at her feet.

Finally, Brenda raised her bulging eyes from the man to Daisy.

"I—I think I killed him," she said.

CHAPTER
2

"Have you noticed any strangers around the premises lately?"

Daisy blinked at the deputy sheriff sitting before her in his starched brown uniform with gold trim. "You mean other than the dead man and his two friends who Brenda saw run off?"

Deputy Johnson—according to the shiny little badge pinned to his shirt—didn't look up from the stack of forms that he was thumbing through. "I mean strangers around the premises this week or last. Strangers are the number-one suspect when it comes to crime, ma'am."

"Doesn't it depend on the type of crime?"

"Crime is crime, ma'am. And strangers are strangers."

That didn't seem particularly helpful or even logical to Daisy, but she didn't argue the point. "Okay. Except we're a bakery, and we're open to the public. So strangers are always going to be around the premises. They have to be around the premises if they want to buy anything from us."

Having apparently located the correct form, Deputy Johnson pulled it from the stack and began filling in the blanks with a stubby blue pencil. "Incident date. Saturday, October fourteenth. Incident location. Bakery called—"

"Sweetie Pies," Daisy supplied.

"I'm aware of that, ma'am," the deputy returned.

His tone was sharp enough that Daisy raised a tetchy eyebrow at him. If he was going to take that sort of attitude with her, then she didn't need to volunteer any further information. He could figure it all out for himself. She shifted in her seat toward Brenda. They were sitting on the tan plastic folding chairs that were ordinarily stacked in the far back corner of the kitchen. The chairs had once belonged to the diner for use at the semiannual barbecue held out in the parking lot. As far as Daisy knew, this was the first time that they had been set up at a crime scene around the refrigerator.

"How are you holding up?" she asked Brenda.

Brenda answered with a gurgle. Although her hands and arms had been scrubbed clean, her bulging eyes had yet to retreat. They were locked on the spot where the man had lain at her feet only a short while earlier. His lifeless body was now gone from the room, but traces of his blood remained. The crimson puddle that had surrounded him on the floor was replaced by dried mahogany smudges and streaks.

Daisy gave Brenda's knee a supportive squeeze. "Try not to think about it. I know it's hard, but just keep reminding yourself it's over. Focus on that. It's over, and nothing so awful like it will ever happen again."

"Oh, Ducky. I pray you're right. I pray that it is over."

"Of course it's over." Daisy squeezed her knee once

more. "The sheriff's office is here now. Sheriff Lowell will take care of everything. He always does."

"But . . ." Brenda swallowed hard. "But what if they come back? The other men who were here. What if they come back later? Or tomorrow? Or the day after that?"

"Don't worry. They won't come back."

"How do you know?"

Daisy didn't know. She could only guess, and hope that she was guessing correctly. But she couldn't think of any reason why the two men would return to the bakery.

"It doesn't make a bit of sense for them to come back here," she told Brenda. "They got what they wanted. Or at least we have to assume that it's what they wanted. Odd as it is. They wouldn't have taken it otherwise."

"You're sure that it's the only thing they took?" Deputy Johnson interjected.

Brenda squeaked in the affirmative.

"There's no money missing? No checks or bank card receipts?"

"No," Daisy replied.

"You're positive?"

She nodded. "I was standing next to the cash register the whole time. They never came out of the kitchen. And we don't keep any money back here."

The deputy sniffed. "So they didn't take anything of value?"

"Well, it does have value—"

"Real value," he cut her off brusquely. "Usable, salable value. At a pawnshop or on the local black market."

Beulah chortled. Up until that point, she had been sitting peaceably in her folding chair, flipping through one of the tattered, yellowed cookbooks that was stacked on the bottom shelf of the wire storage rack next to the refrigerator. "I can't imagine there's much of a black market in Pittsylvania County for stolen cream cheese," she drawled.

Daisy couldn't keep from chuckling with her. Even Brenda had to crack a slight smile. Deputy Johnson, however, didn't share in the amusement. He sniffed once more and scribbled some notes on his form with a grim expression.

"Can you give me a rough estimate as to how much cream cheese was taken?"

"I can give you an exact amount," Daisy said. "We had a delivery earlier this week. Three blocks. Thirty pounds apiece."

The deputy looked up at her. "That's ninety pounds. What could you possibly need ninety pounds of cream cheese for?"

"Frosting. Filling. And most obviously, cheesecake." She frowned at him, annoyed by the inanity of the question. "Cream cheese is one of our staples. As you may recall, we're a bakery. For a bakery, three blocks isn't really very much."

"They took all three blocks?"

"They did."

"And the blocks were kept in the refrigerator?"

"They were. Cream cheese is perishable. It's always in the refrigerator."

"Do you think they knew it was cream cheese?"

Daisy sucked on her teeth, her irritation swelling. "I don't see how they couldn't have known. It says 'cream cheese' in big black letters right on the crates. On every side of the crates. The men could have been half comatose and still figured it out."

"Maybe they took it by mistake," the deputy suggested.

"Or maybe they eat a lot of bagels," Beulah snapped. "Instead of talking like a fool and asking why Daisy and her bakery would have ninety pounds of cream cheese—which is pretty dang self-explanatory, if you stopped and thought about it for even half a second—you should be asking why anybody in their right mind would want to steal ninety pounds of cream cheese. That's a heck of a pile of cheese to be hauling around the countryside."

It was Deputy Johnson's turn to suck on his teeth. He glared at Beulah from behind the smeared lenses of his glasses. "Were you an accomplice to the theft, ma'am? Because only a co-conspirator would know why a criminal does what he does."

Beulah and her very short redheaded fuse slammed the cookbook on the floor. "You better not be accusing me of something—"

Daisy grabbed Beulah's elbow as she started to rise from her chair. "Of course he's not accusing you of anything," she responded swiftly, giving Beulah a stern glance. "He knows that you were with me in the front of the bakery and that we came back here to the kitchen within a minute of each other and saw what had happened."

There was a tense pause, during which Daisy kept a firm hand on Beulah's elbow. She wasn't any less irked than Beulah at the evident ineptitude of the deputy, but she was better able to remember that he was still a deputy. And they had called the sheriff's office for a reason. Brenda did stab a man to death in front of the refrigerator with a chef's knife. There was no doubt whatsoever about it being self-defense. Under normal circumstances, Brenda was about as aggressive as a pudgy slug snoozing under a shady leaf. But she had killed him. An official report couldn't be avoided. The important thing at this point was making sure the report set forth the facts in the most favorable manner to Brenda. That was a lesson Daisy had learned from her estranged husband, Matt. Before Matt decided to drive off one morning nearly five years ago and never come home again, he had on occasion found himself in trouble with the local authorities. As a result, Daisy had a bit of experience with the law.

She shot Beulah another stern glance. When Beulah finally sat back down, Daisy turned to the deputy with a feigned apologetic smile.

"I'm sorry. As I'm sure you can understand, it's been a stressful morning for all of us. I think the shock of it is beginning to catch up with everyone."

Although Deputy Johnson didn't appear entirely appeased by Daisy's syrupy tone, his glare did soften somewhat. Encouraged, she continued.

"When we've had any problems here in the past, we've always talked to Sheriff Lowell. He knows us pretty well, and he's used to our little quirks. So maybe it would be better if we talked to him now too."

"You can't," the deputy said.

"We can't?"

"Sheriff Lowell is gone, ma'am. He's on vacation and won't return to duty until the beginning of next month."

Daisy sighed. She had known that the sheriff was planning on taking a cruise. It was to the Greek isles in celebration of his thirtieth wedding anniversary. Although his wife, Sue, had come into the bakery half a dozen times over the past few weeks to share all the exciting plans, Daisy had forgotten the exact dates. Talk about lousy timing. Sheriff Lowell was smart and reliable. He could have been counted on to clean up the whole mess quickly and efficiently, not only in relation to Brenda and the dead body, but also the underlying question as to why someone would want to steal ninety pounds of cream cheese from them. Unfortunately, if the sheriff was currently sipping ouzo seaside, then she and Brenda and Beulah were stuck with the clearly less smart—and probably equally less reliable—Deputy Johnson.

As though he could sense Daisy's skepticism regarding his abilities, the deputy cleared his throat, straightened his spine, and returned to business.

"Can you give me any description of the two men who got away?" he asked Brenda.

She shook her head. "I couldn't see their faces. They were wearing baseball caps with the hoods of their sweat-shirts pulled up over the top, just like . . . like him." She gestured toward the bloodstains on the floor.

"What about their height? And build?"

"Are you sure they were men?" Beulah jumped in.

"They had to be men," Deputy Johnson said. "They carried out ninety pounds of weight between them. How many women could do that?"

"Except they were only planning on carrying out thirty pounds apiece," Beulah countered. "A lot of women can handle that."

"I can," Daisy agreed. "I was the one who put the blocks in the refrigerator to begin with."

"Laurel can carry thirty pounds," Bobby said.

They all looked at him. It was the first time that he had participated in the proceedings since the law arrived on the scene. He was stretched out on two folding chairs, one arm hanging down to the ground, absently rubbing Blot's portly belly, while both he and the cat dozed.

"It wasn't her, of course," Bobby continued. "Laurel wouldn't want a crate of cream cheese, and she's up in the woods. But she could carry it." He glanced over at Daisy before closing his eyes again.

"Laurel?" Brenda asked in confusion.

"Laurel is a mystery woman," Beulah informed her with a titter. "Although if she's keeping company with Bobby and that weaselly brother of his up in the woods, it's not too hard to guess what kind of—"

Daisy didn't let her finish. She was still curious to learn who Laurel was, but not if it meant discussing Bobby's brother. "Thirty pounds is manageable," she remarked. "But sixty? The whole length of the kitchen, out the back door, and then loading it into a vehicle? It would have to be a heck of a farm girl to do that. There are plenty of guys around here who can't carry sixty pounds all that way. It's too much and too far."

"So it could have been a woman for the thirty and a man for the sixty," Deputy Johnson mused.

"Laurel and the weasel Rick, perhaps."

Still tittering, Beulah said it quietly enough so that Bobby couldn't hear her, but Daisy did. She wrinkled her nose.

"Don't make that face at me," Beulah retorted. "You ignore Rick like he's been wallowing with the hogs whenever you see him. Maybe he was trying to get your attention."

"By stealing ninety pounds of cream cheese? You've lost your mind!"

"I don't think," Brenda said, chewing on her lips

thoughtfully, "there was a woman. They all moved like men."

"But you can't describe them?" Deputy Johnson pressed her.

Brenda went on thinking and chewing. After a minute, she mewed in frustration. "I don't know. Everything happened so fast. I was at the mixer trying to get the dough for the shortcake to come together right. Ducky has shown me how to do it at least a hundred times, but somehow I still always make it too wet. So I turned to get a scoop of flour to dry it out, and all of a sudden, there they were. Three of 'em. With their caps and sweatshirts. Walking straight through the middle of the kitchen." Brenda waved toward the center of the room. "I had the impression that they didn't expect me to be here, because they stopped for a second, like they were just as surprised to see me as I was to see them. Then one of 'em signaled the others. He must have been the leader of the group, because they followed him to the refrigerator. He opened it and began looking around inside. I asked him what he was doing, but he didn't answer me. I told him—I told all of 'em—to leave. Except they didn't listen. They just started pulling out the cream cheese."

"Did they say anything?" Deputy Johnson asked. "Did they speak at all?"

"Not at first. Not until Blot got underfoot."

"Huh?"

"The cat," Daisy explained, pointing at the heap of fur sprawled near Bobby.

The deputy squinted at Brenda. "How did the cat get underfoot?"

She squinted back at him. "The usual way, of course.

Blot's extremely friendly. He went over to the men to greet 'em—not knowing they were bad men—and one of them didn't like it. He tried to shoo him away, but Blot didn't understand. He's a very sweet kitty and used to getting lots of love from everybody. Well, the man tripped over him, crashed into the rack next to the refrigerator, and started cursing up a storm. Blot naturally got scared and hightailed it out of the kitchen."

Beulah turned to Daisy with a grin. "That settles it then. The cat's a genius. That's why he kept coming to us. It wasn't my sneakers or the snickerdoodles that he wanted. He was trying to warn us."

"Blot was trying to warn you?" Brenda's bulging eyes stretched even wider. "You think so?"

"You bet. He was afraid that if there wasn't any more cream cheese, he wouldn't be getting any more carrot cake."

Daisy had to clamp down on her tongue to keep from laughing.

"Carrot cake?" The deputy squinted harder. "What does carrot cake have to do with this?"

"Nothing. Nothing whatsoever." Daisy looked at Brenda. "What happened next?"

"I told 'em to leave again, Ducky. I reminded them that it wasn't their bakery and the cream cheese didn't belong to them. But by that time, they weren't paying a lick of attention to me. It was like I wasn't even there. I might as well have been a spatula hanging on the wall. They each had a block of cheese in their arms. The leader was already carrying his toward the door. They could have all just left without any fuss, except Blot came back into the kitchen. He was really upset—racing around on his little

kitty paws like he was wearing motorized roller skates—
and he did something he almost never does. He bit the
man who had tripped over him before. The man tried to
shove him away with his foot, and Blot bit him again."

Brenda paused, drawing a shaky breath. Her lips were
almost raw from the intensity with which she had been
chomping on them. "The man was awfully angry. He was
cursing somethin' fearful. And then he kicked Blot. It was
so hard, Blot flew right up into the air! That's when I got
mad. I demanded he leave my cat alone. If he wanted the
cream cheese so dang bad, he could have it, but there was
no need for violence against a defenseless kitty. Well, the
other two men turned back from the door and were trying to get the third one—the cat kicker—to come with
them. They didn't talk, but they kept grunting and motioning at him, almost frantically after a minute."

"Standard criminal behavior, ma'am." Glancing up
from the notes that he was taking, Deputy Johnson nodded authoritatively. "They didn't want you to be able to
identify them later based on their voices."

"I would guess they were getting nervous," Daisy told
Brenda. "If you're right about them not expecting you to
be in the kitchen, then they were probably beginning to
worry about how long it was taking them to get out of here.
Somebody else could show up and surprise them. Like me
or a customer or—"

"Or Aunt Emily and her shotgun," Beulah chimed in.

There was a little whimper from Bobby. He was all too
familiar with Aunt Emily's Remington.

"They also must have been getting tired," Beulah added.
"From holding the stupid cheese the whole time."

"The cat kicker put his block down on the rack," Brenda

said, "so he could chase after Blot. I still had that scoop of flour in my hand for the shortcake dough, and I threw it at him. Like flour does, it went everywhere. On the men, on me, on the floor. A bunch of it must have gotten into the kicker's eyes, because he took up cursing again and went crazy rubbing his face. Then he slipped. I don't know how exactly. He stumbled toward me and was yelling. The other men started yelling too. Blot jumped at him, trying to bite him again. The man grabbed my arm, and I grabbed the knife from the counter. Before I could really figure out what was happening, he fell against me, and the knife went into him." She shuddered. "There was all this blood."

"And the other men?" Deputy Johnson asked. "What did they do?"

Brenda shuddered once more. "They said something to each other. I can't tell you what it was. I didn't hear it. I was too busy looking at the blood. There was so much of it. It was all over me—and my hands—and the knife. And it kept coming. Gushing out of the man somethin' terrible. Eventually, the other men took the cream cheese and left. I think they took his block from the rack too, because it was gone. Then Daisy walked in."

"Did you see them?" the deputy said to her.

"No." Daisy shook her head. "The back door was closed when I arrived. There was no cream cheese anywhere."

She glanced toward the storage rack next to the refrigerator. In addition to the old cookbooks, the wire shelves were stacked with supplies: measuring cups and bowls, long sleeves of cupcake liners, assorted jars of colored sprinkles. It all looked a bit tossed about from the man having crashed against the rack, but nothing appeared particularly out of place. There was a thicker dusting of flour than usual from what Brenda had thrown. And the blood smeared on the floor in front of the rack.

"There was no cream cheese anywhere," Daisy repeated, eyeing the mahogany stains. A man was dead, and she was going to have to scrub away the last remnants of his life.

Deputy Johnson added a few final scribbles to his form. "Well, I think that about covers it. For *now*," he emphasized. "If you remember anything more about the other two men, you should contact me immediately."

Brenda nodded. Daisy went on staring at the floor. There was something red on the ground peeking out from under the edge of the wire rack. It wasn't more blood, of that she was certain. The color wasn't right. It was too bright, and the object itself was too solid.

"You should keep a sharp watch for anything out of the ordinary," the deputy continued. "We'll give the place a good once-over. Maybe we'll get lucky and pull a clean print off the refrigerator or back door." He rose from his chair.

Not hesitating, Daisy stood up with him. She had noticed something out of the ordinary, and she wanted to get to it before he did. Beulah yawned. As she stretched in her seat, her sneaker pushed against the cookbook that she had thrown down earlier. Quick to take advantage of the opportunity, Daisy picked up the book and returned it to the bottom shelf of the storage rack. At the same time, she quietly scooped up the enigmatic object from the floor and tucked it into her pocket.

Turning back to the group, she wondered if anyone had spotted her. Apparently they hadn't. Beulah was picking cat hair off her clothes. Bobby was sound asleep. And Brenda was nodding at every sententious word from the deputy.

"Criminals make mistakes," he pontificated. "That's how we catch 'em, especially strangers. Strangers think they're so clever, except they always leave a clue behind. Sometimes it can be hard to find. But that's my job. The first clue is the most important, and I'll be the one to find it."

As he droned on, Daisy's lips lifted into a slight smile. She was pretty sure that she was the one who had found the first clue.

CHAPTER
3

The sun had already sunk below the horizon before Daisy was finally able to lock the bakery doors and return home to the inn. She was mildly crabby and more than a little tired. Normally Sweetie Pies closed for the weekend at noon on Saturday. That way she and Brenda got a much-needed day and a half of rest before once again diving into the cornucopia of flour and sugar early Monday morning. But without Sheriff Lowell leading the charge, his office had moved slower than a confused turtle on the highway with their endless forms and toddling examination of the premises and even more toddling questioning of all the potential witnesses. The only good point from Daisy's perspective was that at least the bakery didn't miss out on a lot of sales. The potential witnesses had grown hungry over time and ended up purchasing just as many cookies, brownies, muffins, and scones as they had on the previous days. And they didn't seem to be overly traumatized by the news that there had been a death by stabbing in the kitchen, which boded well for their return the following week.

Beulah spent most of the drive grumbling. She hadn't been allowed to leave the bakery, so she had missed her chance to have Connor Woodley try to find—and hopefully also fix—the cause of the mysterious flood at the salon. She hadn't been able to contact him on the phone again either, so her only hope was that he might be willing to come by tomorrow, which didn't seem very likely considering that it was Sunday.

Brenda sat in the backseat, clutching Blot under one arm and her overnight bag under the other. She had looked so forlorn and frightened at the prospect of having to go back to her house all alone—with only her feline friend for comfort and protection—that Daisy had insisted on her spending the remainder of the weekend at the inn. Out of collective exhaustion, they had all piled into Daisy's car. After a brief stop at Brenda's to retrieve a few essentials for both her and Blot, they then proceeded to the Tosh Inn.

The venerable Victorian rose up in the gray dusk like a behemoth ghost awakening from its ancient grave. At night the shadows from the gables gave the stately house a forbidding air, but it wasn't in any way a cold or unfriendly place. Daisy had found more hours of joy and solace than she could count sitting in one of the white-pine rocking chairs on the wraparound porch. Although she and her momma had moved to the inn out of necessity, they never lamented staying there.

"I'll take Brenda upstairs and get her settled," Beulah said, as they turned off the main road and traveled up the long driveway. "Meanwhile, you can share all the exciting news with Aunt Emily."

Daisy gave a little snort. "Thanks so much."

"Hey, it's your bakery. That makes it your story."

The snort repeated itself. "You can spin it however you like, but I know what you're trying to do."

"Me?" Beulah responded with exaggerated incredulity. "What am I trying to do?"

"You're trying to avoid being in the room when I tell Aunt Emily that Deputy Johnson thinks strangers were involved."

She groaned. "I can't listen to another one of her speeches on strangers lurking."

"That makes two of us."

They shared a sigh as Daisy pulled the car into the row of parking spaces at the side of the inn.

"I do think steering clear of Aunt Emily tonight is a good idea," Daisy said, shutting off the engine and climbing out. "After what happened today, a heavy dose of her could very well be the straw that breaks the camel's back. Somebody's nerves," she motioned surreptitiously toward Brenda, who was talking in a low tone to Blot, trying to keep the scaredy-cat calm while she prepared to remove him from the backseat, "might crack completely."

Beulah took Brenda's overnight bag, so that she had both hands free to carry Blot up the flagstone path to the house. "Now if we could only get inside without Aunt Emily hearing."

"Fat chance. It's why she keeps the front steps creaky and the screen door squeaky."

"Maybe she's on the back porch with your momma."

Daisy shook her head. "Momma's out this evening. She went to a lecture at the Pittsylvania Historical Society. It's some sort of fund-raiser. I guess they're really struggling to keep the doors open."

"Aren't we all these days? But I'm glad your momma felt up to doing that."

"Me too. Except she'll probably have to spend the whole next week in bed trying to recover from it."

Beulah limited her reply to a sympathetic nod. They had reached the last flagstone on the path to the house. It was safer not to speak while standing directly before the porch. Old Southern homes had notoriously thin walls, and old Southern aunts had freakishly good hearing. The porch lights were on, but that meant very little. The porch lights were almost always on. Of more interest were the parlor lights. The parlor was the first room to the right of the front door. Its windows were fully lit. Although Daisy and Beulah would have dearly liked to see inside, they couldn't. The lace sheers were drawn closed.

They leaned forward and listened. Voices. A conversation. It was too quiet to make out the words, but it was definitely coming from the parlor. Aunt Emily was entertaining. The two shared another sigh. There was no way to get through the entrance hall to the stairs without passing by the parlor. Aunt Emily would see them for sure. Their only hope was that she might be too engrossed in her company to pay much attention to them.

"I can't think of an alternative, can you?" Daisy whispered to Beulah.

"No, I'm sorry to say."

"We might as well just get it over with then. But let's try to make it quick. As soon as we're done with all the obligatory niceties to whoever is in there, you get out and take Brenda upstairs. No lollygagging or extra talking."

"Sounds like a plan. If you can just keep Aunt Emily occupied until we're—"

"I can't hold him much longer," Brenda interjected, struggling to keep the desperately squirming and yowling cat in her arms.

They hustled Blot onto the porch before he could break free and race off into the night. As expected, the aged steps creaked under them. Daisy pushed open the front door with another heralding squeak. The response from inside the house was almost instantaneous.

"Ducky? Ducky, is that you?"

She took a deep breath. "It surely is, Aunt Emily."

"Oh, good. I was wondering where you were. We were almost beginning to think you had gotten lost."

"Is my momma back? How was the lecture? Is she feeling okay?"

"Lucy hasn't come home yet. She's still at the fundraiser— Mercy me! What is that racket?"

If there had been any remaining possibility of sneaking Brenda by unnoticed, Blot unequivocally spoiled it. The kitty started shrieking like a furry banshee, no doubt just as tired and unsettled from the day's troubling events as the rest of them. On top of that, he was now in a strange place—with strange smells and strange voices—and he was vociferously expressing his frustration in the only manner available to him.

"It sounds like a couple of sick sea otters that ate some bad clams for breakfast. You didn't see anything skulking near the porch when you came in, did you, Ducky?"

Daisy couldn't help chuckling. "No, Aunt Emily. There were no sick sea otters skulking near the porch."

Aunt Emily whipped around the corner of the parlor into the entrance hall a moment later. She might have been closing in on seventy, but there wasn't any evidence of it in her speed. There wasn't even much evidence of it in her appearance. She was always fashionably dressed. Her silver hair was invariably well coiffeured. And her makeup was beyond reproach. Wrinkles or not, Emily Tosh was a handsome woman with shrewd blue eyes. Very shrewd.

"Mercy me!" she exclaimed again. "What a wonderful surprise! Why didn't you telephone me, Ducky? You should have called ahead and told me that Brenda was coming along with you. I would have made something fancy for supper."

"It wasn't planned," Daisy explained, truthfully enough. "We just decided at the last minute. I invited her to spend the weekend. I hope that's not a problem. I was pretty sure there were empty rooms."

"Of course it's not a problem. We always have a room for Brenda—and Blot. But what on earth is wrong with him? Why is he crying like that?"

"Rough day. Kitty tantrums." She nudged Beulah with her elbow.

Beulah moved closer to Brenda and started guiding her down the hallway. "Maybe once we get him upstairs," she said. "Where there isn't so much noise and people and excitement—"

"Is he hungry?" Aunt Emily asked. "Should I go dig around the kitchen? We must have something he likes to eat."

"I think Beulah's right," Daisy responded swiftly. "The car ride over here was a tad much for him. Some quiet time in a room is probably just the thing he needs to—"

Although Beulah did an excellent job of standing in between Brenda and Aunt Emily, and she continued to herd Brenda and Blot toward the stairs, Aunt Emily was just too hospitable to the cat.

"You poor dear. So upset about a drive to the inn. How about a snack? Would you like a snack, Blot? Would that make you feel better?"

Taking a step forward, she reached out her hand to comfort the kitty. That was when she saw it.

"Is that blood on your sleeve, Brenda? Did he scratch you?"

There was a pause. Beulah looked at Brenda. Brenda looked first at Blot, then at Daisy. Daisy closed her eyes and waited.

"Hold up a minute," Aunt Emily went on. "There's blood all over your blouse. That can't be from Blot scratching you. Are you okay, Brenda? Did you hurt yourself?"

The pause continued.

"Did you hurt yourself?" she repeated, her brow furrowing.

Brenda didn't seem capable of answering. Her face was so wan and strained that she appeared to be on the verge of collapse. Daisy knew that she could no longer avoid giving Aunt Emily a full explanation, but Brenda certainly didn't need to be part of it. In fact, Daisy had the distinct impression that if Brenda did become part of it, she would end up having to take her to the hospital for a nervous breakdown.

Daisy nodded at Beulah, who wrapped her arm around Brenda's quivering shoulders and led her the rest of the way down the hall. Aunt Emily was astute enough to realize that something was seriously wrong and didn't protest. She turned to Daisy.

"Ducky?"

"Let's sit down, please."

They headed toward the parlor. Aunt Emily glanced back at the staircase as Beulah, Brenda, and Blot disappeared up it.

"I hope she didn't hurt herself too badly," she mused.

"She'll be fine," Daisy replied. "I think she just needs a good night's sleep. We all do."

"You're beginning to worry me, Ducky. Did something happen at the bakery?"

They turned the corner into the parlor. In the excitement of trying to get Brenda and Blot quickly and quietly to a room, Daisy had forgotten about Aunt Emily's company. When she had first heard the traces of conversation outside the house, she had assumed that it was a neighborhood acquaintance who had dropped by for a cup of coffee and some friendly gossip. She didn't expect to find Richard Balsam instead.

He was sitting in the scuffed leather smoking chair across from the settee, holding an etched crystal tumbler filled with ice and a generous serving of a chestnut brown liquid, most likely bourbon. Aunt Emily kept a well-stocked bar, but she liked to pour particular bottles at particular hours on particular days. Saturday evening was usually bourbon.

"Hello, Daisy."

She gave a slight nod of acknowledgment. "Rick."

Rick was Bobby's brother—two years older and infinitely cleverer, dangerously so. Bobby may have been born a dim bulb, but he was a predictable dim bulb. Rick, on the other hand, was a wild card. He enjoyed playing games, trading favors, and holding an ace up his sleeve at all times. To his credit, Rick was good at keeping secrets. He was also good at philandering, carousing, and distilling corn whiskey. He supplied half the eastern seaboard with his illegal moonshine, making him quite wealthy and allowing him to buy huge tracts of Pittsylvania County land. That included Daisy's childhood and ancestral home, which stuck deep in her craw no matter how hard she tried to be at peace with it. But copious money and property aside, Rick still drove an old pickup truck, wore construction boots and faded jeans, and slept in a dilapidated trailer so far out in the backwoods that there was no actual need for either his large number of dogs or his even larger arsenal, at least not in terms of personal protection.

"Why don't you sit down and have a drink?" Rick said, giving Daisy an appraising gaze. "You look like you could use it."

"Golly, thanks," she muttered.

"Come on now. I didn't mean it like that. You know I always think you're mighty fine."

She didn't respond. It was safer not to. Rick was an undisputed snake charmer, and she didn't have enough energy left to be as careful as she needed to around him.

"He's right, Ducky," Aunt Emily agreed. "You're awfully pale. Take a seat, and I'll get you a glass."

Daisy sunk down on the settee. An instant later, she had an etched crystal tumbler in her hand. She didn't bother asking what it contained. She didn't care. After the day that she had had, any liquor was good liquor. She took a drink. It was indeed bourbon. Sharp and bracing, exactly what she needed.

Aunt Emily pulled over a straight-backed chair from the tea table and settled herself on it. "Now let's get down to business, Ducky. Does Brenda need a doctor? Should we call someone? How bad are those cuts?"

"Brenda cut herself?" Rick asked.

"No." Daisy shook her head. "Brenda doesn't need a doctor, not for that, at least. She didn't cut herself."

"But that blood . . ."

She took another drink. Long and slow. A mellow caramel flavor lingered on her tongue. It made her think that maybe she should come up with a few more items for the bakery that featured spirits. A brandy butter for the scones, perhaps. And something with rum. Rum and peaches would make a nice combination.

"But that blood," Aunt Emily said again. "Brenda had all that blood on her blouse. If she didn't cut herself—"

"It's not her blood."

"Not her blood?" Aunt Emily echoed.

Rick raised a curious eyebrow.

"It's not her blood," Daisy repeated. "And I can't tell you whose blood it is, because he's dead, and nobody's been able to identify him yet."

The eyebrow went higher.

She shrugged. "Three men broke into the bakery this morning. There was a bit of an altercation. Brenda picked up a knife and sort of stabbed one of 'em. It's his blood."

"Holy hell." Rick shot forward in his seat. "Are you all right?"

"I'm okay."

"Are you sure?" He leaned toward her and put his hand on her knee. "They didn't hurt you, did they, Daisy?"

As much as she distrusted him, there was something so very warm and soothing about his touch at that moment, she didn't push his hand away.

"I'm fine, Rick. Really."

His dark eyes looked at her intently. "If they did anything—"

"They didn't. You can ask your brother. He was there. So was Beulah."

"Bobby was there? I knew that he was going to the bakery this morning to talk to you, but I haven't heard from him since."

"That's probably because he was trapped all day in the kitchen with us and Deputy Johnson."

"Deputy Johnson?" Rick frowned. "Not Sheriff Lowell?"

"Sheriff Lowell is on vacation, so we're stuck with Deputy Johnson until he comes back. The timing really stinks."

His frown deepened. "Maybe. Or maybe the timing was perfect."

"What?" Daisy blinked at him in surprise. "You think those men planned it? They waited until Sheriff Lowell was gone to break in to Sweetie Pies? Why?"

"I don't know." Rick's lips curled into a smile. "But I do know enough about crime to understand that three boys coming into your bakery to make trouble during the middle of the day isn't some random act. It was definitely planned."

Daisy found herself smiling back at him. "I can't argue with you there, Rick. You certainly know plenty about crime." Then she laughed. "And I can't believe I'm about to say this—because comparing you to the law is like comparing a hornet to a moth—but you sounded almost like Deputy Johnson just then. He's got lots of theories about criminals. Criminals and strangers."

As soon as the word came out of her mouth, she wanted to suck it back in. She hadn't intended on mentioning anything regarding strangers. It was a subject that dear Aunt Emily could go on about ad infinitum, especially when it came to strangers lurking, just waiting for an opportunity to prey on helpless females. The fact that Brenda hadn't turned out to be helpless—far from it, considering that she had managed to single-handedly stick a chef's knife into a man's chest and kill him—wouldn't make the tiniest difference. The strangers were still there, and they were still lurking.

Wincing in anticipation, Daisy glanced over at the straight-backed chair. To her relief, Aunt Emily didn't seem to have noticed her slip of the tongue. On the contrary, she was sitting completely still, with her head tilted to one side, as though she was listening very closely to something else instead.

"Aunt Emily?" Daisy said.

She raised a silencing forefinger.

Daisy looked at Rick. He seemed to be listening also.

After a minute, Aunt Emily whispered, "You heard that, right? It came from outside, didn't it?"

"By the windows," Rick responded in an equally low tone. "Trying to see in here probably."

Aunt Emily gave a small nod.

They listened for a few more seconds. This time Daisy listened along with them, and she realized that they were right. There was a light scratching noise outside by the windows. Lifting his hand from her knee, Rick reached around to his back. She stiffened, knowing full well what he was doing. Rick was going for his gun.

CHAPTER
4

The revolver appeared an instant later. Even without trying, Rick was a fast draw. It was a mixture of innate skill
and a great deal of practice. All the Balsam babies began
playing with pistols before they were out of diapers. Rick's
concealed carry weapon of choice was a Ruger .44 with a
rosewood grip. He was rarely without it, and in Daisy's
experience, he tended to have an itchy trigger finger, especially when he had been drinking.

"Rick—" she began.

He rose from the leather smoking chair.

"It's a skunk or a possum," she said. "There's no need
to blow the poor critter's head off."

"Get behind the sofa," he replied.

With a sigh, she stayed on the settee.

"I'm not going to tell you again, Daisy. Get behind the
sofa."

"Oh, Rick—"

Rick cocked the hammer on the Ruger.

Daisy turned to Aunt Emily for support, but she should

have known better. Aunt Emily was no longer in her chair either. She had scurried to retrieve her shotgun and the needlepoint bag in which she stored her extra boxes of shells. Cracking open the breech of the double-barreled 20-gauge, Aunt Emily dropped in two new shells. With a satisfied smile, she snapped the breech shut again and stroked the Remington like it was a faithful old bluetick.

"Crazy people," Daisy muttered.

There was some more scratching by the windows—slightly louder this time—and it gave the impression of moving, possibly in the direction of the front door.

"Get behind the goddam sofa right now!" Rick thundered at her.

She rolled her eyes but grudgingly complied. It was considerably easier and more prudent than arguing, especially when both he and Aunt Emily were waving around loaded firearms. Glass in hand, Daisy stood up, walked around to the back of the settee, and plopped herself down on the floor.

Rick pointed a stiff finger at her and growled, "Stay there."

Rolling her eyes again, Daisy took a drink. At least the crazy people could be relied upon to provide ample liquor. As she sipped the bourbon, she listened to the unidentified noise outside. The scratching had now become more of a shuffling, and it was definitely moving. There was a thump on the front porch. It was a thump that sounded an awful lot like a footstep. A heavy human footstep. Not the soft paw of a skunk or possum.

She frowned. But if it was a footstep, why didn't the person come inside? Why were they out there creeping around in the dark? It suddenly occurred to her that maybe Brenda had been right to be worried. What if the men really had come back to the bakery—and followed them to the inn—and were looking for revenge for what had happened to their friend? Daisy found herself sinking a little lower and leaning a little more closely against the back of the settee.

Peeking around the corner of the fabric, she saw Rick and Aunt Emily standing just inside the parlor at the edge of the entrance hall. They were listening attentively to the intermittent sounds out front. There was some additional shuffling, followed by another footstep or two. Somebody was clearly on the porch.

Daisy felt her heart beat a little harder in her chest. At least Brenda and Beulah were safely upstairs. Hopefully they would both stay in their rooms for the time being. She wished that she could somehow get upstairs too. Her gun was there. It was a small Colt—a .380. Her daddy had given it to her momma the Christmas before he passed, but it belonged to Daisy now. And she would have liked to have it in her hands right about then.

The porch steps creaked. Whoever was outside was standing near the front door. Daisy bit her lip. Maybe they would knock. Maybe it was just a confused guest. Maybe it had nothing to do with the men from the bakery after all. The screen door squeaked. It was just a slight squeak. The door didn't actually open. But that made it worse. It was like somebody was testing the door, or they had brushed against it as they shifted into a better position.

It was enough to get Rick into a better position. He glanced first at Daisy. If he was checking to see whether she was still behind the settee, he didn't need to be concerned. She had absolutely no intention of vacating the location until the identity of the person prowling outside the inn was confirmed. Motioning to Aunt Emily, Rick moved with a quick step from the parlor to the opposite side of the entrance hall. The screen door squeaked a second time. The Ruger went up.

There was more squeaking, and the door started to open. Daisy couldn't see it, but she could hear it. Aunt Emily tucked the butt of the Remington against her shoulder and raised the barrels. Her aim wasn't generally the greatest, except it didn't have to be, not from that distance. It was only a few short yards from the corner of the parlor to the front door. That was sufficiently close for the shotgun to pulverize the door, along with anything else that happened to get in the way.

"Hey, Daisy," Beulah called, trotting down the stairs. "Do you know where the extra towels—" Her words and feet stopped in the same instant, no doubt when she saw Rick and his revolver in the entrance hall.

Without taking his eyes or the gun off the door, Rick directed sternly, "Go back upstairs, Beulah."

Beulah didn't ordinarily respond well to commands—especially not those issued by a Balsam brother—but she wasn't any more eager than Daisy to end up in the middle of a gunfight. Retreating several steps, Beulah sat down on the top of the stairs. She leaned over and looked at Daisy on the floor in the parlor.

Daisy could only shrug. She didn't know what was happening either. As she swallowed the last of her bourbon, the ice cubes rattled against the sides of the glass. They sounded loud in the tense stillness. The screen door had stopped squeaking. Based on Rick's intent expression, Daisy assumed that the door was ajar, but no one was yet in sight.

"You've got two seconds to show your face," he barked in warning, "before I start shooting."

The door immediately slammed open.

"Jesus, Mary, and Joseph!" Rick hollered. "That's a damn good way to get yourself dead!"

He promptly lowered his Ruger, and Daisy breathed a sigh of relief. Apparently it wasn't anyone whom Rick considered a threat. Standing up, she started toward the entrance hall. To Daisy's surprise, Aunt Emily remained stationed at the corner of the parlor. She didn't lower her Remington.

"You're not welcome here," she said brusquely.

Not welcome? But Aunt Emily was always the perfect hostess.

"I thought I made that clear the last time you came into this house uninvited." Her finger tightened on the trigger of the shotgun. "But I guess you need a refresher."

There was a whimper from the direction of the front door. Daisy smiled. She knew that whimper. It was Bobby Balsam.

Aunt Emily sucked on her teeth. "Don't you have anything to say for yourself? Or are you just going to stand there sniveling like a half-drowned chipmunk?"

With a chuckle, Daisy turned away from the hall and headed toward the liquor cart. Now was a good time for a refill.

Beulah rose from her seat on the stairs. "Pour me one too, would ya, Daisy?"

"My glass could sure use a dividend," Rick chimed in.

Daisy wrinkled her nose. "Just because I used to be a waitress at the diner doesn't mean that I'm the official barmaid of the inn."

"The bourbon is in the decanter on the far left, Ducky," Aunt Emily said. "I wouldn't mind a snort myself."

"Better make it a short snort," Beulah chortled, as she sauntered down the steps to the parlor. "Otherwise your aim might suffer."

Bobby whimpered again.

"Oh, for crying out loud, Bobby," Daisy called to him. "She's not going to shoot you, at least not before you tell us why you're here. So spit it out already."

"I . . ." He gurgled. "It's about that red velvet cake, Daisy."

"What is it with you and red velvet cake!" Beulah snapped. "Is it some new hunting bait that nobody has ever heard of? Red velvet instead of a salt lick?"

"I . . ." Bobby gurgled some more.

"For all those interested, drinks are served." Taking her own drink from the row of crystal tumblers that she had filled, Daisy returned to her former spot on the settee.

Beulah picked up a glass and joined her. Also grabbing a glass, Rick went back to the leather smoking chair. Although she glanced wistfully at the liquor cart, Aunt Emily and the Remington maintained their position.

"I know it's a tough decision," Beulah grinned, "but you're going to have to put down the gun if you want the bourbon."

"I think we can trust Bobby not to do anything silly." Daisy looked at Rick.

He nodded. "Don't worry," he told Aunt Emily. "Bobby knows that he's got to be on his best behavior here."

Aunt Emily responded with a dubious grunt but finally lowered her firearm. After collecting her drink, she sat down on the straight-backed chair, laying the shotgun across her knees. It took a while for Bobby to muster enough courage to pop his head around the corner of the parlor.

"Did you follow us from the bakery, Bobby?" Daisy asked. "Have you been outside the whole time?"

He answered with a halfhearted shrug.

She frowned at him. "What is going on with you? You've been acting weird all day."

Eyeing the shotgun warily, Bobby took no more than two shuffling steps into the room. "I—I'm gonna need a red velvet cake, Daisy."

Beulah slammed her glass on the tea table and stuck out her hand toward Aunt Emily. "If you're not going to shoot him, can I?"

"Don't tempt me," Aunt Emily replied.

Daisy was inclined to agree with Beulah. She didn't have enough bourbon in her system to listen to Bobby prattle on interminably about red velvet cake.

"Come by the bakery on Monday," she said. "There are probably a couple of slices in the freezer. You can have as many as you want, Bobby, if you stop talking about it now."

"I don't need a slice," he protested. "I need a cake."

Growling like a badger that was about to chew its own foot off, Beulah reached for the Remington a second time. "Please, Aunt Emily? No one has to know. We can bury him under the cellar. That groundhog has dug a pretty good hole on one side already. It wouldn't take much to make it big enough for a body."

Aunt Emily cackled so hard that a bit of her drink sloshed over the top of the glass. Bobby's brow furrowed in confusion.

Daisy glanced at Rick. "Are you planning on helping him out? Because I'm not."

"Have you told them why you want the cake?" Rick asked his brother.

Bobby shook his head.

Both Beulah and Aunt Emily turned to Rick with interest. Daisy sunk her head on the back of the settee. She couldn't have cared less why Bobby wanted the cake.

Rick took a sip of bourbon, then he smiled. "He wants it for the wedding."

The tumbler fell from Daisy's fingers, hitting the Persian carpet beneath her with a thud. A cluster of melting ice cubes, mixed with the chestnut brown liquid, darkened the yellow floral pattern.

Beulah jumped up. "I'll get a napkin."

"There's a stack next to the decanters." Aunt Emily pointed toward the liquor cart.

Grabbing a handful, Beulah dropped them on top of the puddle and pressed them down with her foot.

"I'm sorry." Daisy stared at the rug. "I don't know how that happened."

Unruffled, Aunt Emily clucked her tongue. "It's not worth fretting over, Ducky. Just a little liquor and water. That carpet has seen a lot worse over the years. When it dries, it won't even be noticeable."

"Not noticeable at all," Rick drawled. "Means nothing."

The implication behind his mocking manner was unmistakable, and Daisy raised an eyebrow at him.

He raised his eyebrow right back at her. "Are you going to pretend you don't understand me? Well, I understand you perfectly, darlin'. I spooked you just now. That's why you dropped your glass. You don't want me gettin' married."

"Why would I care if you got married?" she retorted. "As you may recall, I'm married."

His smile grew. "We both know that is entirely different. How many years has it been since you've seen Matt?"

Daisy scowled.

"You're the one getting married?" Aunt Emily interjected. "I thought you said that it was your brother's
wedding."

"It is Bobby's wedding." Rick gave Daisy an arch glance.
"And his charming bride has decided on a red velvet cake."

Beulah's mouth sagged open. Only slightly less surprised, Daisy looked at Bobby. She didn't have to ask him
if it was true. His telltale cheeks were as red and swollen
as a pair of overripe tomatoes. She turned to Aunt Emily.

"Since when did you become a wedding coordinator?"

"Don't be snide, Ducky," Aunt Emily chastised her. "I
haven't been keeping secrets if that's what you're suggest-
ing. Rick just told me about it tonight. That's why he came
over. He wanted to know if they could have it here, on the
back porch."

Daisy blinked at her.

"I haven't given an answer yet if that's your next question," she went on. "I was waiting to talk to you girls—and
your momma, Ducky—about it first. It's your home too.
You should have a say in any events that take place here."

That was a bunch of baloney. Aunt Emily scheduled
all sorts of events without discussing them with anybody,
and there was no reason why she shouldn't. It was her inn,
after all. She could hold every wedding in the Commonwealth of Virginia on the back porch if she wanted to.
Except this particular wedding was different. It involved
the Balsam brothers. And when Daisy met Aunt Emily's
shrewd blue eyes, she knew that the hesitation in this instance was solely for her benefit.

"It's very thoughtful of you, Aunt Emily." She gave an appreciative nod. "But I'm sure that my momma wouldn't object. She likes any party with lots of pretty flowers. I'm more concerned about you. You do realize that you just held the prospective groom at gunpoint?"

"These things sometimes happen, Ducky."

Although the words were light and jocular, the shrewd blue eyes were earnest. Daisy could see that Aunt Emily was looking for confirmation. Before making any commitment to Rick and Bobby, she wanted her approval. Daisy was admittedly a little taken aback by the idea of a Balsam wedding at the Tosh Inn. Her own wedding reception had been held there, but that was a long time ago. And she certainly didn't want Rick to think that she had any qualms because of him.

She nodded at Aunt Emily again. "The bride would probably be grateful if you didn't pull out your Remington during the middle of the ceremony."

Beulah snickered. "Unless it's a shotgun wedding."

"It can't be that," Rick remarked. "Bobby only met her two weeks ago."

"Two weeks!"

"It was love at first sight. Isn't that right, Bobby?"

Bobby and his tomato cheeks grinned.

"You can't be serious." Beulah gave a derisive snort. "Love at first sight?"

"Not a believer? How about you, Daisy?" Rick said it in a taunting tone, but he didn't wait for her to respond. "Bobby sure believes in it. Him and Laurel both, at least that's what she says."

"Laurel?" Beulah frowned. "That's who the mysterious Laurel is? Your fiancée?"

Bobby went on grinning like an arthritic old hound that had found a comfortable hearth with a nice warm fire to curl up in front of.

Beulah's nose twitched. "So maybe she's the one who stole the cream cheese. Maybe she wanted to make her own red velvet cake."

It was Bobby's turn to frown. "I told you already. Laurel's up in the woods. She had nothin' to do with the cream cheese."

"The cream cheese?" Rick echoed.

"Didn't Daisy tell you about the bakery?" Beulah replied.

"She said three guys broke in, and Brenda stabbed one of 'em."

"They also stole a hundred pounds of cream cheese."

"Ninety pounds," Daisy corrected her.

"Ninety pounds of cream cheese?" Rick shook his head slowly, then he looked at Daisy. "The bakery's not open tomorrow, is it?"

"No," she answered tersely.

"Good. That will give me a chance to improve your security."

"I don't need you to improve my security."

"Considering what happened today, you could obviously use some better locks on the doors and windows."

"Mind your own business, Rick," she said.

"Your business is my business, darlin', if you're making my brother's wedding cake."

He was lucky that she had dropped her glass on the rug, because if it had still been in her hand, Daisy would have chucked it at his head.

CHAPTER
5

"I really appreciate you giving up your Sunday afternoon to come here, Connor," Beulah shouted toward the utility closet at the back of the salon. "Especially since it's getting worse. Yesterday it was two feet. Today it's three. By tomorrow, the water might be halfway up to the ceiling."

"Can't let ya get flooded out," Connor hollered back. "The missus wouldn't like that. She's not happy when her hair's no good. 'Course, it always looks good to me."

Daisy smiled. "His wife sure has him well trained."

Beulah nodded. "The secret to a happy marriage is proper training."

"Says the woman who is single and has never been in a relationship longer than six months."

"I was quoting Aunt Emily."

"Also a woman who's single and hasn't been in a relationship in decades."

"Maybe so, but that doesn't make it any less true."

"It's not something I can argue either way," Daisy remarked flatly. "My marriage certainly hasn't been full of bliss and tranquillity."

"At least yours was okay for a while. I doubt this crazy thing between Bobby and Laurel will last more than a week."

"But you forget—it's already lasted two weeks!"

Beulah laughed. "Can you imagine having Bobby Balsam as your husband?"

"Lordy, no." After a moment, Daisy shrugged. "There are worse people in the world, though. Bobby isn't mean or violent."

"And he has access to all of Rick's lovely money."

Daisy let out a low whistle. "I hadn't thought of that."

"No? It was the first thing that went through my mind."

"Do you think Laurel knows? About how much Rick's got?"

"I wouldn't be surprised. It's not too hard to find out, especially if you're interested. And that nonsense about love at first sight? Talk about setting off alarm bells. Love at first sight with Bobby looking like a scruffy goat wanderin' down from the hills?" Beulah scoffed. "More like love at first sight with Rick's immense bank account and land holdings."

"You could be right."

It was Beulah's turn to shrug. "Or I could be wrong. Laurel might be just the same as Bobby. She might look like a scruffy goat wanderin' down from the hills too."

"I wonder what Rick thinks of her. He did call her a charming bride."

"I'd give him credit for being a little less weasel-like than usual by asking Aunt Emily if they could have the wedding at the inn, except I doubt it was for Bobby or Laurel's benefit. I would wager that Rick did it as an excuse to see you."

Wrinkling her nose in response, Daisy pulled out a small red clay circle from her pocket. "Speaking of wagers, what does this look like to you?"

Beulah took the object from her and turned it over in her hands. "It looks like a poker chip."

"I agree. Now look at the center."

"Is that some kind of engraving?" Squinting at it, Beulah rubbed the center of the chip with her thumb. "Are those initials?"

"*TS*—or at least that's how I read it."

"Do we know a TS?"

"Not that I can think of."

Beulah frowned. "Don't tell me that you're considering taking up gambling?"

"Of course not! Do you remember how bad it got with Matt? He would lose more in a week than we both earned in six months. And then the really nasty stuff started. The calls in the middle of the night. The threats. I've wondered so many times if that could have been some part of why he left. The gambling and the debts and the—" Daisy broke off, shaking her head, trying as best she could not to dredge up any more painful memories of the past.

"Did you find the chip in Matt's old stuff?" Beulah asked quietly.

"No. I found it yesterday at the bakery, in the kitchen. It was under the wire rack next to the refrigerator."

"Yesterday in the kitchen?" Beulah blinked at her. "Do you think it could be from those men?"

"I do. Brenda said the one she stabbed crashed into the rack after tripping over Blot. My guess is that he dropped it then, or when he fell to the floor."

"But couldn't it have been there before they came?"

"I swept the kitchen myself early that morning. There was no poker chip. And it couldn't possibly belong to Brenda. She doesn't even like betting pennies at pinochle."

Beulah went on blinking at her. "Does Deputy Johnson know about it?"

"You think he'd let me take evidence from a crime scene?"

She gave a little snort. "I'm not sure he's smart enough to even realize it is evidence."

"That's precisely one of the reasons I took it. I don't care if he's with the sheriff's office or not. Sweetie Pies is mine, and Brenda's my friend. I can't be having people stealing from me or scaring the heck out of her without trying to figure out why."

"You can count me in." Beulah rubbed the center of the chip again. "These initials look professionally done."

"They do, don't they? No one did that fiddling with a knife while rocking on their porch swing."

"I hate to ask but . . . did Matt have anything like this?"

"I never saw it if he did. He didn't usually bring home poker chips, or any other kind of counter. It was either a full wallet or an empty one." Daisy sighed. "Mostly empty."

"If those men had cleaned out your cash register," Beulah mused, "or taken something more . . ." She hesitated.

"More marketable and less perishable?"

Beulah nodded. "Then I'd say they were trying to make a quick buck to pay off a debt. But cream cheese?"

"I'll be the first to admit that it's not quite as lucrative as electronics or gold jewelry—"

Daisy was interrupted by the sound of a car parking outside the salon. Beulah quickly handed the chip back to her, and she slipped it into her pocket. In unison they swiveled around on the styling chairs they were sitting in. The front door was propped open by a broom, allowing the water to flow out and tumble down over the stoop in a series of cascades.

A woman in her late twenties walked toward the building. Daisy didn't recognize her, but she knew that she wasn't a client. Beulah didn't make appointments on Sundays. The woman had long black hair, even longer legs, and a thick tan that was rosy enough to be natural. When she saw the water spilling from the salon, she stopped and gazed at it for a moment. Then she looked up and smiled.

"If I had known about this, I would have put on my galoshes."

It was a warm, friendly smile—the type that instantly put a person at ease. Both Daisy and Beulah smiled in return.

"You don't need 'em." Beulah waved at her own bare feet. "The water isn't cold."

"Trust me," the woman laughed, "you don't want me to take off my shoes! I've been wearing the same pair of hiking boots for three straight weeks, and my toes look like they've been chewed on by piranhas."

"Hiking boots?" Daisy thought of the swarm of hiking boot–clad customers that she had had in the bakery over the past week. "Does that mean you're part of the hunt?"

She nodded. "I'm one of the organizers, actually."

Beulah frowned. "I didn't know it was a hunt. I thought it was some sort of meeting. Isn't only archery open right now?"

"It's not that kind of hunt," the woman replied. "We're geocaching. And that's why we scheduled the event now instead of a month or two later, when all the seasons are open."

Daisy nodded back at her. "If you rustle through the

woods then, there's a pretty good chance that somebody who has had a few too many beers and feeling a bit jumpy might mistake you for a bear or turkey."

"It wouldn't be the first time that a geocacher got shot for poking his head around a tree and not wearing fluorescent orange in fall."

"A geo-what?" Beulah said.

"Geocacher. Different groups in different places have their own little variances," the woman explained, "but basically geocaching is the grown-up version of hide-and-seek outdoors. Somebody puts a logbook—and sometimes a small prize—in a waterproof container and buries or conceals it somewhere. You get clues and try to find the cache using GPS."

"You're doing that around here?" Beulah's frown deepened. "But you can't find anything around here using GPS, not reliably at least. The mountains are always getting in the way."

"It's one of the reasons we picked this area. Great mountains, good hiking trails, and plenty of dark nooks and crannies to use as hiding spots. We have so many experienced participants at this event. The fickle GPS makes it a lot tougher for them."

Daisy remembered what the woman had said a minute ago about wearing the same pair of hiking boots for three straight weeks. "The hunt hasn't been going on for three weeks already, has it?" she asked. "I thought it just started last week and had one more week to go."

"It did start last week. And you're right, it ends officially on Friday, assuming that all the caches haven't been located before then. But my brother and I came early to check on the arrangements and make sure everything was set up properly for the hunt."

Beulah sucked on her teeth. "Hunt doesn't sound right. It doesn't . . . fit."

The woman chuckled. "That's what Bobby says too. According to him, you can't call it a hunt unless somebody's bagged an eight-point buck."

"Bobby?" Daisy gaped at her in surprise. "Bobby Balsam?"

She answered with a nod. "I'm sorry. I should have introduced myself earlier. I'm Laurel. Laurel Page."

This time Daisy gaped at Beulah. This was Laurel? Bobby's Laurel? She didn't look at all like a scruffy goat wandering down from the hills. On the contrary, she looked much more like a sleek, spruce Thoroughbred trotting confidently around the track.

Laurel chuckled harder. "I can see what you're thinking. You have the exact same expression Chris—my brother—did when I told him I was going to marry Bobby. I might just as well have said I was moving to Antarctica for the rest of my life to study frozen algae. I'm not delusional. I know that Bobby and I have our differences. I also know that we're going to have some troubles now and again. But together, we're like peas and carrots. And I happen to love carrots."

The comparison of Bobby to a carrot made Daisy smile. "Well, welcome to Pittsylvania County then. I'm Daisy, and this is Beulah."

"How do you do?" Laurel replied with well-mannered politeness. "It's a pleasure to meet you both. I would come inside and shake your hand, but . . ." She gestured toward the water on the floor. "I've heard so much about you."

"I bet!" Beulah muttered. "Don't believe a word that comes out of the weasel's mouth."

"The weasel?"

"She means Rick," Daisy explained. "And she's joking."
Beulah snorted.

Laurel's brow furrowed. "I don't understand. I thought you and Bobby and Rick grew up together. Aren't you all old friends?"

"Friends!" Beulah snorted again.

"But Bobby told me such nice things about you. Rick too."

It took Daisy some effort to restrain herself from snorting along with Beulah. Clearly Rick and Bobby had put on quite a show for Laurel, making it sound like the four of them were terrific pals.

"We did all grow up together," she responded lightly, not wanting to open the door to a full-blown discussion regarding their tortuous history. "But since we've known each other for so long, sometimes the line between friends and enemies can get a bit blurry."

The furrows softened. "I can understand that. Although usually I adore Chris, every once in a while he does something that makes me want to rip out his throat with my bare hands."

Daisy grinned. She often felt like ripping out Rick's throat.

Laurel sighed with relief. "I'm so glad I came here. I wasn't sure if I should. But I really wanted to thank you for agreeing to make my cake. I know it's such short notice."

"Bobby said you need it for this upcoming Saturday?"

Her cheeks reddened. "I realize that's not much time. . . ."

"No worries," Daisy assured her. "It's plenty of time. Except I will have to get some new cream cheese."

"New cream cheese?"

She glossed over the remark. It didn't seem good form to tell a blushing bride that the old cream cheese, which would have been used for her wedding cake, had been stolen the day before and a man stabbed to death because of it. "Bobby also said you wanted it to be red velvet. I can make a red velvet groom's cake if you'd like. That way you could have a more traditional white wedding cake."

"What a nice offer!" Laurel exclaimed. "Rick's right. You are sweet as sugar. But to be honest, I'm not much of a traditional girl. I don't plan on wearing a shiny dress with lace or satin. And I told Bobby we should skip the champagne and stick with moonshine instead."

Beulah and Daisy exchanged a glance. That answered one question. Laurel obviously knew about Rick's business.

"So I'd rather have the red velvet cake," she continued. "I hope that's okay?"

"Of course," Daisy replied. "It's your wedding."

"And of course, you're both invited to it," Laurel returned cheerfully. "While we're on the subject of invitations, Chris and I are planning on having a little party tonight. It's nothing fancy, just a barbecue at the campground where most of us are staying. Do you know Fuzzy Lake Campground?"

Daisy nodded.

"Then you'll come? I would love for you to meet my brother and the rest of the group."

Beulah and Daisy exchanged another glance, and this time they both nodded.

"Great! Around seven? We've got nearly all the cabins rented, so we've pretty much taken over the place. You can't miss us."

With a parting smile, Laurel turned on the heels of her hiking boots and walked back to her car. "See you tonight!" she shouted through the open window as she pulled out onto the road, a cloud of gravel and dust flying after her.

There was a brief silence, which Daisy was the first to break.

"I don't care if she is marrying Bobby for Rick's money. I like her."

"Me too!"

"Bobby sure wasn't exaggerating when he told us she was up in the woods."

"Or that she likes his dirty old jeans and boots."

After another short silence, Daisy added, "But I won't be able to stay long tonight. Monday is always my super-early morning at the bakery."

Beulah grimaced in sympathy. "If it makes you feel any better, I switched the appointments I had yesterday to tomorrow, so I won't—"

She stopped as Connor emerged from the utility closet and waddled over to them looking like a short, wide, wet penguin that had eaten some bad fish.

"It's not in here," he said with a glum expression. "The pipes and connectors are all fine."

"Fine? They can't be fine." Beulah pointed at the water.

"It's not in here," he repeated. "It's the line."

"Please tell me that you don't mean the line from the well."

Connor bobbed his chin apologetically, and Beulah groaned.

"Duke and I can start on it in the morning if you want. We got some other folks on the list ahead of ya, but you got it worse than them."

"Thanks, Connor. That's awful nice of you."

He bobbed his chin again. "You may want to tell Emily before we go digging. It's a safe bet that she'll have something to say about it."

Beulah groaned even harder, until Daisy cut her short. Connor's quip reminded her of the poker chip in her pocket, and she pulled it out.

"You wouldn't by any chance know where this comes from, would you, Connor?"

She didn't expect him to have much of a response. Connor was a subdued man of few words who tended to mind his own business. But to Daisy's surprise, he took one look at the chip and nodded.

"Sure do. Duke made a delivery there just yesterday."

"Yesterday?" Beulah echoed. "When I called yesterday you told me Duke went down to Tightsqueeze."

"Yup. That's where he was."

Daisy raised a questioning eyebrow. "Is that what the initials on here stand for? The *TS*? Is that Tightsqueeze?"

"Sure is."

"I thought the initials were for a person," Beulah said.

"So did I," Daisy agreed.

"But Tightsqueeze is a town. Why would a town have a chip?"

Daisy gazed at Connor curiously. "Does it belong to a place in Tightsqueeze? Do you and Duke do plumbing and electrical work for them?"

"I don't go there no more," he replied. "The missus doesn't like it."

"She doesn't approve of gambling?"

Conner frowned. "Gambling?"

"Gambling." Daisy held up the chip as evidence.

"There's no gambling."

It was her turn to frown.

"It's not a counter," Connor explained. "It's a marker."

"A marker?"

"That one's for a jar."

Daisy's mouth opened in astonishment. "You mean it's a—"

"White's a drink. Red's a jelly. And blue's a canning."

"How patriotic," Beulah sneered.

Patriotic indeed. Daisy could only shake her head. A patriotic nip joint.

CHAPTER
6

"So are you going?"

"Where?"

Beulah drummed her fingers impatiently on the steering wheel. "Don't play dumb with me. I know that you're thinking about it. You've been thinking about it ever since Connor told you how to get there."

Daisy answered with a shrug.

"You shouldn't. You really shouldn't go, Daisy. Those places can be scary."

"And you know this because you've been to so many nip joints in your life?"

"I read the news!" Beulah protested. "Last summer they tried to shut one down over in Lynchburg, and three people ended up dead."

"That wasn't a nip joint," Daisy corrected her. "It was one of those slapdash painkiller clinics."

"Close enough."

"Moonshine isn't a prescription drug."

"It is according to Aunt Emily."

That made Daisy laugh. Aunt Emily had a gift for creating superior brandies—particularly her gooseberry brandy—and she loved to refer to them as medicine. In her mind they could cure almost any ailment, at least temporarily if you drank enough of them.

Beulah swerved around a group of vultures clustered along the edge of the highway. "It's not the likker that worries me, Daisy."

"I know. It's the people who might be there."

She nodded. "If you're right, and that chip did come from the man Brenda stabbed—"

"Then the other men—his friends—could be at the nip joint."

"Is it really worth the risk? Sure, you might get some information about them, but you could also meet them!"

"Except I wouldn't know them if I saw them," Daisy countered. "I don't even know if they'd know me."

"We have no idea if they know any of us," Beulah said.

"Rick thinks it was planned—the men wouldn't just randomly come into the bakery during the middle of the day. So I have to assume that they did some sort of surveillance in preparation. They knew how to get in the back door and about the cream cheese."

Beulah clucked her tongue. "Don't get me started on the stupid cream cheese."

"Well, it doesn't matter right now anyway. The nip joint will have to wait. We've got a geocacher barbecue to go to."

"I wonder," Beulah clucked her tongue again before turning into the entrance of the campground, "if any of those geocachers are single."

Fuzzy Lake Campground wasn't actually adjacent to Fuzzy Lake. The two were separated by a mountain and several hundred acres of dense forest. There weren't many campgrounds in Pittsylvania County, primarily because there weren't many tourists, and for the most part the locals already lived in the middle of nature. Recreational vehicles weren't allowed. Neither were campers or trailers. Visitors could choose between a dozen sites to pitch their own tent and twenty rustically outfitted cabins. To some, the amenities might have been considered primitive. There was no swimming pool or media room, and the nearest sit-down restaurant was a solid forty-five-minute drive. But it was a pretty campground—with long paths through pine-scented woods, meadows covered in rainbow carpets of wildflowers, and lots of outstanding opportunities for bird-watching and other wildlife viewing.

Laurel had chosen well. It was a good place for the geocachers to stay during their hunt. They obviously enjoyed being outdoors, and the campground was much better situated than any of the area motels, which were even farther away than the restaurants. Daisy now also understood why the group had been frequenting her bakery since their arrival. Sweetie Pies was without a doubt the closest spot for a hot cup of coffee.

They drove slowly down the stony, snaking road, occasionally catching a glimpse of a red or yellow tent through the trees. The low rays of the setting sun didn't have much strength left. There were more shadows than light.

"It's going to be a pain coming back this way later," Beulah groused. "I hate these pitch-black places at night."

"I hope that Bobby doesn't go walking around here after dark. With his rotten sense of direction, he could easily get turned around and make it halfway over the mountain before dawn."

"But then Laurel could come and rescue him." Beulah tittered.

Daisy laughed with her. "Maybe that's how they met. He was roaming around the countryside in his camouflage— rifle in one hand, jelly jar in the other—drank too much, got miserably lost, and all of a sudden there she was. An angel in hiking boots to help him find his way home."

"So instead of love at first sight, it was actually drunken fatigue!"

"We should really ask her about it. It might be an awfully good story."

"Do you think Bobby will be here?" Beulah said.

"Probably."

"And the weasel?"

"Aw, jeez." Daisy groaned. "I forgot all about Rick."

As they reached the center of the campground, where the cabins were situated, she looked at the vehicles parked along the side of the road. To her relief she saw neither Rick's nor Bobby's pickup.

"Laurel wasn't kidding." Beulah pulled the car onto an open patch of grass. "They have taken over the place."

Ahead of them was a group of about fifty people gathered loosely around a blazing fire pit. Blue and amber flames leapt upward, crackling and popping from exploding pine sap. It was a splendid night for an inferno. The air was damp and chilly, and the sky was clear, with the first few stars just beginning to show themselves. As she and Beulah approached the others, Daisy recognized some of their faces from the bakery. He liked buttermilk doughnuts. She was fond of macadamia nut cookies. They were all eating, mostly hot dogs and hamburgers while passing around mammoth bags of potato chips. There were also a lot of beer cans and what appeared to be wine in translucent plastic cups.

"Oh, good." Beulah sighed. "It's relaxed."

"It's a barbecue at a remote campground on the edge of Appalachia. What did you imagine they would have? Baby quiches and cucumber sandwiches on silver salvers with doilies?"

"No." Beulah scrunched up her nose indignantly. "But I've never been to a party with geocachers before—"

She was interrupted by Laurel, who emerged from the crowd holding a wine bottle in each hand and two plastic cups hanging from the tips of her pinkies.

"Hooray! I'm so happy you came," she exclaimed. "Red or white?"

Daisy took a cup of the red, while Beulah took a cup of the white.

"There's plenty of food over there." Laurel motioned toward a rickety folding table piled with plates, buns, and condiments. "And somewhere . . ." She glanced around. "There he is! Chris? Chris!"

A man turned at her shouts. The family resemblance was immediately evident. He had the same long legs as Laurel, the same black hair—although cut short—and the same warm, friendly smile.

As he walked over to them, he bestowed the smile on his sister. "You bellowed?"

"He loves to pick on me," Laurel said to Daisy and Beulah. "It's the price one pays for having a big brother."

Introductions were made. Chris Page was as polite and well mannered as his sister. Daisy found him just as easy to like.

"Laurel told me that she met you today and you were coming tonight." Chris's smile grew as he spoke. "I have to confess I wasn't quite sure what to expect."

Daisy chuckled, understanding full well what he meant. For all he knew, she and Beulah might have looked like a couple of scruffy goats wandering down from the hills too. "Is Bobby here?" she asked.

Laurel shook her head. "He had to help Rick with something this evening."

Silently, Daisy cheered. Now she could relax.

Chris also shook his head but for a different reason. "I'm having a hard time believing that you and those Balsams come from the same zip code."

"I'll take that as a compliment," Daisy drawled.

"Oh, it's most definitely a compliment," Chris returned suavely.

Beulah gave her a surreptitious nudge with her elbow, and Daisy felt her cheeks flush. If she needed an excuse, she could always blame the heat from the fire.

"Please don't start picking on Bobby." Laurel's tone was one of weary exasperation. "Not tonight, Chris. Not again."

"But he doesn't do anything." Chris shook his head once more, sternly this time. "He just sits around all day in that broken-down trailer, playing with his dogs and cleaning his guns. At least his brother has a job. It may be making illegal hooch, but it's still a business. Or sort of a business—"

Eager to avoid the subject of Rick and his hooch, Daisy interjected, "What do you do for a living, Chris?"

Laurel glanced at her gratefully.

"I teach history at a college up in Maryland."

"You're a professor?" Beulah raised an eyebrow at Daisy. It carried an unmistakable message: *Pay attention to this one! A reputable college professor is a heck of a lot better than a rough-and-tumble moonshiner.*

"What type of history?" Daisy asked, genuinely interested.

"American. Nineteenth-century mostly. I did my
graduate work on the Civil War."

Beulah coughed. "You mean the War of Northern Ag-
gression?"

With a grin, Daisy added, "Or the War for Southern
Independence?"

"The War Between the States," Chris answered diplo-
matically.

"Have you been to Danville?" Daisy said. "It's not far
from here, and as I'm sure you know, it was the last capital of the Confederacy."

"Has he been to Danville?" Laurel moaned. "That's all
he ever wants to do—drive around endlessly in search of
old things. 'Look!'" she cried, parodying her brother in
the manner of a bookish archaeologist. "'This is the outline of some long-forgotten building. Over there is the
spot of a teeny-tiny unmarked battlefield. And here's one
crumbling stone left from a ruined monument'—"

"Thanks, sis. You make me sound about as interesting
as sawdust."

"But it is interesting," Daisy replied. "At least I think
so. When I was little, I used to love driving around on
Sunday afternoons with my daddy. He was a big fan of historical markers, and he turned it into a game for us, to see
how many we could find. We stopped and read every single one. I didn't understand what half of 'em were talking
about, of course. When you're eight years old, every mili-
tary regiment and semi-famous statesman's gravesite
seems pretty much the same."

Chris smiled at her so warmly that Beulah nudged her

again. For all of Beulah's cynicism regarding love at first sight—and every other form of love, for that matter—she was still an inveterate matchmaker.

Topping off their cups with her bottles, Laurel smiled too, giving Daisy the distinct impression that she had a bit of matchmaker in her as well.

"Are there a lot of historical markers in this area?" Chris asked. "I've only seen one. It was for a tavern."

Daisy laughed. "Throughout every century—regardless of world events—the citizens of Pittsylvania County have always enjoyed raising a glass."

He laughed with her. "I would be interested in seeing some of the other markers. . . ."

She took the hint as he hesitated. "I'd be happy to show them to you."

"Would you? I'd really like that."

"My bakery closes at two during the week. Any time after that is fine by me."

"How about Tuesday?" Chris looked over at his sister. "Do we have anything on the schedule for Tuesday afternoon?"

Laurel's nose twitched. "Nothing that can't happen without you."

He turned back to Daisy. "Tuesday then?"

She nodded in agreement.

Shifting slightly closer to her, Chris gestured toward a hewn log bench that was set away from the group. "It's kind of warm so near to the fire. Would you like to go over there?"

Nodding once more, Daisy glanced at Beulah, but she was already sashaying in the direction of several agreeable-looking men. Equally quick to catch a hint, Laurel was also in the process of disappearing into the crowd.

They sat together on the bench for a long time—talking, admiring the night sky, thoroughly enjoying each other's company. When Beulah finally came over and told them that the party was breaking up, it was much later than Daisy had originally planned on going home, but she didn't mind. Spending a pleasant evening with a pleasant man was well worth being a little more tired the next day.

As he walked them to Beulah's car, Chris put his arm around Daisy's shoulders and told her how much he was looking forward to Tuesday. She was looking forward to it too, and for the first time in as long as she could remember, Daisy felt a touch of gratitude toward Bobby. If he hadn't met Laurel, then she would never have met Chris.

CHAPTER 7

Daisy found herself whistling along with the teakettle song of a Carolina wren as she unloaded a heap of supplies from her trunk the following morning in the parking lot of the bakery. The little bird was merrily singing its heart out even though it was barely dawn, and she felt equally auspicious toward the approaching day. There would be plenty of geocaching customers. There would be a delivery of new cream cheese. There would be . . . a strange man standing in front of the bakery door.

Her whistling stopped with a startled squawk. The man was about as wide as the oversize refrigerator in the kitchen. His expression was about as steely too. In his black shirt and black jeans, he looked like one giant, bulging, formidable muscle—the type that ate an entire pound of bacon along with half a dozen lard-fried eggs for breakfast, not one of her petite, heart-healthy blueberry bran muffins.

"Um . . ." Daisy's brow furrowed. He didn't appear to be waiting for Sweetie Pies to open, but she could think of no other legitimate reason for him to be on the premises. "Are you here for the bakery?"

"No, ma'am."

She breathed a small sigh of relief. Although his tone was too stiff to be affable, it wasn't threatening either.

"Can I help you with something?" Daisy asked politely.

"No, ma'am."

"Do you need directions somewhere?" She glanced around for his vehicle but didn't see it.

"No, ma'am."

It was the third time that he had given her the exact same answer, and Daisy was starting to get irritated.

"What do you want then?" she said, less courteously.

"Nothing, ma'am."

At least that was a slight variation, albeit an uninformative one.

"Well, I own this place—" Daisy began.

"I am aware of that, ma'am."

"So if you have no business here, I'm going to ask you to leave."

"I can't do that, ma'am."

She frowned at him. "You can't do that?"

"No, ma'am."

"Would you care to tell me why not?"

"No, ma'am."

"You'd rather have me call the sheriff instead?"

It was his turn to frown, just faintly. "I wouldn't recommend that, ma'am. Mr. Balsam wouldn't like it."

Daisy's irritation promptly swelled like a helium balloon. It wasn't difficult for her to guess which Balsam he was referring to. Bobby never commanded that much respect.

"What's Rick got to do with it?" she snapped.

"I'm only following Mr. Balsam's orders, ma'am."

"His orders?"

"I was told you need protection, ma'am."

She blinked at him in surprise. "I need protection?"

"Yes, ma'am."

"Protection from what exactly?"

"Mr. Balsam didn't specify, ma'am."

In an effort to restrain herself from calling Rick one of several names that her momma took strenuous objection to, Daisy drew a deep breath. Then she reminded herself that it was far too early in the day to get so exercised about a Balsam brother.

"You can go," she said after a minute. "I don't need protection."

The man didn't respond.

"You can go," Daisy repeated, more sharply. "I don't need protection."

Still no response. She growled.

"You're really beginning to get on my nerves."

"With all due respect, ma'am, I would much rather have you angry at me than Mr. Balsam."

He spoke with such gravity that Daisy knew there was no point in her arguing any further. She could have begged, bribed, cried, and threatened, and it wouldn't have done her a lick of good. Rick not only commanded respect, he could also be extremely intimidating.

"Mr. Balsam directed me to give these to you." The man handed her a ring of glossy gold keys. "He put new locks on the doors and windows last night."

For an instant, Daisy was inclined to throw a fit, but then it occurred to her that perhaps she should be appreciative instead. Laurel had said the reason Bobby didn't come to the barbecue at the campground was because he had to help Rick with something. If she had been spared their company and spent a lovely evening with Chris free from the Balsam brothers' annoying antics as a result of them installing better locks on the doors and windows of her bakery, she had no cause for complaint.

"Well, if you're going to stay," Daisy said, turning toward the supplies that she had unloaded from her trunk, "could you at least help me carry some of this stuff inside?"

The man ended up carrying almost all of it, which was a nice change of pace. He and his enormous biceps also managed to move a work table topped with a thick marble slab that Daisy and Brenda had been trying to reposition for the last month without an inch of success. From a professional standpoint—as Sweetie Pies opened and the morning wore on—the man proved to be an excellent guard. He didn't share any information, not even his own name. He expressed almost no emotion. And he kept a close eye on everybody, while at the same time seeming nearly invisible himself. Best of all in Daisy's view, Brenda found his presence exceedingly reassuring. Over the weekend she had told Daisy repeatedly how worried she was about returning to the bakery on Monday, but after meeting their hulking protector, Brenda went humming into the kitchen, relaxed and happy like a baby kangaroo tucked safely inside its parent's pouch.

Business was even brisker than Daisy had anticipated, and she was so busy filling coffee cups and bagging biscotti that after a while she forgot about the man stationed watchfully in the corner. She jumped when she suddenly heard him speak. Looking over, Daisy found Rick standing beside him, watching her also.

She grimaced. "When did you get here?"

Rick grinned at her. "About a dozen doughnuts ago."

"Now's not a good time, Rick."

"I'll wait," he replied equably, wandering over to the back of the large glass display case and perusing his options.

"Here." She grabbed a piece of waxed paper. "Use this."

The grin grew. "Thank ya, darlin'."

"Just take what you want and get out of the way. I'm working."

He ended up picking two chocolate chip cookies, which didn't surprise Daisy in the least. Just like his whiskey, Rick preferred his food neat and simple. Frilly desserts didn't interest him. He didn't have to wait long for a lull either. All at once the geocachers headed out for their daily adventures, and Sweetie Pies became empty and silent.

As Daisy cleaned the used napkins and stray crumbs from the counter, Rick settled himself on a green vinyl stool across from her.

"If you're expecting me to gush about how grateful I am to you for improving the locks in here," she said, "you're going to be disappointed. I told you to mind your own business."

"And I told you that your business is my business if you're making my brother's wedding cake."

"Keep it up, and Bobby can get his cake from the Dairy Queen."

Rick raised his hands in mock surrender.

"And while we're on the subject of you minding your own business, you can take him," Daisy gestured toward the man still stationed in the corner, "with you when you go."

He shook his head. "That's not happening."

"We don't need a guard, Rick."

"It's just a little extra security, Daisy."

"We don't need a little extra security."

"You want your customers to feel safe, don't you?"

"*My* customers don't need to worry," she replied tartly. "I cook up pastries, not likker."

His gaze narrowed slightly.

"Having a guard around makes it look like Brenda and I've joined the Pittsylvania County mafia," Daisy added.

Rick cocked his head at her. "Never heard of it."

"Sure you haven't," she drawled.

He drew out a brown paper bag the size of a lunch sack and set it on the counter. "This is for you."

She looked at it and then at him, raising a wary eyebrow. "What is it?"

"Open it and see."

Daisy hesitated. Rick was impossible to trust. Leaning forward, she lifted the top of the bag gingerly and glanced inside. The eyebrow went higher.

"Rick—"

"Just another little precaution," he told her.

"I can't accept this."

"Yes, you can."

Daisy looked in the bag again, longer this time. A revolver lay at the bottom. It was a snub-nose Smith & Wesson, nickel with walnut grips—a .38 Chiefs Special.

"I already have a gun," she reminded him.

"I know. Your momma's Colt. But that's for the inn. This is for the bakery."

"I can't accept it," Daisy said once more.

"Yes, you can," Rick repeated.

His tone was uncompromising. She tried to use a light touch.

"But I don't know where it's been," she argued jocularly. "What crimes it may have committed."

He gave her a tolerant sort of half-smile, as though he

were placating a silly toddler. That provoked Daisy enough to pull out the big weapon in her arsenal.

"Matt wouldn't like it. He wouldn't want me taking gifts from other men."

Rick's eyes darkened like a menacing sky before a torrential storm. Just as he was about to unleash his fury, the rusty bell strung up above the front door of the bakery clanked. Grabbing the paper bag, Daisy shoved it hurriedly under the counter. But it turned out that there was no need to hide the sack from the inquisitive scrutiny of a customer. Bobby and Laurel walked in instead.

"G'morning all," the younger Balsam pronounced cheerfully.

"It's past noon," his fiancée corrected him, with a peck on the cheek. Then she turned to the others. "Hi, Rick. Hi, Daisy!"

Daisy greeted her with equal warmth. "Hey there, Laurel!"

Although Rick barely blinked at Bobby and Laurel's arrival, the fact that Daisy and Laurel were acquainted clearly surprised him.

"You two know each other?" he asked, looking back and forth between them. "You've met already?"

"Yes, we've met," Daisy responded dryly. "The world does carry on even when you're not present, Rick."

"I stopped by Beulah's salon yesterday to introduce myself," Laurel explained. "And we were all at the barbecue last night. That was a good time, wasn't it?"

Daisy grinned. "Best time I've had in a long time."

Laurel grinned back at her. "Chris said the exact same thing."

"Too bad we didn't go," Bobby whined to his brother. "It sounds like it was fun."

Busy glaring at Daisy, Rick didn't answer. She ignored him.

"So you aren't together with your fellow geocachers today?" she said to Laurel.

The grin faded. "Bad news there. Chris and I found out a couple of hours ago, and he's breaking it to the rest of the group now: the event is over."

"All the caches have been found?"

"No. We had to call off the hunt. We were kicked out."

"Kicked out?" Daisy squinted at her. "I thought you were on public land."

"We were, but it's been closed."

"I told her that was a load of hogwash," Bobby protested. "They should just ignore it."

"We can't ignore it," Laurel replied with an air of patient forbearance, giving him another peck on the cheek. "It's the whole area around Fuzzy Lake, and that's where the final caches are located."

Daisy was puzzled. "I've never heard of anyone closing that area before."

"From what I understand, it's a sort of emergency measure. The state biologist who I talked to this morning said they needed to block all access immediately. Apparently there are bat colonies living in the caves by the lake, and they discovered a fungus . . ." Laurel paused. "I can't remember what he called it. 'White' something."

"White-nose syndrome?" Daisy suggested.

"That's it!" Laurel nodded. "He told me that they found it on the bats in one of the bigger caves, and they're afraid it will spread to the others. I guess it's lethal to them."

"Extremely lethal," Daisy agreed. "It's killed more than ninety percent of some infected colonies. A lot of the caves along the Virginia–West Virginia border have been shut off in the hopes of containing it. They're pretty sure the fungus is transmitted bat to bat by contact in shared hibernation spots, but they don't want to take any chance that the clothing or equipment from people might contribute to the spread."

"You know so much about it—are you a spelunker?" Laurel asked her.

"No. I don't go digging in caves," Daisy said. "But my daddy was a farmer, and he taught me about the many benefits of bats at a young age. They're fantastic insect eaters, which means fewer pesticides, higher yields in the field, and lower costs at the grocery store. Great for agriculture, the environment, and consumers all around. Even moonshiners and their precious corn," she added under her breath, with a sideways glance at Rick.

He didn't appear to hear her. He was looking at Laurel.

"Well," Laurel responded, "beneficial insect eaters or not, the bats and their fungus have definitely put an end to our hunt. I've requested permission to go into the area and collect the remaining caches."

"Why bother?" Bobby muttered. "They're not hurting anybody. I say leave 'em where they lie."

Laurel's patient forbearance reappeared in the form of a gentle smile. "I can't just leave them. That would make me an awfully bad geocacher. It would be like dumping trash on a hike or not cleaning up a campsite."

Bobby nuzzled against her shoulder like a tractable puppy that was in the process of being housebroken. Daisy couldn't keep from chuckling. Laurel was right. Together she and Bobby were like peas and carrots. Odd as it was, they did seem to make a good match, at least temperament-wise. She glanced again at Rick, curious whether he thought so too. She found him still looking at Laurel. Ordinarily Daisy wouldn't have paid much attention to it. Rick never failed to admire an attractive woman. But in this instance—considering that the attractive woman was soon to be his brother's wife—he was admiring her a little too long and a little too intently. It made Daisy wonder. She still didn't know how Bobby and Laurel had met. Perhaps Rick had met Laurel first. She couldn't remember a time when the Balsam boys had ever been interested in the same girl.

The rumble of a truck down the road reminded Daisy that she was still waiting for her cream cheese delivery. "Does the hunt ending so soon have any impact on the timing of the wedding?" she asked, thinking of the red velvet cake that she was supposed to make.

"Not a bit. We're still full steam ahead for Saturday." Laurel squeezed Bobby's arm. "That's the good news in all of this. Now I'll have more time to focus on the wedding. As soon as I get those last caches taken care of, and the rest of the group heads home."

Her words struck Daisy. "Heads home? Is Chris going back to Maryland right away?"

It was Laurel's turn to chuckle. "Of course not. He's really excited about the trip with you tomorrow."

Finally breaking his gaze from Laurel, Rick turned to Daisy. "You have a trip tomorrow?"

"It's not an actual trip," she explained. "I'm just showing Chris some of Pittsylvania County's historical markers."

Rick's jaw twitched. "I think you're right, Bobby. It is too bad that we didn't go to the barbecue last night. It seems everybody there had so much fun organizing sightseeing expeditions."

Daisy scowled at him.

He smirked and with dripping sarcasm imitated what she had said earlier. "Matt wouldn't like it, darlin'. He wouldn't want you showing historical markers to other men."

Pulling out the bag with the revolver, Daisy slammed it down on the counter. "Is this gun traceable? I need to know so that I can dispose of it properly after I shoot you."

The burly man in the corner took a step forward. Although he was ostensibly there to guard Daisy, Brenda, and the bakery, Rick's protection evidently took precedence over all else. Rick raised his hand, and the man stopped.

"No worries, Caesar," Rick drawled. "Daisy's just playing around. She wouldn't ever shoot me."

"Famous last words," she retorted.

"Is there . . ." Laurel frowned at the sack. "You don't actually have a gun in there, do you?"

Daisy would have answered in the affirmative, until she saw Bobby's face. It was contorted in horror like he was about to be stung by a thousand hornets. Apparently his fiancée wasn't quite as fond of firearms as he was, at least not those sitting unlocked and immediately accessible on Sweetie Pies' counter in a brown paper sack.

Judiciously removing the bag from sight, Daisy switched to a more pleasant subject, one that had more to do with Chris and absolutely nothing to do with Rick. "So if the rest of the group is leaving, will you still be staying at the campground?" she asked Laurel. "Because if you're interested, you could come to the inn. It's very comfortable, and I know that Aunt Emily—she's the owner—would love to have you."

"I couldn't leave poor Chris out there all alone," Laurel objected.

"I meant him too, of course. There's plenty of room."

Rick coughed. "How convenient."

"It would be convenient," Daisy returned, feigning the expression of an innocent lamb who was in no way referring to the intriguing possibility of having Chris's bedroom just a few short steps down the hall from her own bedroom. "Since the wedding is going to be at the inn, you'd save yourself a lot of driving."

"That's true." Laurel appeared thoughtful.

"It's a great plan!" Bobby proclaimed with enthusiasm. "I don't like the idea of you being at the campground with nobody else around."

"Chris is there," she reminded him.

"The inn isn't as far away." Bobby stuck out a pouty lip. "I'll be able to see you more."

"But the campground is so much closer to the caches," Laurel responded pragmatically. "I'll be able to retrieve them that much quicker."

"That decides it then," Rick said. "Clean up from the campground, and when you're done, go to the inn with your brother."

He spoke with such definitive firmness that it ended the discussion on all sides. Daisy looked at him in surprise. Why did Rick care whether—or when—Laurel and Chris were at the campground or the inn? He looked back at her with an unmistakably devious gaze. It sent a warning chill snaking down her spine. Rick had an agenda, and there was always trouble when Rick had an agenda.

CHAPTER
8

If Rick's agenda in any way included keeping Daisy and Chris from their scheduled expedition, it didn't work. The next day Chris arrived at the bakery just as Daisy was putting the finishing touches on a grand banana pudding.

"Wow." His eyes widened like those of a kid holding a crisp fiver in front of an ice cream truck. "That looks awesome."

Daisy smiled to herself. It was nice whenever someone admired her creations, but it was especially nice if that someone also happened to be a well-groomed, well-educated, well-employed male who was just plain interesting.

"Could we skip the markers," Chris said, "and eat instead?"

"If you like, but this pudding isn't ready. It's got to chill overnight."

"Tomorrow then?"

That made Daisy smile even more. He was asking for a second date before the first one had barely begun.

"The pudding won't be here tomorrow afternoon," she told him.

"So we'll have it for breakfast."

Daisy felt her cheeks warm. Chris Page was a bit of a flirt. Apparently that was another thing he had in common with his sister. Laurel had to be a bit of a flirt too, considering that she and Bobby were getting married after knowing each other for a whopping two weeks.

"I'm afraid the pudding is already spoken for," Daisy replied lightly. "It's going to the Pittsylvania Historical Society."

"The county has a great history of pudding?"

"No." She laughed. "They're having a lecture. They've been having a lot of teas and lectures lately—as fundraisers. The pudding is my contribution to the cause."

"That is awfully nice of you. It's often been a topic of debate between me and my colleagues."

"What has?"

"If more citizens had contributed banana puddings, would the Confederacy have fared better?"

Daisy laughed harder. "I guess that teaches me for talking about a historical society with a history professor."

"You can talk about whatever you want," Chris responded smoothly, "as long as you don't tell me that anything else is already spoken for."

He could have meant the nectarine torte that was sitting on the work table alongside the banana pudding, but this time there was more than a bit of flirting in his tone, giving Daisy the distinct impression that he was referring to her.

She hesitated. Although she certainly hadn't dated much since Matt left, she always made a point of being open and honest about the fact that she was still legally married. It wasn't usually an issue with the local boys, because in many ways rural southwestern Virginia was a small place. Everyone found out quickly—and easily—who was attached, who was unattached, and who was having dalliances at the motel over in Gretna. But today Daisy didn't feel like sharing. It would have spoiled the mood somehow. If not for Chris, then at least for her. Matt McGovern was never an enjoyable subject.

Evidently not requiring an answer, Chris wandered to the window. "It's kind of ironic, really. Now that the geocaching is done, the weather has turned perfect. Sun shining. Good temperature. Last week it was boiling hot, freezing cold, or pouring down rain—sometimes all three in the same day."

"I'm sorry you had to cut the hunt short," Daisy sympathized.

"I'm not. Truth be told, I'm glad that it's over. It's been a pile of work from start to finish, too much juggling."

"Well, now you can relax." She picked up the pudding and carried it to the refrigerator. "And enjoy the wedding."

"Relax?" Chris snorted. "How relaxed could you be if you were about to be related to those Balsams?"

"Oh, Bobby's not such a bad guy. A little rough around the edges, of course, but he seems to really adore your sister."

"And Rick?"

Rick was a decidedly different story. Daisy remembered his devious gaze from yesterday. Yes, he was going to be trouble. Somewhere. Somehow. But definitely before the big event. She had no doubt about that.

"Let's just hope," she said, carefully sliding the nectarine torte on the shelf below the pudding, "you don't see much of Rick Balsam this week."

Chris turned from the window. "I can't imagine that he regularly visits historical markers."

Daisy chuckled at the idea. "There's only one that would interest him. Clement Hill. In honor of Captain Benjamin Clement, first maker of gunpowder in Virginia."

"We better skip that one then—be on the safe side."

They ended up skipping quite a few of them, mostly because Chris was right about the weather. It was a beautiful day to be outside. An azure sky. A soft breeze. The sort of day that made you want to spread out a blanket and watch fluffy clouds in the shape of animal crackers float by. And that's precisely what Daisy and Chris did. They pulled off the road at the third marker and settled themselves down on the former site of a Revolutionary War–era blacksmith shop turned debtors' prison. The grass beneath them was warm. The smell of French lavender drifted over from a nearby meadow. Chris's chest became a comfortable pillow for an afternoon nap.

When they woke up, the sun was descending in a hazy golden glow as the afternoon was switching to evening. Chris suggested an early dinner, and Daisy in turn suggested pizza. It was the only option for some distance, unless chips and soda from the gas station were included on the list. The nearest town was Tightsqueeze, although it was hard to consider it a town. It was more a sad little cluster of dilapidated stores, most of which were shuttered.

"Fine by me," Chris agreed. "But seriously? It's called Tightsqueeze?"

"If you think that's a good one, head down Highway 40 and you'll hit Climax. Try having that as a mailing address."

His brow wrinkled with a mixture of amusement and concern. "Poor Laurel. We used to be so close, but we haven't seen much of each other over the last year or two. I keep trying to figure out where her head is. I don't think she has any clue what she's gotten herself into."

Daisy couldn't agree with him there. Laurel seemed pretty smart and aware to her. But then again, Chris obviously knew his sister much better than she did. Daisy did wonder whether the happy couple would remain in the area long-term. She had a hard time picturing Bobby in the glitz and speed of the big city. It was like trying to slap a rusty horseshoe on a Ferrari.

Leaving the historical marker behind, they drove toward Tightsqueeze on a small road that Daisy couldn't remember ever having traveled before. A couple of miles outside of town, they passed an even smaller side road with a tilting brown street sign that caught her attention— COTTON PATCH ROAD.

"Do you mind if we turn here?" she said.

"A shortcut?" Chris asked.

"Not exactly. Something I need to see."

It was a good thing that he didn't object, because Daisy would have turned regardless. Her initial inclination upon seeing the sign had been to eat a quick dinner, then drop Chris off at the campground and return alone, but her curiosity was simply too great to wait. And there was something about that sign and that road suddenly appearing before her the way that they did. It seemed like an omen— just hopefully not a bad one.

A few hundred yards down Cotton Patch Road, the asphalt ended and was replaced by a pitted combination of mud and stones. To keep the bumping to a minimum,

Daisy steered the tires into a pair of densely compacted ruts. After a few hundred yards more, the road narrowed to the point where it was only wide enough to hold about a car and a half, or one bigger pickup. If another vehicle approached, she would have to pull over onto the scrubby shoulder, which was mostly a sloping ditch filled with towering weeds.

Chris surveyed the surrounding fields. They were yellowed and dried after being harvested a month or so earlier. Remnant of cornstalks stood in jagged rows. "We're not going for pizza anymore, are we?"

"We are," Daisy answered somewhat absently, "except I have to find something first."

"Find something?" he returned dubiously. "Like what? A crow? A haystack?"

He had a point. The fields did stretch out in every direction in an endless, meandering fashion. But he was thinking urban, not country. He equated empty fields with empty land. Daisy, on the other hand, equated empty fields with quiet, secluded land that was the perfect spot for a nip joint.

The directions that Connor Woodley had given her at the salon were simple—go to Tightsqueeze, two miles west of town was Cotton Patch Road, follow it to the red rooster. There she would find the home of the clay chip that she had discovered.

Daisy hadn't intended on going there tonight, but the timing was so fortuitous. She was west of Tightsqueeze. She had stumbled upon Cotton Patch Road. Now all she had to do was follow it to the red rooster. Except she wasn't entirely sure what Connor meant by that. Was it a name? She had never heard of a house or property called the Red

Rooster. Could it be some type of an emblem? Or maybe it was an actual rooster? This was farm country, after all—chickens aplenty.

There was no question that she was looking for a private building. Nip joints were not public. They didn't advertise with billboards or flashing neon placards. They weren't located in strip malls between the dollar store and the Laundromat. On the contrary, they were tucked away as discreetly as possible. A little residence on a tranquil street. A slightly larger garage or shed, perhaps. Inconspicuous and low-key. That was of prime importance. No cause for attention. No reason for the law to come knocking. Just 'shine.

She couldn't have asked for a better hour of the day for her visit. It wasn't dark out yet, so she could still see where she was going. At the same time, it was late enough for the nip joint to be open, or at least she thought it was. Although Daisy didn't personally have much experience with such places, her husband had been fond of one in Danville. For better or worse, nip joints were neither new nor a novelty in Appalachia.

At every bend in the road she slowed in anticipation of a sign, but there was no red rooster—live or otherwise. The rolling fields on both sides continued, broken up occasionally by a low wire fence. Mottled dots of cattle moved off in the distance. Deer browsed on the edge of a pine windbreak.

"If you tell me what you're looking for," Chris volunteered, "maybe I could help."

Daisy's mouth opened, but she found herself reluctant to use the phrase *nip joint*. It sounded so horribly hillbilly, especially after the comment that Chris had made regarding his poor sister not having a clue what she was getting into. Daisy wanted him to have a good impression of her and Pittsylvania County. It was one thing to appreciate the history of the area, which he obviously did. It was quite another to be driven around the outskirts of nowhere in search of a possible shanty serving up white lightning.

"I'm all for admiring the scenery," Chris shifted in his seat, "only . . ."

He had had enough of dried cornstalks. That was clear. The pleasant, intimate mood from earlier was now gone. Although they both might have been thinking about markers, Daisy was pretty confident that only hers was in relation to likker. She would have to come back some other time to continue her search. Maybe with Beulah instead.

"I'll turn around at the next opportunity," Daisy said.

It was difficult to use the shoulder for that purpose, because the ditch had grown steep, but she did see what appeared to be a tractor road up ahead. That would work much better. Suddenly a thick cloud of dust rose before them. Daisy squinted at it. A large silver pickup emerged, driving fast. She watched it throw up stones and more dust as it tore onto the tractor road. A coincidence? It was a mighty strange coincidence then, considering that it was the first vehicle they had encountered the whole way.

She slowed down in case the truck intended on turning around too. It didn't. It went racing along the tractor road. Daisy slowed further. The dust swirled away from the entrance of the road, and she stopped. At the far corner—on a flat-topped rock the size of a small coffee table— stood a red rooster.

The rooster was actually more green than red. It looked to be the upper portion of an old barn weathervane. Worn and battered by decades of wind and rain, the copper had developed an attractive verdigris. Daisy's first thought was how much Aunt Emily would have liked it. She was extremely fond of folk art and spent countless hours perusing the neighborhood antique shops and estate auctions in search of it.

As she pulled onto the tractor road, Daisy debated with herself. Turn around or go straight? She was sorely tempted to choose the latter. She was, after all, already there. Her date with Chris was already washed up. And if the silver truck could be used as any sort of a guide, the nip joint was already serving its wares. She wouldn't spend all evening there, just long enough to take a good look at the place, see for herself if the clay chip in her pocket really did equal a jelly jar of corn whiskey, and possibly nose around for some information regarding the men who had broken into the bakery.

Making up her mind to stay the course, she glanced at Chris. He was frowning but didn't say a word. Should she explain? How much should she explain? Daisy wasn't overly eager to tell him that her dear friend and business partner had stabbed a man to death last Saturday in Sweetie Pies' kitchen. It sounded, well, odd. Homicide—justified as it may have been in this particular case—was certainly not the most romantic of topics, especially since Daisy still had hopes for a second date. Murder in relation to the theft of cream cheese seemed like a conversation much better left for the third or fourth date.

She trailed after the cloud of dust. The truck itself was no longer visible. It was going much too fast for her to keep up, at least from a comfort standpoint. The tractor road was even rougher than Cotton Patch Road had been, and

Daisy figured that if she was going to force Chris to keep her company, then she should do it without turning his insides to apple sauce.

"You won't be stuck out here for long," she promised him. "I just need a few minutes."

He started to respond, but they hit a depression that sent them flying in their seats and the car swerving. The road had changed to crumbling dirt—dirt and potholes. The dirt was comparatively smooth, but the potholes were big enough to hold bowling balls. Daisy avoided them as well as she could, anxious to keep her automobile and its axles in one piece. It was like skirting land mines.

Chris didn't speak again. He was obviously annoyed, and Daisy couldn't blame him. She was annoyed too—with the road, with Connor Woodley, and mostly with herself, for following the road and Connor's directions. She was beginning to think that Connor didn't have a clue what he was talking about. The clay chip wasn't a marker. The initials on it didn't stand for Tightsqueeze. It had not the slightest connection to a nip joint. And wherever Duke had made a delivery, it wasn't on this road.

What kind of deliveries was Duke making out here anyway? Plumbing and electrical? There was no plumbing or electrical for miles, at least not that Daisy could see. Aside from the silver truck that had disappeared long ago, there was no one around—not a single sign of life or land ownership. Even the entrance to the tractor road had been empty. No gate, no chain, no PRIVATE PROPERTY or NO TRES-PASSING postings. If anyone was drinking, gambling, or just plain wandering around that stretch of acreage, there wasn't any evidence of it. Just a lot of dirt and one green-red rooster perched on a rock.

Wishing that she had never noticed Cotton Patch Road, Daisy looked for a wider, flatter spot to make a U-turn. The car dipped down between two squat hills. When it rose on the opposite side, she slammed on the brakes.

She had caught up with the silver truck. It was parked on the edge of a field next to a dozen more trucks. There were also about half a dozen cars. None of the drivers was present. But two other men were. They were standing smack in the middle of the tractor road, holding a pair of shotguns pointed straight at her.

CHAPTER
9

The men were good ol' country boys, lanky and unshaven, with sunburned skin and tousled hair. Their uniform was standard—blue jeans, work boots, and raggedy shirts, all with an assortment of multicolored stains. Their shotguns weren't quite as standard. They were Mossbergs. Matte black, 12-gauge, pump action, pistol grip.

Those were not hunting guns. Those were security guns. With no stock, they were short and narrow like a baseball bat, perfect for concealing under a trench coat. Except in this instance, no one was wearing a coat and the guns weren't concealed in the slightest. They were staring Daisy right in the eye.

With her fingers wrapped tightly around the steering wheel, she weighed her options. She couldn't go forward. The men were completely blocking the road. Nor could she turn around. She could drive backward, but she wasn't so sure she wanted to try that, not with the way the men were holding the guns—waist high, one hand on the grip and the other on the slide. It was a fighting stance. There was no doubt about that. Daisy also had no doubt about who would win the fight. The Mossbergs, not her.

There was a long pause, with everybody warily watching everybody else. Chris didn't move or make a sound. Finally Daisy shifted the car into "park" and turned off the engine. It seemed to her to be the most prudent choice. It gave the impression of calm innocence. She would get out and peaceably talk to the men. She would explain the situation with a cute little story about driving around in circles, ending up utterly lost. And then—with a bit of luck—she and Chris would be allowed to go on their merry way, without any further involvement of the Mossbergs.

Slowly, Daisy opened the car door. In unison both men pulled back the slide and chambered a shell. It was a sharp, painful sound. She winced.

"Hey there." Standing up, Daisy forced her heartiest Southern twang. "I haven't a clue where we are or how we got here, but I'm hopin' y'all can help. We're tryin' to get to the pizza parlor over in Tightsqueeze."

She held her breath as she looked down the pair of barrels. What a lovely way to end the date—and the day.

"Sweetheart, ya ain't nowhere near Tightsqueeze. And I reckon ya know it."

They chuckled. Daisy tried to think of a witty response but failed. She glanced over at Chris, hoping that he might make a helpful contribution. He didn't. He just went on sitting in the car like a mute, moldy sack of onions. She assumed that he was suffering from a certain degree of shock. This wasn't the historical, theoretical study of firearms that he was accustomed to inside the protective walls of higher education. This was the practical, everyday use of such weapons out on the hinterlands.

The men continued chuckling. It was with such giddiness that Daisy began to wonder whether they were slightly drunk. She remembered the clay chip in her pocket and pulled it out. The men recognized it instantly.

"If ya got that, sweetheart, what in tarnation are ya waitin' for?" one of them said. "Go 'head." He motioned an elbow toward the line of trucks.

Daisy turned to where he was gesturing. Just beyond the trucks she could see the gray corner of a roof. It appeared to belong to a building, which she couldn't see. Neither the roof nor the building had been visible from her car.

"But ya can't stay parked where ya are," the other man added. "Ya gotta get outta the road."

Climbing back into her car just as slowly as she had climbed out, Daisy deliberated what to do next. Clearly she was in the right place. Connor Woodley did know what he was talking about after all. This was where the chip had come from. So was the building with the gray roof the nip joint? She couldn't be sure unless she went there.

Daisy restarted the engine and crawled off the road onto the grass. Should she go there? She had passed the first test—the armed guards. Her concern was whether there would be any more tests. But what other tests could there possibly be? This wasn't a Napa Valley vineyard. Corn whiskey enthusiasts didn't hold double-blind taste comparisons. They drank their likker. They didn't play with it or dress it up in ribbons and bows.

There was also the issue of Chris. Daisy glanced at him again. He was gazing blankly through the windshield like a salmon lost somewhere downstream. She couldn't even begin to guess what he was thinking. Should she encourage him to go with her, or was it better for him—and her—if he stayed behind?

"I'm going to check out a building by those trucks,"

she said, letting him decide for himself. "Do you want to come along?"

"All right."

Pulling up next to the other cars parked on the edge of the field, Daisy waited for him to continue, but he didn't. That was it. He asked no questions, gave no argument, and offered no observations. There wasn't even any sort of intonation behind his words. Whatever was ticking through Chris's brain, he kept it well hidden. Or maybe he was still in shock. Pistol-grip shotguns did tend to have that effect on the uninitiated. Daisy was just glad that they were no longer pointed in their direction.

The men and their Mossbergs remained in the middle of the tractor road while she and Chris got out and headed toward the line of trucks. They walked at the same speed, neither outpacing the other. Daisy couldn't tell if Chris was keeping up with her or if she was keeping up with him, but regardless, they did it in silence. She would have offered an apology for the unexplained and unscheduled detour, but she was too busy peering in between the trucks, trying to get a better view of what lay on the other side of the line.

Finally she saw it. It was a one-story rectangular building that was made entirely of cinder blocks. They hadn't been painted, so the whole place was a dull gray. A short stovepipe chimney stuck out from each end of the roof. Looking at the building, Daisy realized why it wasn't visible from the road. It sat snuggled down in a gully just like a shorebird huddled low in its nest in the sand. If it had been constructed that way intentionally, it was brilliant. Without the men in the road and the vehicles in the field, the building simply vanished—no hide or hair of it if anyone unwelcome happened to drive by after hours. Very clever for a nip joint.

And it was definitely a nip joint. The front entrance consisted of a double sliding patio door, without the patio. A man stepped out holding two clear glass jars in his palms. They were filled with a colorless liquid. There was no mistaking its identity. It was 'shine. No one in southwestern Virginia would ever use a canning jar as a water bottle.

Daisy thumbed the clay chip in her pocket. Connor had said that the white marker was a drink, the red a jelly, and the blue a canning. She was there, so she might as well collect her jelly jar. That was the only way to talk to someone, and talking to someone was the only way to find out anything about the men who had broken in to her bakery.

She didn't recognize the fellow carrying the canning jars. Clasping the mountain dew to his chest like he was guarding a pair of million-dollar diamonds, he passed her and Chris with a slight nod. Just before they reached the sliding door, Daisy stopped and put her hand on Chris's arm. She didn't know quite what to say, but she wanted to prepare him for what they might find inside. The equivalent of a squalid animal stall came to mind.

"I've never been here before," she began, "but my guess about what we'll see—"

Not waiting for her to finish, Chris pulled open the door. "After you."

His tone was courteous and absolutely nonchalant, void of any nervousness, any bewilderment, or even any curiosity. Daisy blinked at him.

"After you," he said again, blinking right back at her.

Confused, Daisy half stepped and half stumbled through the doorway. She felt like she was missing something—something important—but she was too startled by the

inside of the nip joint to ponder it further. It wasn't anything like she had expected. The interior of the cinder block
building was the complete opposite of its exterior. There
were no dull gray walls or a concrete patio-style floor. No
threadbare sofas or rickety bar stools. No plastic jugs
stacked up in the corner or dirty, chipped glasses lying on
a makeshift table.

The place was fancy, really fancy. It could have easily
been the smoking lounge at a hunt club—a seriously ex-
clusive hunt club. Mahogany paneling lined the walls.
There was gorgeous parquet flooring, burgundy leather
chairs and ottomans, pecan card tables, and an intricately
carved matching pecan bar. Even the twin set of wood-
stoves on either end of the room were spotless and ornate,
with glossy enamel and shining brass.

Irrespective of her limited experience with such lo-
cales, Daisy was fully confident that this was an aberration for nip joints—an extreme aberration—otherwise
her husband would have spent a lot more time at the one
in Danville. If the Pittsylvania Historical Society's accom-
modations had been even half as lavish, it wouldn't have
had any trouble fund-raising, especially if a snort or two
of home brew were served alongside the tea and pudding.

In one regard, however, Daisy had anticipated correctly. The moment that she and Chris entered the building, every activity ceased. Laughter stilled, stories were cut
short, sentences trailed away. Men stopped moving about,
stopped shuffling cards, and stopped drinking. And they
were notably all men. There wasn't a female in the bunch.
Daisy couldn't help but wonder whether that was mere
chance, or downright deliberate.

"That Beulah has got a real mess on her hands."

Daisy's head snapped around. Standing at the edge of the pecan bar—unloading fresh, full jars from a wooden crate—was Connor's hardware store buddy, Duke. Apparently, Duke was making a delivery today in addition to the one that he had made last Saturday, and neither one had any relation to plumbing or electrical.

"I was at the salon all morning working on it," Duke said, with the placidity of a stolid old fisherman who was no longer the least bit staggered by whatever odd or unexpected creature happened to flop into his boat. "Connor thinks it's the line from the well, but I ain't so sure."

"No?" Daisy mumbled. Far less stolid and more staggered, she was trying to process what she was seeing. Since when did Duke dabble in wet goods? She had always considered him a consumer—an inveterate consumer—not a producer.

"We're going to have to talk to Emily," he replied. "We're going to have to do more digging."

"You are?"

"I can't think of a way around it. We gotta take a look at what's going on down there."

Aunt Emily would not be happy. She was very protective of her home—understandably enough—and she wasn't keen on people digging parts of it up. But Daisy couldn't worry about that now. She had to focus. She was at the home of the red clay chip, and she might never get there again.

"Duke," Daisy reached into her pocket, "who do I cash this in with?"

As she held up the chip, a man who at the time of her arrival had been stacking sparkling shot glasses on the opposite end of the bar moved toward a door in the corner.

The door blended in so well with the mahogany paneling that Daisy hadn't noticed it before. The man knocked once—quietly—then slipped through, closing the door quickly behind him. It was done with such furtiveness that it gave her a nervous twinge.

Scratching his mostly bald head, Duke frowned at the chip in Daisy's hand. "How did you get that?"

"What does it matter?" she answered. "I've got it, and I'd like my jelly jar."

"How did you know it's for a jelly?"

Daisy restrained a smile. Although Duke didn't realize it, it was a funny question coming from him, considering that his buddy Connor was the one who had given her the information. But she certainly didn't tattle on him. Without Connor, she wouldn't have a clue about the chip.

"What does it matter?" Daisy repeated. "It's not all hush-hush, is it?"

"Naw." Duke shrugged. "I just ain't seen you in here before."

"Well, I'm in here now."

He glanced at the door in the paneling, as did the other denizens of the nip joint. Daisy's gaze followed theirs. She was curious about what lay behind the door. The man had gone through it so swiftly that she hadn't caught even a glimpse of the other side.

"May I have my jar, please?" she prodded Duke after a minute. "Or will you tell me who I can get the jar from?"

The place wasn't at all like a normal pub or tavern. There wasn't an obvious bartender. Nobody was taking money or pouring drinks. Interestingly enough, there wasn't any money in sight. There were some other markers, though. A couple of white chips on the border of one of the card tables. A blue chip on the arm of a leather chair. But none of the men appeared to be purchasing chips, or even re-deeming them. It was a strange secret society, and Daisy couldn't figure out the rules.

Duke glanced at the door in the paneling a second time. He—along with all the others—seemed to be wait-ing for something, or someone. The boss, perhaps? Maybe it was the door to the owner or manager's office. That would make sense. Then Duke wasn't actually a producer, which made even more sense. He was just a delivery chap. Plumbing and electrical by day, bootlegging at night, evi-dently.

"All right," he said at last. "I'll get you the jar."

Heading toward the center of the bar, Duke squatted down out of sight. As Daisy waited for him to reappear, she looked at Chris. He didn't look back at her. Just like in the car when they had been stopped by the men and their Mossbergs, he didn't move or speak. No one else in the nip joint spoke either, but they were all looking at her. Daisy could see it from out of the corner of her eyes. And she was beginning to feel exceedingly unwelcome.

Clearly there was an issue. These men didn't like strangers—or women—or a nonmember of their strange secret society holding one of their precious little chips in her fingers. But regardless of the reason for it, their gross lack of geniality confirmed to Daisy that she wouldn't learn a thing about the previous holder of the chip, at least not from them, not voluntarily.

Duke surfaced with two jars. He set them down on the bar in front of Daisy. Both were standard-size glass jelly jars with metal screw-top lids. One was filled with a clear, colorless liquid, and the other with a clear, amber liquid.

"Which do you want?" Duke asked her.

Daisy motioned toward the amber jar. "Is it aged, or is it applejack?"

He responded with a derisive snort. "Ain't no applejack here. Ain't no applejack ever here."

Apparently the men were particular about their likker, very particular. If applejack wasn't considered acceptable, then neither would Aunt Emily's gooseberry brandy. Which was a shame, because Aunt Emily made a darn fine gooseberry brandy.

"I'll go with the aged then," Daisy said.

Having selected her jar, she offered Duke the red chip. He didn't take it from her. She offered it again, almost pressing it into his palm, but he moved his hand away. It was as though he wouldn't—or couldn't—touch the chip. Daisy's brow furrowed. She had never seen Duke act so peculiar. He was usually about the same as Connor. He fixed the lamp or the tub, maybe gossiped a little about whoever else's lamp or tub he had recently fixed, and was all-around friendly and helpful. Something was decidedly off.

She didn't know what it was—her being there, or Chris being there, or the boss behind the door in the mahogany paneling being there. Except Daisy did know that she didn't want to make it any worse, especially not for Duke, who she ordinarily liked and was evidently making every effort to fix Beulah's flood. That meant it was time for her to leave. She hadn't gotten what she came for, not a stitch of information about the men who had broken in to Sweetie Pies, but that couldn't be helped.

Sliding the chip back into her pocket, Daisy picked up the amber jar and turned to Chris. "Are you ready to go?"

He was just starting to nod in reply when the door in the paneling suddenly swung open.

"He better as hell be ready to go, because I told him the last goddam time he was here never to come back!"

CHAPTER
10

"The last . . ." Daisy's jaw sagged. "The last time you were here?"

That explained it. That explained everything. Why Chris didn't make a single remark about the cinder block building or what they were doing there. Why he didn't appear surprised—or flummoxed—or the least bit inquisitive about any of it. It turned out that he hadn't been in shock at the sight of the men and their Mossbergs in the middle of the tractor road. He had seen them before. He had seen it all before.

Except that raised a whole new set of questions. If Chris knew the entire time where she was going, why didn't he say so? The farther she had driven down Cotton Patch Road, the more antsy and uncomfortable he had become. Daisy had assumed that it was because he was tired of staring at dried cornstalks. But now it seemed a lot more like he hadn't wanted her to find the red rooster and the tractor road. Why? Why hadn't he just told her that this wasn't his first visit to the nip joint?

Chris didn't respond. He turned toward the opening in the mahogany paneling. Daisy followed suit. Two men emerged. One was the fellow who had knocked on the door earlier and then disappeared behind it. The other was Rick. Daisy's jaw sagged lower.

Paying no attention to her, Rick spoke to Chris. "You better have a damn good explanation."

If he had one, he didn't share it.

Rick's gaze hardened. "Don't act like you don't know what the hell I'm talking about. We both know that you've been here, and we both know that you weren't supposed to come back."

"It wasn't my idea," Chris answered in a sullen tone.

"Oh, no?" Rick retorted. "Then whose idea was it?"

"Mine," Daisy said.

Both Rick and Chris looked at her.

"It was my idea," she confirmed.

Rick frowned. "What are you doing, Daisy?"

"I—" She stopped. What was she doing? She wasn't so sure anymore. The original purpose of the expedition had been to get some information, but everything that she had learned so far was more troubling than helpful.

Turning back to Chris, Rick said, "You shouldn't have brought her."

"I didn't," he replied. "Weren't you listening? She brought me."

Daisy watched Rick's fingers curl into fists. She didn't understand why Chris had kept his previous visit to this place a secret from her, nor did she understand why he had been banned from visiting again, but she did know that Rick had a seriously short temper. And it was typically even shorter when he had been drinking, of which there was an extremely high likelihood, considering that they were in a nip joint. There was also an extremely high likelihood that Rick was armed—along with nearly every other man in the room—so it was best not to let things escalate. Her date with Chris had already ended on a sour enough note. There was no need to add a gunshot wound and a hospital visit to it.

"He isn't making it up," Daisy told Rick. "I drove. My car, my plan." Then she glowered at Chris. "You could have mentioned somewhere along the way that you had been here before and gotten kicked out. I don't appreciate being played for a fool."

"You're wrong." Chris shook his head. "I didn't play you for a fool. I would never do that."

His words sounded genuine, and he joined them with a deeply apologetic smile. It was such an earnest and charming smile that Daisy found her irritation retreating somewhat. Perhaps she had been too hasty to judge him. Maybe he wasn't really keeping secrets. Maybe it was all a misunderstanding.

Rick gave a dubious grunt. "You need to be more selective in your choice of company, Daisy."

"My choice of company?" She raised an eyebrow at him. "That's rich coming from you. Where are we standing? Who are your friends?"

"They include *your* husband."

"You . . ." Chris stammered, staring at her. "You have a husband?"

Rick chortled. "Didn't share that morsel, now did you, darlin'?"

Daisy's hands tightened around the jelly jar. She felt a strong urge to hurl it at Rick's simpering face but managed to restrain herself. It would be a terrible waste of good likker.

He looked at the jar. "Who did you get that from?"

It sounded so similar to what Duke had asked her that Daisy responded the same way she had to him, only with a bit more bite. "What does it matter to you, *darlin'*?"

"It matters to me," Rick informed her, "because this is my place you're standing in and that's my jar you've got in your lil' paws."

That surprised Daisy enough to silence her for a moment. It annoyed her, because she knew that she shouldn't be surprised. She should have guessed who the owner might be. If there was any country boy who could create a country club nip joint, it was Rick Balsam. It wasn't because he was so highbrow, certainly not. There wasn't a highbrow muscle in all of Rick's pretty body. His rusty pickup with bullet holes in the sides of the bed and his ramshackle trailer with more blueticks and coon hounds in the yard than grass were proof enough of that. But Rick had an undeniable talent for making—and selling—corn whiskey. If that talent extended to an exceedingly lucrative distribution network along half the eastern seaboard, then it surely also included a cinder block building much closer to home.

"I gave her the jar," Duke confessed. His previous placidity had vanished. Now there was a quiver in his words that betrayed a significant degree of anxiety, as though he feared Rick's potential wrath.

"No worries." Rick nodded at him without any sign of ire. "I know how persuasive our dear Ducky can be."

Daisy growled. Rick smiled.

"She had a chip," Duke went on.

"Did she indeed?" The smile widened.

"A red one. I didn't take it from her. I didn't know if I should. I didn't want you to think . . ." Duke didn't finish the sentence.

"You did the right thing." Rick nodded again, then gestured toward the crate that Duke had been unloading when Daisy first walked in. "Did you get everything moved and organized like we talked about?"

"Yes, sir."

"Good. That's real good."

Daisy let out a low sigh. So Duke wasn't just a delivery chap. He was Rick's delivery chap. One of Rick's trusty bootleggers. Heaven help him.

Rick looked at her. "Something on your mind, darlin'?"

"For starters," she snapped, "you can quit calling me *darlin'*."

"But Matt used to call you that all the time. I remember it well." Rick cocked his head. "Don't you?"

If she had been a cobra, she would have spit at him for that remark. Daisy figured that her next best option was leaving.

"Well, this has been heaps of fun," she muttered. "And now I think it's about time for me to go on home."

She began walking toward the sliding door, but Rick stopped her.

"Aren't you forgetting something?"

With reluctance Daisy turned back. He held out his hand.

She clutched the amber jar protectively. "I earned this, and I'm keeping it."

"You earned it?" Rick echoed with a grin.

"I drove all the way out here, didn't I?" She added under her breath, "And I had to deal with you."

The grin continued. "I'm glad you think so highly of my product."

As much as she would have liked to, Daisy couldn't argue with him there. Rick's moonshine was second to none. And she could definitely use a drink after this cheerless adventure.

Moving closer to her, Rick dropped his tone so that only she could hear him. "All you have to do is ask, Daisy. I'll give you whatever you want."

His voice was soft and sweet, almost caressing. She swallowed hard. Rick could be very difficult to resist. It was why he was never lonely at night. Her husband had been the same way, and when Daisy reminded herself of that, she found it much easier to take a step backward. There was no chance on this earth that she was going to suffer through that again.

"Thank you for the kind offer," she replied, pretending not to understand him, "but one jar will last me for quite a while."

"You know that's not what I meant." Rick moved closer to her again. "You know I wasn't talking about 'shine."

Daisy dearly wished that he wouldn't stand right next to her, not when he was purring at her too. He was like a leopard—slinking soundlessly through the brush—right before the ambush and the kill. Except she wasn't a clueless gazelle.

"Aunt Emily's liquor cart is always full." This time Daisy took two steps backward. "So whatever I need, I'm sure she'll have it."

Rick's dark eyes gazed at her.

"Speaking of Aunt Emily," she went on, trying to force a change in his predatory mood, "she's not going to be very happy with you."

"Aunt Emily loves me," he responded simply.

"She won't when she finds out that you don't serve brandy here."

He shrugged.

"Or that you don't serve anything to women."

"We have women," Duke interjected. "Rick's always bringing them in."

Daisy laughed—hard. "I'm sure he is."

Rick turned his dark gaze on Duke, and this time it was full of murder, not seduction.

Duke paled like a man who had just caught sight of the gleaming guillotine blade hovering above his neck. Grabbing the empty crate, he hustled to the sliding door. "I—I'll put this in my truck."

He was gone as quick as a mouse fleeing the talons of a hawk. Daisy didn't think that he would be back any time soon. She was grateful to him, however. He had done a marvelous job of switching the subject—albeit unintentionally—to Rick's philandering habits.

Still laughing, she followed in Duke's fleet footsteps and headed toward the door. "Would you like me to take you back to the campground?" Daisy asked Chris.

"Does that mean dinner is no longer on the menu?" he said.

She hesitated. For the last hour she had been convinced that their date was not only over but that there wouldn't be a second one. Now suddenly they might pick up where they had left off before turning onto Cotton Patch Road? The tidbits that they hadn't shared with each other regarding him having been to the nip joint previously and her having a husband currently were to be forgotten?

"Daisy," Rick began, "you should—"

"Don't," she interrupted him crossly. She was hungry, weary, and not at all interested in hearing his criticisms of the company that she might—or might not—be keeping, as well as more snide comments in relation to Matt. Reaching into her pocket, Daisy pulled out the red chip and tossed it onto the bar. "I believe that belongs to you."

Rick frowned at it, then at her.

"It covers the jar, doesn't it?" She frowned back at him. "I don't want you claiming later on that I owe you for it."

"You need to tell me where you got that," he demanded.

Daisy rolled her eyes. Both he and Duke acted like the chip was some priceless piece of stolen art instead of a clay marker for hooch. The only reason that it had any importance to her was because of the place where she had found it. But the more time that she spent at the nip joint, the more reluctant she became to share that fact, at least so publicly. The whole thing had become a spectacle. She was no longer quietly asking for information, as she had planned. She was broadcasting it instead. There were too many men listening and watching from their leather chairs and pecan card tables. And Daisy didn't know them. Beulah was right. One of the men from the bakery—one of the friends of the man who had died and left the chip behind—could be there right now, sitting a mere foot away from her, and she wouldn't have a clue. She needed to be careful.

"What darn difference does it make?" Daisy shrugged in an exaggerated fashion, like she couldn't remember exactly how the chip had come into her possession and it wouldn't matter even if she did. "You've got it back. I've got my jar. We're all happy, so let's just—"

A throat cleared from the direction of the sliding door.

In unison, everybody looked over. To Daisy's surprise, Duke had returned. He was standing at the very edge of the door, twitching like a skittish squirrel.

"What is it?" Rick barked.

"I—uh—I was about to head on back to the hardware store, and I saw those other crates sitting around the side, and I didn't know if I should take them too."

"What other crates?" Rick asked. "What side?"

"Outside," Duke explained. "Around the corner of the building."

Not interested in either the location or the disposition of Rick's bootlegging crates, Daisy took advantage of the distraction to make a quick exit. She nodded at Chris as she went.

"I'm leaving, so you better decide if you're coming."

Chris promptly accompanied her.

"We're not done with this conversation, Daisy," Rick informed her gruffly, following also.

Brushing past Duke at the sliding door, she responded over her shoulder, "You know how to find me."

"Yes, I do. And don't you ever forget it."

It sounded so much like a rather thinly veiled threat that Daisy spun around on her heel, ready to lash out at him, except she discovered that Rick was already walking with Duke toward the corner of the building.

"You see?" Duke pointed at the ground.

The daylight was failing, but there were still enough ocher streaks along the horizon to make out the small collection of crates piled haphazardly on the grass. Daisy squinted at them.

"Where did those come from?" Rick said.

"I don't know. I thought you'd know," Duke replied. "They ain't like the ones I usually use."

Instead of heading to her car, Daisy found herself abruptly heading to the crates. Duke wasn't mistaken. Although the crates on the grass were also made of wood, they weren't the same as the crate that he had emptied on the bar. There was one very large, very noticeable distinction, and when Daisy saw it, the blood drained from her face.

"There's writing on the side." Rick leaned down for a better look. "What does it say?"

"'Cream cheese,'" Daisy whispered. "It says 'cream cheese.'"

CHAPTER
11

"'Cream cheese'?" Rick echoed. "What the hell are crates for cream cheese doing out here?"

That was a question Daisy would have loved to be able to answer, but she couldn't. She could only stare at the crates in utter perplexity.

After a moment's reflection, Rick turned to her. "Isn't that what you had stolen from the bakery—cream cheese?"

She nodded.

"Are those your crates?"

The nod repeated itself.

"You're sure?"

Daisy was positive. What she had told Deputy Johnson immediately after the incident was true. The cream cheese couldn't have been mistaken for anything else. The words were stamped in big black letters right on the crates, on every side of the crates. *CREAM CHEESE. CONTENTS PERISHABLE. KEEP REFRIGERATED.* And that was exactly what the crates piled on the grass at the corner of the cinder block building said. Three wooden crates for three blocks of cream cheese, except the cream cheese was gone.

"Damn, that's strange," Rick murmured.

She couldn't have said it any better herself.

"When did you first see them?" Rick asked Duke.

"The crates? Just a couple of minutes ago, while I was putting our crate in the back of my truck."

"Then you don't know how long they've been sitting there?"

Duke shook his head. "I ain't been here since Saturday— since my last delivery—and they weren't there when I left at noon."

Daisy drew a deep breath. Saturday had been quite a busy day all around. Duke delivering jars. Beulah's salon flooding. The theft and stabbing in the kitchen. Sometime, somehow between then and now, the crates— but not the cream cheese, apparently—went from her bakery to Rick's nip joint. If only those crates could talk.

"I wonder where that cheese ended up," Rick mused.

So did she.

"What about you?" Rick turned to Chris. "You were here Saturday too. Saturday night. Were the crates sitting there on the grass?"

"I . . ." Chris shifted his weight from one foot to the other. "I didn't see. It was too dark."

Rick snorted. "It had nothing to do with being dark. You didn't see, because you were too drunk."

Chris didn't deny it. Daisy looked at him curiously.

"I don't know what happened." His brow furrowed. "I didn't think I drank that much."

She couldn't help chuckling at his moonshine naivete.

"When it's corn whiskey, you don't need to drink that much."

"I learned that lesson the hard way."

"Did you also learn the lesson about not dealing from the bottom of the deck?" Rick remarked sharply.

Chris shifted his weight again. "I was drunk. It wasn't intentional."

"That's bull, and we both know it."

"I don't cheat," Chris protested. "At least not when I have any brain cells still functioning."

"Except if there's cash involved?" Rick retorted.

This time it was Daisy's brow that furrowed. "Connor said there wasn't any gambling."

Rick raised an eyebrow at her. "So that's how you heard about this place—Connor?"

She winced slightly. She hadn't meant to snitch on him, especially after seeing how nervous Duke had gotten with Rick in relation to her having a jelly jar and the red chip.

The eyebrow remained elevated. "Was the chip from Connor too?"

"No," Daisy answered firmly. Then she added, back-pedaling as well as she could, "There's no need to get mad at him, Rick. Connor didn't bring up the subject. I pushed him on it."

Duke's shoulders slumped as he exhaled. He was clearly relieved by what she had said.

"I don't care about Connor," Rick replied. "I care about where you got that chip."

"And I care," Daisy countered, "about whether you're gambling here."

"You saw the card tables, didn't you? Sometimes people play cards."

"Of course I saw them. But there's playing cards, and

then there's gambling. Don't pretend there's not a difference."

Rick didn't respond.

A thick lump swelled in Daisy's throat. It was a combination of sadness, disappointment, and anger—mostly anger. "That's great, Rick," she spat. "Just great. You know how bad it got for Matt. You were there. You saw it. For God's sake, you were part of it! And now you're running the same kind of operation here? What the hell is wrong with you!"

He met her fuming gaze without flinching. Rick's own expression was unreadable. Daisy couldn't tell if he was amused, or sorry, or mad himself.

There was a short pause, then he said—still without discernible emotion—"I'm not running any kind of operation. It's just cards and a little cash. No big deal. All friendly and easy-going. At least until that one," Rick stuck a stiff thumb toward Chris, "and his pals decided to start cheating last Saturday night. As I'm sure you can imagine, some of our local boys didn't take that too well. So I tossed him," the thumb went back to Chris, "and his pals. And I warned them never to show their faces here again. Maybe I shouldn't have done it. Maybe I should have just let them get what was coming to them."

Daisy understood what that meant. With sufficient likker joined with sufficient provocation, the local boys could have very easily deposited Chris and his pals in a ditch over in the next county, possibly with several appendages missing.

"You should thank him," she told Chris. "If Rick hadn't thrown you out, there's a mighty good chance that you wouldn't be in one piece for your sister's wedding."

He cringed. "You won't tell Laurel, will you?"

"She didn't notice that you came back to the campground wobbling like a newborn calf?"

"She didn't see me. She wasn't there."

"Of course. I forgot. She would have been with Bobby—"
Daisy stopped. "Wait a minute. Last Saturday night?" She
looked at Rick. "You and Bobby were at the inn Saturday
night."

"I came here after leaving there, when I got a call about
certain folks," Rick snickered at Chris, "not being able to
handle their hooch and trying to be card sharks. I don't
know where Bobby went. I lost him somewhere along the
way."

"That's no surprise." Daisy's lips reluctantly curled into
a smile. "We both know how good your brother's sense of
direction is. After the sun goes down, Bobby can find his
trailer and the inn, but that's only because he's been to
both of them so many times. Other than that, he might as
well be trekking blindfolded through the Amazon. Laurel
probably had to help him get to the campground."

"He got lost a couple of days ago trying to find her
cabin," Chris said. "I saw him wandering in circles, and he
told me that he'd gone into the wrong cabin even though
he'd been sure it was the right cabin, except it wasn't."

Daisy's smile grew, partially because she could well
imagine Bobby ambling around the campground like a disoriented sheep in search of his fiancée's cabin and partially
because she now had a much better understanding of Rick
and Chris's animosity. Chris didn't care for Bobby, because
he wasn't keen on his dear sister marrying a disoriented
sheep. He also didn't care for Rick, because he was embar-
rassed about getting drunk, getting caught cheating at
cards while being drunk, and consequently getting kicked
out of the nip joint. And Rick didn't care for Chris, be-

cause he had had to kick him out of the nip joint. The good news was that none of it was her problem.

But her smile faded an instant later when Daisy remembered that she did have a problem, and it was a big one in the form of the three wooden crates that were sitting on the grass at the corner of the nip joint. The ochre streaks along the horizon had grayed to a pale charcoal. Soon she wouldn't be able to see the crates anymore, let alone transport them safely to her car. Spinning around, Daisy walked quickly toward the line of trucks.

"Not even a good-bye?" Rick called after her.

She waved absently.

Chris called after her too. "Uh, Daisy, can I still get a ride?"

"Don't expect one from me," Rick rejoined brusquely.

"Yes, you can have a ride," Daisy shouted over her shoulder. "Just give me a minute."

Returning within the promised time frame, she found both Rick and Chris still standing where she had left them. Duke had disappeared.

"I'm sure you won't mind me taking these," Daisy said to Rick, as she bent over the crates with the spare blanket that she had retrieved from her trunk.

He shrugged. "They're yours."

"I'm confused." Chris shook his head. "They're your crates—and they were taken from your bakery—and now you're taking them back?"

"That's correct," she answered him.

"And you're letting her do that?" Chris snapped at Rick in the tone of an aggrieved gentleman. "You're making *her* clean up the garbage at *your* place? You can't haul it to the dump yourself?"

"I don't think she considers it garbage," Rick retorted

with equal crispness. "And I'm pretty sure that she's not hauling it to the dump."

Chris went on shaking his head. "Do you need some help?" he asked her.

She was carefully stacking the crates together using the blanket, and as she did so, Daisy found some irony in the fact that it was the same blanket she and Chris had shared that afternoon for their cozy nap. Now she was trying to protect evidence with it instead.

"Don't touch those crates!" Rick barked at Chris.

Daisy's eyes flicked up. She could tell that Rick looked back at her, but it had grown too dark for her to make out more than the outline of his face.

"Fingerprints," he said to her. "That's the point of the blanket, isn't it?"

Rick was right. That was the point of the blanket, although she was skeptical that there would be any fingerprints on the crates—or at least any useful, legible ones. Maybe an unidentifiable smudge, or her own prints from when she had originally put the crates in the refrigerator. While Daisy was certainly no expert on the subject of fingerprints, she knew two things. First, according to Brenda, the men who had stolen the cream cheese wore gloves, so unless they had removed them after leaving the bakery, they didn't deposit their fingerprints on the crates. Second, the crates had likely been in their present location outside the nip joint for a while, possibly even since Saturday afternoon. Anyone could have touched them after they were deposited on the grass, where they were also exposed to the deleterious effects of the elements. In the last three days that included rain, wind, sun, dew, and plenty of humidity. Chances were awfully slim that anything useable remained behind.

But regardless of how futile it seemed to be, Daisy still felt that she had to give it a try. The crates were the only clue that she now had. The clay chip from under the wire rack in the kitchen had proved to be a bust, unless she considered that the chip had led her to the crates. Unfortunately, she couldn't do anything with this new clue herself. She had to hand it over to Deputy Johnson. So far he hadn't managed to come up with a single clue, or even any helpful information, but maybe—with a little luck—the crates would at last provide some sort of breakthrough in the investigation.

"Fingerprints?" Chris echoed. "Seriously? You want to dust a bunch of empty cream cheese crates for fingerprints?"

He sounded amused, like it was one of the wackiest ideas that he had ever heard of. But his sniggering reaction didn't bother Daisy, because he didn't have the full story about what had happened at Sweetie Pies—most important, of course, that there was a corpse involved. Rick, however, was less forbearing.

"You won't be laughing when they find *your* prints on them," he snarled.

"What!" Chris exclaimed. "*My* prints?"

"Are you denying—"

"Stop, Rick," Daisy cut him off. "Just stop. You're being ridiculous."

Rick clicked his teeth together. "Are you so confident, Daisy? It couldn't possibly have been him and his pals? He knows about your bakery. He knows about this place. He was here Saturday night. Where was he Saturday morning?"

"Oh, for the love of bacon, now you're getting beyond ridiculous—" This time she cut herself off.

Was Rick being ridiculous? Could there be some truth

to his words? Could Chris have been one of the men who broke in to her bakery? On the surface it seemed absolutely incredible. Chris was so nice, and polite, and—aside from a smidge of trouble after consuming too much likker—upright. Furthermore, she didn't think that he had even known about the theft until a few minutes ago. And he still didn't know about the stabbing. So if Chris hadn't known about either of the events, then he obviously couldn't have been a part of them. Unless he was a darn good actor.

Was Chris a good actor? Daisy had never considered it before, but the instant that the first drop of doubt entered her mind, a deluge followed. Had he offered to help her with the crates so that he could explain why his fingerprints were on them? Maybe that was the reason why he hadn't wanted her to find the red rooster and the tractor road. If she didn't find the nip joint, then she wouldn't find her crates. And if she didn't know that he had been there before, then she couldn't put him together with any of it. It wasn't a misunderstanding at all. Chris really had been keeping secrets—huge secrets.

The more Daisy thought about it, the more it occurred to her that it actually could have been Chris. But not only Chris, or some stranger who was a career criminal, as Deputy Johnson presumed. It could have been anyone. Anyone who knew both about her bakery and the nip joint. That included Duke—and Connor—and even Rick. Beulah had said it at the outset. Rick could have stolen the cream cheese to get her attention. He clearly had enough men working for him to pull it off. The crates were sitting outside his nip joint, where he hadn't expected her to go and find them. And now he was trying to push the blame onto Chris.

It sounded outrageous, and it probably was outrageous. Except it made Daisy realize that she didn't only need to be careful of the men inside the nip joint; she needed to be careful of just about everybody. Her momma and Aunt Emily were excluded, naturally. Brenda, Beulah, and Bobby were all accounted for in Sweetie Pies. And Laurel had been up in the woods. But otherwise, everybody in the area could have done it. They all could have taken the cream cheese, and they all could be looking for revenge for what had happened to their friend. There were so many possibilities, another with each passing second in Daisy's mind.

She understood that her best chance of narrowing down the list was to figure out why. Why walk off with ninety pounds of cream cheese? It couldn't honestly be an attempt to get her attention, either from Rick or anybody else. Not when Brenda was the one who had been in the kitchen. It was far too silly and simplistic, especially considering that a man had ended up dead on the bakery floor as a result. There had to be more to it. A lot more.

If only she had something to go on. But the cheese itself was so inane and worthless, not to mention perishable. It wouldn't last long without refrigeration, particularly in southwestern Virginia in the middle of October. The days were still plenty warm, and the nights weren't nearly cool enough to offset the warmth. Nor was it really feasible to buy and store a sufficient quantity of ice for the amount of cheese involved. That translated into a great pile of melted, mushy, stinking cream cheese rotting out there.

Although Chris vehemently argued his innocence— while Rick just as vehemently scoffed—Daisy didn't listen to them. She was too focused on loading the crates wrapped

in their protective blanket cocoon into her trunk. No one
but the law was going to touch those crates. No one was
even going to get near them. They were her only chance
for answers. And she had a very bad feeling that if she
didn't find some of the answers soon, much more than
cheese was going to turn rotten.

CHAPTER
12

"I was thinking that maybe we should have a little get-together for Laurel," Aunt Emily proposed.

Daisy nodded.

"A sort of combination bridal shower and bachelorette party."

She nodded again.

"As far as I can gather," Aunt Emily went on, "none of her friends or family are in the area—other than her brother, of course. And he can't be expected to host anything, not properly at least."

"Uh-huh."

"How about Friday in the afternoon? After the bakery closes. Would that work for you, Ducky? I figured we could have a few drinks and some snacks here at the inn, and it could go on for as long as everybody was interested, with the older ladies bowing out early if the younger ladies wanted to get a bit more rowdy or take things elsewhere later on."

The nodding continued.

"Are you planning on being open on Saturday at all?"
Aunt Emily asked, as she patted her head to check for any
wayward silver strands. Even at the crack of dawn, her
hair was perfectly done and her raspberry lipstick was in
place. "I wasn't sure if you and Brenda were going to try
to squeeze in a couple of hours of business before the
wedding, or if you needed that time to finish the cake."

"I'll have the cake ready on Friday," Daisy answered
distractedly.

"In that case, should we make it later on Friday afternoon or in the early evening instead for the get-together? I
don't want to rush you if—" Breaking off, Aunt Emily
tapped the toe of her shoe against the scrolled table leg impatiently. "Are you paying attention to a word I'm saying?"

"Of course I am."

"Then why do you keep looking out that window?"

When she didn't immediately respond, Aunt Emily
rose from her chair and circled around the dining table,
stopping at the set of french doors nearest to Daisy's seat.
She stood so close to the doors that her nose nearly touched
the glass.

"There isn't anything interesting out this way. The
blue asters—that old hand pump from the well—your car.
What are you staring at, Ducky?"

She was staring at her trunk. She had left the cream
cheese crates inside it, and they had bothered her the
whole night. Daisy had woken up every hour, thinking
that she heard noises outside. Someone had followed her
from the nip joint and was now breaking in to her car to
steal the crates. But it ended up being a lot of wasted worry,
because with the light of day she found her car, the trunk,
and all three crates untouched.

"I would say that you were hiding a man." Aunt Emily's shrewd blue eyes turned to her. "But then you'd be looking at the stairs leading up to the bedrooms, not at the flagstone path heading down to the parking spaces."

Daisy smiled. Aunt Emily had a remarkable ability to bring romantic trysts into the most unromantic of conversations.

"Oh, honey! What a wonderful surprise to find you here this morning!"

Her smile flew to the doorway leading to the hall. "Hey there, Momma!"

Lucy Hale entered the dining room with slow but steady steps. She had the thin limbs and sunken cheeks of long-suffering illness. Her hair was a pale blond that matched her pallid skin. Unlike Aunt Emily, she wore no jewelry or makeup. But she was dressed for the day, and even in her sickly state, she carried herself with grace and confidence. The ghost of a once stunning woman lingered beneath the decaying body.

"Such a treat! We so rarely get to eat breakfast together," Lucy said to her daughter.

"I know." Daisy sighed. "I wish we could do it more often, but unfortunately, the goodies don't bake themselves."

"Just imagine if they could!" Her momma laughed. "The world would be overrun by poppy seed bagels."

"Cement doughnuts," Aunt Emily retorted. "That's what bagels are. Nothing more than cement doughnuts."

Still laughing, Lucy began to pull out a chair at the dining table. Daisy promptly stood up.

"No, no," her momma chided her. "Sit down, honey. I don't need any help. I'm entirely capable of buttering my own toast, thank the Good Lord."

Daisy hesitated. Putting a firm hand on her shoulder, Aunt Emily pressed her back into her seat.

"You stand enough during the day, Ducky." She walked over to the buffet and picked up the china teapot with its gold-leaf trim. "I can certainly pour your momma a cup."

"Have you decided to start opening the bakery later on Wednesdays?" Lucy asked, shaking out a starched linen napkin and spreading it on her lap. "Or do I have my days confused? It is Wednesday, isn't it?"

"It is," Daisy confirmed. "And no, we're still opening at the same time. But I'm going in a little later this morning. The geocachers are gone now—or most of them are—so we aren't nearly as busy. I prepped everything yesterday afternoon, and Brenda volunteered to be the early bird today."

Aunt Emily clucked her tongue. "How is poor Brenda doing? Better, I hope?"

"Much better. She's not jumping like a spooked jack-rabbit at every noise anymore."

"I don't blame her one bit for being spooked," Lucy said. "I do wish they would hurry up and figure out who's responsible. It makes me worry so. I've been worrying ever since you told me about it."

"There's no need to worry," Daisy responded hastily, not wanting to cause her momma any extra stress. She was weak enough already. "We have new locks on the doors and windows and a temporary security guard."

Lucy's eyes flickered in surprise.

"A security guard!" Aunt Emily cried.

Daisy wasn't eager to explain, but she didn't have much of a choice. "Courtesy of Rick," she said dryly.

Although the two women glanced at each other, neither spoke a word. Aunt Emily poured the tea, while Lucy reached for the honey pot.

"Before I forget," Daisy added, happy to switch the subject, "I finished the banana pudding for the lecture at the historical society this evening. I can drop it off there in the afternoon, if that's convenient."

"That would be great!" her momma exclaimed. "Thank you, honey. The timing couldn't be better. After what happened over the weekend, we really need this fund-raiser to be our best yet."

"What happened over the weekend?"

"Somebody smashed in one of the society's windows with a beer bottle."

"Hooligans," Aunt Emily declared.

Daisy frowned at her momma. "You didn't tell me this before."

"It wasn't a crisis," Lucy replied calmly, stirring the honey into her tea. "Just one window. Except the insurance deductible is so high, the society will have to pay to fix it itself. That's more money we simply don't have."

"When was this exactly?" Daisy asked.

"Well, it was only discovered yesterday. The window belongs to the back conference room, and that room rarely gets used. But the inside of the frame and the rug on the floor were wet from blowing rain, so it probably happened Sunday night. As you may recall, we had that heavy shower early Monday morning. At least that's Deputy Johnson's best guess."

At the mention of Deputy Johnson, Daisy's frown deepened. "Was anything taken?"

Her momma nodded. "A couple of maps that were hanging on the walls."

"Maps? Were they valuable?"

"Not at all. At least, nobody at the society who knows about these things thinks so. They're old, but apparently not really old for maps—mid-or late-nineteenth century. I'm told they aren't anything special. Just some parts of Pittsylvania County, mostly around the mountains. Even the society wasn't particularly interested in them, which is why they were put in the back room to begin with."

"If they're not collectible," Aunt Emily mused, "then it sure is an odd thing to steal."

"Collectible or not," Daisy returned, "stealing semi-old maps still makes a heck of a lot more sense than stealing cream cheese."

Lucy nodded again. "Deputy Johnson thinks that it might be the same people."

"Right!" Daisy burst out laughing. "An evil cream cheese–Pittsylvania County map syndicate."

Aunt Emily gave her a stern glance. "Strangers lurking in the neighborhood and causing trouble is no joke, Ducky."

"Oh, Aunt Emily," she groaned, "please don't start with the strangers lurking—"

"Mercifully," Lucy interjected, "there wasn't anyone harmed at the historical society, unlike that sad soul at Sweetie Pies. Not that I'm blaming Brenda for it in the slightest. She was right to protect herself the way that she did."

"What makes Deputy Johnson believe the two thefts might be related?" Daisy asked. "The places aren't at all near each other. It was the same weekend, but aside from that I don't see the connection."

"I don't honestly know." Her momma took a sip of tea. "Maybe it's because neither one seems the least bit logical. Together they somehow become more rational."

Daisy remembered the crates in her trunk. "I was going to call him today besides, so I guess I can ask him about it then. Even though I doubt he's going to tell me anything new. Last I heard, they hadn't even identified the man who died yet."

"Not yet!" Aunt Emily echoed in amazement. "How hard can it possibly be? He's still got his hands and teeth and face, doesn't he? Can't they use one of those to figure out who he is?"

Both mother and daughter grimaced.

"It isn't like Brenda flambéed him," she continued.

"Not at breakfast, please," Lucy reproached her.

Aunt Emily smiled.

Although she made an effort to maintain a somber expression, Daisy said, "Brenda never did care for crème brûlée."

Not even her momma could keep from cracking a grin at that.

"Speaking of desserts," Aunt Emily remarked after a moment, "I don't want you to think that you need to do any baking for the get-together on Friday, Ducky. I'll take care of everything, food included."

Reaching for an apple in the fruit bowl, Daisy nodded gratefully.

"But I was hoping that you could be the one to talk to Laurel about it. You've had the most contact with her, after all. And she'll probably be more excited if the invitation comes from a person nearer to her own age, instead of a shriveled biddy."

"Gracious!" Lucy chortled. "If you're a shriveled biddy, what on earth does that make me? A withered and molting hornworm?"

"Pish, pish. You're a good ten years younger than I am, Lucy. Not to mention ten times lovelier, even on the worst of days. So I don't want to hear any such nonsense. And furthermore, hornworms don't molt."

"They don't? I always thought . . ."

Taking a bite of apple, Daisy checked her watch. She had no time for hornworms, molting or otherwise. It was time for her to get to work. As she rose from the table, her momma interrupted the speech that Aunt Emily had just commenced on the myriad differences between the equally fascinating tomato hornworm and tobacco hornworm.

"Must you leave already, honey?"

"I'm afraid so."

"You'll ask Laurel, won't you?" Aunt Emily prodded her.

"I will," Daisy agreed. "This afternoon." She looked at her momma. "After I drop off the pudding." Then she added silently to herself, *And I bring the crates to Deputy Johnson.*

"I didn't see Beulah last night," Aunt Emily said. "Did you, Ducky? Do you know how the repairs on the salon are coming?"

"I didn't see her either, but I did see Duke." She headed toward the doorway that led to the hall. "I think he and Connor need to speak with you."

"They did already—yesterday morning. They wanted permission to dig in the yard. They think the problem has to do with the line from the well."

Daisy's feet moved a little faster, anticipating the ill-fated direction of the conversation. "Apparently there's some question about that now, and they have to do more digging to figure out what's going on."

"What!" Aunt Emily screeched like an agitated barn owl. "How much more digging?"

"I have no idea."

"They sure as heck better not be expecting me to shut off the power to the well for all that digging. The inn uses the same well as the salon, you know. No power means no water for us."

Not able to restrain the mischievous imp perched on her shoulder, Daisy gestured toward the french doors and said with a chuckle, "There's always that old hand pump out there, Aunt Emily. If you start soon, you should be able to get enough buckets for your bath this evening."

Lucy nearly spit out her toast in amusement. Aunt Emily's nostrils flared.

"You won't find it so funny, Ducky, when you don't have water to make your coffee tomorrow morning."

"Don't worry," Daisy responded in an attempt to mollify her. "If you do have to shut off the power to the well—which I highly doubt—I'll get the guard at the bakery to come over and do the pumping. You should see Caesar's arms. They're as big as rain barrels. I'd wager that he could fill up every tub, sink, pot, and ice cube tray in the whole inn before you even finished your first glass."

The nostrils quieted. The only thing that comforted Aunt Emily more than her Remington was her nightly snort.

Daisy glanced at her watch again. Now she was really getting late. Just as she was about to hurry out of the dining room, her phone rang.

"Hey, Brenda," she said, answering it. "I'm awfully sorry. I'm leaving the inn right this second, so I'll be there

in—" She was cut off by what sounded like extremely labored breathing.

"D—Daisy—"

"Brenda?"

"Daisy!"

She instantly stopped moving. "What's wrong, Brenda?
Are you all right?"

Both Lucy and Aunt Emily turned to her with wide,
anxious eyes.

"I—I think somebody's here," Brenda whispered in a
terrified tone.

"At the bakery?" Daisy felt suddenly terrified too.
"Where are you?"

"I'm in the kitchen."

"Where are they?"

"Outside." Brenda gulped. "I—I think they're trying
to get in. They rattled the back door."

"Where's Caesar?"

"I don't know."

"Brenda, you listen to me. Get the cleaver. It's next to
the work table in that box of utensils left over from the
diner."

She whimpered.

"Get the cleaver," Daisy repeated, her voice rising.
"You get it right now, and you go to the far corner of the
kitchen. That's the best spot. It's the most protected. If
anybody comes in who you don't know or you don't like,
you hack off whatever you have to that will keep 'em away
from you."

"Go for the groin!" Aunt Emily shouted. "That's the
most bang for the buck."

Daisy ignored her. "Brenda, I'm going to hang up now

and call Deputy Johnson. Then I'm going to drive as fast as I can. Just hang on for a couple of minutes. That's all it'll take me to get to you."

Still whimpering, Brenda began to reply, but she got out no more than a syllable before there was the sound of shattering glass and the connection went dead.

CHAPTER
13

Although Daisy had little confidence in how quickly Deputy Johnson would get to Sweetie Pies, she arrived there in record speed. Her tires threw up fistfuls of gravel as she swerved from the road into the parking lot. She had already shut off the engine, jumped out of the car, and was racing toward the building when she slammed on her internal brakes. Who was there? What was happening?

Nothing and nobody. That was what Daisy saw when she stopped and actually looked at the bakery. The front door was closed. It appeared entirely normal, neither battered nor ajar. The front row of windows was similarly undamaged. All the glass was in one piece. The frames were intact and unbent. Nothing seemed to have been jimmied or otherwise tampered with. Rick's new locks had evidently worked very well.

She listened. Aside from two squirrels chattering back and forth between a pair of neighboring oaks, there was a peaceful silence. Nobody screaming, crying, fighting, or fleeing. Maybe the new locks hadn't worked so well. Maybe they hadn't worked at all, because there was no need for them to. Brenda was mistaken. Her nerves were simply playing tricks on her. There wasn't anyone there. She had just imagined that they were trying to get in, rattling the back door. But what about the shattering glass? And the abruptly ended phone call?

With slow, cautious steps, Daisy circled around the building. The near side was fine, but she had assumed that it would be. With no doors or windows, it was relatively impenetrable—at least without a bulldozer or an assortment of explosives, neither of which Brenda had mentioned. Coming around the back, she saw Brenda's car, which looked fine. And the back door, which also looked fine. If anyone had seriously tested it, they left no marks.

Daisy thought of Caesar. The prior two days he had been at the bakery much earlier than this. Where was he now? There wasn't a vehicle for him, but he also hadn't parked at Sweetie Pies previously. He said it was better for security. She wasn't entirely sure why. Maybe because then people wouldn't know when he was there and when he wasn't. That obviously worked, considering that she didn't know either. Or maybe Rick had recalled him. He might have been so annoyed with her for showing up at the nip joint yesterday uninvited that he decided to punish her by removing the guard from the premises. If that was the case, she couldn't really complain about it. Rick had every right. He was the one paying Caesar's wages, after all.

Pulling out her key, she was about to unlock the back door when it occurred to her that she hadn't completed her loop around the building. There was no door on the far side, but there was one window, which led to a tiny interior storage room. Daisy took a few more steps and popped her head around the corner. She was no longer expecting to find anything out of the ordinary, so it startled her when she discovered that the lone window was broken.

She hurried over to it. Other than a couple of jagged pieces that were sticking out of the corners like shark's teeth, the pane was gone. There were some shards of glass on the ground at her feet, but not enough of them. That meant the window had been broken from the outside. A gaping square was left, sufficiently large for someone to climb through.

Careful to avoid cutting herself on the shark's teeth, Daisy leaned toward the opening, which was about shoulder high. "Brenda?" she called.

Brenda didn't answer. The storage room was dark, but based on the rays of sunlight that were creeping inside, there was no visible disturbance.

Pulling back, Daisy ran to the front door and grabbed the handle. It moved. Either Brenda had already unlocked it for the day, or an intruder had. She threw open the door.

"Brenda!"

Still no answer. She took a hasty survey and to her considerable surprise saw nothing amiss. The cash register was shut. The large glass display case was full and unharmed. Both the floor and the counter were clean. And all the bags of sweet treats on the shelves along the wall were still organized in their neat rows.

Daisy squinted from one corner to the next. She was thrilled, of course, that her place of business hadn't been ransacked and torn apart, but at the same time she was confused. The shattering glass that she had heard on the phone clearly came from the window to the storage room, except the perpetrator didn't appear to have accompanied it. So if Sweetie Pies was safe, where in the world was Brenda?

Continuing to look for some sign of disorder and not finding any, Daisy walked to the end of the counter. Just beyond it was the door to the storage room. She tried the knob. It should have been locked, but like the front door it wasn't. Her confusion grew. Had Brenda opened it, or had the person who broke the window opened it? In theory that person—or persons—could have gone through the storage room, out the storage room door, through the main portion of the bakery, and out the front door. That would explain why both doors were unlocked and unscathed, but it didn't remotely begin to explain why someone would want to do it.

Not sure whether she should be more relieved or concerned, Daisy turned the knob and looked inside the storage room. Her eyes outside hadn't deceived her. The contents of the room were indeed undisturbed. The brooms and mops were all standing where they had been left the day before. The buckets were still stacked politely together. Not even a package of extra napkins had been shifted out of place. The only thing that wasn't as it should have been was the floor. Glittering shards of glass lay on the tile reflecting the strengthening sunlight that was flooding into the room in a rainbow of colors.

Some darker, less reflective glass caught Daisy's attention, and she bent down for a closer inspection. It wasn't from the window. There was no doubt about that. The glass from the window was clear and had broken into lots of thin fragments. This other glass was brown, and there were only a few, thick pieces of it. Daisy reached for one and promptly sliced open the skin on her hand. With a yelp of pain, she stuck the wounded finger in her mouth to slow the bleeding.

Standing back up, she was about to toss the offending shard into one of the nearby buckets so that she wouldn't cut herself on it again later during the obligatory cleanup when she suddenly realized what it was—the chunky round bottom of a bottle. She examined the other brown pieces. The smooth side, the narrow neck. They were all pieces of a bottle. And not just any bottle. It was a beer bottle.

Daisy stared at it. Someone had smashed in one of the bakery's windows with a beer bottle, just like someone had smashed in one of the windows at the historical society. Maybe Deputy Johnson was right after all. Maybe the two thefts were related. First the cheese, then the maps— and now this. But what was this? Breaking a window to come in, unlocking a pair of doors, and then leaving again without apparently taking anything or doing anything else? That made even less sense than stealing perishable cream cheese or trivial county maps.

Regardless of how little sense it made, there had to be a connection. Daisy's instinct told her that. If not a connection between the two thefts, then at least between the two broken windows. They couldn't just be a coincidence. The timing was too close, and the beer bottles were too much of a matching modus operandi. Of course it could have been merely hooligans, as Aunt Emily had so eloquently put it. Except hooligans tended to wreak havoc, and in neither instance with the broken windows had any sort of havoc been wreaked. Maps aside, the historical society had been left essentially untouched, as had Sweetie

Pies. But if it wasn't hooligans, then who else would do something so ridiculously illogical, without the slightest benefit?

That was a question which Daisy's instinct couldn't answer. She did reach one conclusion, however. No locks—no matter how new, or fancy, or expensive—did a lick of good in keeping a window from getting smashed in or a door from being opened from the inside. That was an excellent reason to have a security guard. Unfortunately, her security guard had vanished, along with Brenda.

Brow furrowed, Daisy turned away from the storage room and headed toward the kitchen. It was the only area that she hadn't checked yet. With uneasy anticipation, she pushed through the swinging door. Unlike the rest of the place, the kitchen was well lit and messy. But the jumble wasn't from someone breaking in and pillaging. It was the normal morning chaos in a bakery. Dirty bowls and sticky spoons. Crowded baking sheets lined up in wait for the oven like ants marching to a picnic. Flour and sugar strewn everywhere.

Something was burning. It hadn't progressed far enough to send out billows of smoke and trigger the fire alarm, but Daisy could distinctly smell the first stage of overbrowning. Hurriedly switching off all the appliances, she threw open the oven doors. It was the biscuits, and they were well past overbrowning. They were as black and shriveled as lumps of charcoal. Too worried about Brenda, she left them where they were. They had to cool off before she could discard them anyway. Brenda had clearly disappeared in a rush. Although she could be a bit scatterbrained on occasion, it was never so much as to let the biscuits burn, especially not to the state of briquettes.

Daisy's sharp gaze traveled around the room. She was looking for a clue to tell her where Brenda had gone. Thankfully, there was no evidence of a struggle or any form of violence. Her eyes paused at the work table. There was a large box next to it on the floor, flipped on its side. It was the box of utensils left over from the diner, the one from which she had told Brenda to get the cleaver.

Kneeling down next to it, she rummaged around inside: warped spatulas, rusty meat tenderizers, and crooked tongs. All had seen much better days and were now generally useless, hence the box. The cleaver—also somewhat warped and rusty—was no longer there. Brenda had obviously taken it, as per her suggestion. But where had she taken it? Not the far corner of the kitchen, as Daisy had also suggested. It really was the best spot, the most protected if someone threatening came in.

Although Brenda wasn't in the far corner, her phone was. Daisy went over and picked it up. It was a bit dinged from the fall to the floor, but it still worked. The last number dialed was hers. Brenda hadn't called Deputy Johnson. She felt as though she should be comforted by that fact somehow. Except maybe Brenda had been counting on her to make the call, which she had indeed done while leaving the inn. Not that either of them could rely on the law getting to the bakery swiftly. Even with the best of intentions, the distances in Pittsylvania County were just too great. It was like that old saying—when seconds count, the police will be there in minutes.

Anxiously searching for something that would lead her to her missing friend, Daisy's eyes circled around again, and this time they stopped at the refrigerator. It reminded her of the crates that were still sitting in her trunk waiting to be delivered to Deputy Johnson, and she suddenly wondered if they could be the reason why the person—or persons—broke the window in the storage room. It was a fairly easy way to get in to the bakery and find the crates, if they had been there. Nothing had been rummaged, but that was precisely the point. Nothing would need to be rummaged if someone was looking for the crates. They were too big to hide effectively, especially in a little place like Sweetie Pies, where there were few cupboards and no secret compartments. The crates would stand out just the same as the vinyl-topped stools or electric mixers.

But why would someone look for the crates? They were even more worthless than the cream cheese they had once contained. The only possibility that Daisy could come up with was a desire to wipe them clean of fingerprints. Except that seemed a stretch, because if someone was so concerned about fingerprints, then they would have wiped the crates clean before depositing them outside the nip joint. Furthermore, why would anybody even think that the crates were at the bakery? There were only two people who knew that she had taken them from the nip joint—Rick and Chris—but neither one knew she had brought them back to Sweetie Pies.

The more Daisy turned it over in her mind, the more perplexed she became. It was a crazy, convoluted puzzle—none of the pieces matched or fit together in any sort of rational manner. There was nothing about it that she understood. But she also had a nagging, growing, irrepressible feeling that the pieces actually did fit together somehow and there was something rational behind it all. Only she couldn't find the right piece to slide into the puzzle the right way to make it coherent and whole.

Off in the distance, she heard the wail of a siren. Deputy Johnson was finally coming. Agitated over the crates and frightened for Brenda, Daisy hurried through the kitchen and out the back door to meet him. She heaved a frustrated sigh toward Brenda's car in the parking lot, dearly wishing that it could tell her what had happened to its owner. With the car still there, Brenda couldn't have gone very far. Not unless she had been kidnapped, and then she surely would have put up one heck of a fight in the process. She would have given somebody's fingers a good whack with the cleaver, or at an absolute minimum, there would be scuff marks on the ground from wrestling and dragging.

Daisy studied the gravel for the tiniest hint, straining to find a drop of blood, a telltale track in the stones, or a scrap of torn clothing. But she hadn't missed anything the first time through. There was nothing and nobody at the bakery. The two squirrels had even ceased their chattering. They had been replaced by the wail of the siren—and a low voice.

The voice hadn't been there before. Daisy was certain of that. She could barely make it out now. It was ineffably soft, like the whisper of blowing sand. She could only catch a trace of it beneath the siren. Where was it coming from? She looked around the rear of the property. The Dumpster was latched to keep out animals, the shed was chained, and the gravel ended in a thick row of raspberry vines. Nobody was hanging out in those thorns, either voluntarily or forcibly. At the far side of Sweetie Pies—the side where the window had been broken—there was an old dirt farm road. It was still used occasionally during planting and harvesting, but there was no traffic on it this morning.

Focusing as hard as she could, Daisy blocked out every noise other than the voice. It was talking. Not a whimper or a hum, but actual words. It didn't sound like anybody was responding to it, however. She tried to pinpoint the direction. Although it didn't seem to be near to her, it also didn't seem far away. Maybe that was because she couldn't hear it well enough. The siren was getting louder, and Daisy knew that soon she wouldn't be able to hear the voice at all.

Perhaps someone was walking along the edge of the dirt road, and she just couldn't see them. There were a lot of tall weeds and camouflaging brush that hadn't been cut down since midsummer. The person could be farther down the road, and their voice could be echoing back to her. That wasn't particularly unusual. All of southwestern Virginia echoed in one way or another—either you were on the top of a mountain or at the bottom of a valley.

Daisy followed the sound. She took several steps toward the dirt road. The voice seemed a tad louder. She took several more steps, and it became distinctly clearer. It was asking for something, or possibly pleading for something. Daisy quickened her pace. What if it was Brenda pleading? What if she was in trouble and begging for help? The voice was light enough to belong to Brenda. And the closer Daisy got to the road, the more it sounded like Brenda.

Then she saw her. At the spot where the gravel from the bakery met the dirt from the road. The grasses were thick, browned, and at least four feet high. Brenda was crouched on the ground in the middle of them. She looked almost the same as she had when Daisy found her in front of the refrigerator in the kitchen with the dead cream cheese thief at her feet. Brenda's apron was falling from one shoulder. The tortoiseshell clip that ordinarily held back her hair was sagging at her neck. And there was red on her hands—bright crimson blood. The only difference was that she wasn't holding a chef's knife.

She wasn't holding a cleaver either. It sat on the soil by her knees. The marred blade was gray, not scarlet. But the person lying next to her was coated in scarlet. It covered his chest, and his stomach, and his shoulders. With stiff elbows and outstretched palms, Brenda pressed down on him hard—near his heart—obviously in an effort to keep the scarlet from spreading further. She was speaking to him, telling him that it would be all right, promising him that help was on its way, imploring him to live.

"My God," Daisy exhaled in horror. "Is that Caesar?"

With blanched cheeks and tearstained eyes, Brenda looked over at her.

"I didn't do it," she wept. "I didn't kill him."

CHAPTER

14

"Of course she didn't do it," Deputy Johnson said. "Of course she didn't kill him."

With a gulp, Daisy nodded.

"He wasn't stabbed—or cleaved."

She nodded again.

"He was shot."

This time Daisy only gulped and answered, "Brenda doesn't own a gun."

In his starched brown uniform with gold trim, the deputy turned toward Brenda, who was slumped on the ground in front of him. "Is that correct, ma'am?"

She lifted her gaze to him with an expression of overwhelming exhaustion. Although Daisy had tried to get her to rise—if only to wash the blood from her palms—Brenda had remained on her knees in the middle of the grass and gravel. All of her strength had gone into trying to stop Caesar's bleeding, and now she had nothing left. Her eyes were blank. Her lips were eerily translucent. The number of graying strands in her black hair seemed to have tripled in the past ten minutes.

"Is that correct?" Deputy Johnson repeated. "You don't own a firearm?"

Brenda shook her head in confirmation, then looked over at the shrouded figure being lifted into the ambulance.

"You did everything you could," Daisy said emphatically, trying to boost her spirits. "You can be proud of that."

"It's not fair," Brenda sniffled. "He died because he was here, and he was here because he was protecting us. I know it was his job, but . . ."

"His job?" Deputy Johnson inquired when she let the sentence trail away.

"Caesar was a security guard," Daisy explained. "Or at least," she corrected herself, not sure what exactly his employment with Rick had included, "he was a security guard for us. After the other incident, on Saturday—"

"He was very comforting to have around," Brenda interjected. "Such a nice man. So helpful too. He moved that heavy table with the marble slab for us."

"You felt it necessary to hire a security guard?"

There was such a strong note of doubt and suspicion in the deputy's tone, it rankled Daisy.

"Obviously we needed one," she snapped, gesturing toward the recently deceased.

"But there was no cheese taken this time?" he asked.

"There wasn't anything taken. Not that I could see." Daisy turned to Brenda. "Did you see anything taken?"

"I didn't see anything at all."

Deputy Johnson squinted at her from behind the permanently smeared lenses of his glasses. "That can't be true, ma'am. You must have seen something."

"I didn't," Brenda insisted. "They broke the window, came in, and then left again."

"If you know that, you must have seen them."

"No. They never entered the kitchen, and that's where I was."

"So they came into the storage room," Daisy mused, matching Brenda's account to what she had already guessed from her own inspection of Sweetie Pies' interior, "went through the main part of the bakery, and out the front door?"

"That's how it sounded to me," Brenda said. "The window broke. I threw down the phone and ran to get the cleaver from that box, like you told me. I heard footsteps—and I was sure they were going to find me—but they didn't. They didn't even take a peep into the kitchen. They just walked out the front door. The bell clanked with 'em."

"And your guard?" Deputy Johnson questioned her. "Where was he during all of this?"

"When I arrived, Caesar wasn't here yet. I came in extra early this morning, since I knew Ducky was planning on coming in a bit late. I thought Caesar still hadn't shown up when the ruckus began, but just a few seconds after the bell clanked, he shouted. He was outside, and he yelled at the people to stop."

"Did they answer him?"

"I didn't hear it if they did. Caesar shouted again. I heard running, a car door slammed, and the car—or it might have been a pickup—started up. They were trying to get away fast. The tires spun on the gravel. And then," Brenda's translucent lips quivered, "there was a shot."

Daisy let out a sigh of sympathy and sadness.

Brenda nodded. "It was awful, Ducky. Just awful. I

knew it was Caesar. I knew in an instant that he was the one who had been shot. The car—or truck—didn't even slow down. It kept on going like nothing in the world had happened, like putting a bullet in a man was the same as tossing a gum wrapper from the window. They went along the dirt road. I was already hurrying outside, but all I saw was a big ball of dust."

"Not any sort of make—or model—or color?" Deputy Johnson pressed her. "A guess, even?"

"Just dust," she responded, echoing Daisy's sad sigh.

"And the guard?"

"Caesar was on the ground." Brenda pointed toward the flattened grass at her knees. "He had this pit in his chest. It was like a hole in a pipe, and I tried to plug it. I tried to close it up until someone came to help, but it didn't work. The blood didn't stop." She raised her stained hands and stared at them. "I couldn't get it to stop."

Although Daisy dearly wanted to comfort her, she knew that it was impossible. Caesar had died in front of her. Brenda had felt his last breath beneath her palms. She had witnessed his final, suffering seconds on this earth. And she had desperately tried to save him but couldn't. There was no comfort for that.

"We'll do a search around the building for the gun," Deputy Johnson pronounced after a moment, "but they probably took it with them."

"And they'll probably throw it away somewhere along the road, so it won't ever be found," Daisy remarked pragmatically. "That farm road goes on for five miles, with two ponds both less than a hundred yards off the road within the first mile. What are the chances the gun doesn't end up in one of them, or some other pond farther down the line? That road connects to another half a dozen unused, secluded farm roads. You could send an army through that area and not come up with the gun."

"Standard criminal behavior," the deputy replied. "They tend to be good at disposing of their weapons."

Daisy frowned. "But it doesn't seem like standard criminal behavior."

Deputy Johnson gave her a startled look. "You don't consider a person being shot in cold blood in the parking lot of your business to be criminal behavior?"

She glowered at him with irritation. "Of course I do. I didn't mean it like that. What I meant was climbing through a broken window into the bakery—and then walking straight out the front door without doing anything else along the way—doesn't seem very standard to me."

He straightened his glasses. "You may be on to something there."

"For goodness' sake," Daisy added to emphasize her point, "they didn't even take a cookie."

"The biscuits!" Brenda exclaimed, jumping abruptly to her feet. "I forgot the biscuits!"

Daisy grabbed her arm just as she was about to sprint toward the back door. "Don't worry about the biscuits, Brenda."

"But they'll burn!" she cried. "And then they'll burn the whole place down!"

"The biscuits are already burnt. Except I turned off the oven, so they won't be burning anything down."

Brenda looked greatly relieved. Daisy was too when she saw that some color had crept back into her friend's cheeks. She no longer appeared quite so forlorn or teetering dangerously on the edge of a despondent abyss.

"If you can't tell me about the vehicle they drove away in," Deputy Johnson said to her, "can you at least tell me how many of them there were?"

"One," Brenda answered.

It was the deputy's turn to frown. "One? That's all?"

"Well, I can't be absolutely positive, because I didn't see it. But it only sounded like one car—or one truck—starting up and one set of tires spinning on the gravel."

The frown became an exasperated grimace. "Not the number of vehicles. The number of people!"

"Oh." Brenda paused. "I'm not sure about that. I assumed it was three, since there were three the last time. But," her brow furrowed, "it couldn't have been three, could it? It could only be two after . . ." She paused again, no doubt thinking about the dead cream cheese thief.

"You referred to them in the plural," Deputy Johnson reminded her. "You said *they*, not *he*."

"You're right." Brenda's brow furrowed some more. "I did."

"I think it could have been just one person," Daisy interjected. "In fact, I think it probably was just one person."

Both Brenda and the deputy turned to her with interest.

"Two people would be much more likely to do something inside the bakery," she surmised. "Two people wouldn't break a window to get in. Two people would break open a door."

"And two people would talk." Brenda continued the line of reasoning. "But I didn't hear any talking. I didn't hear two sets of footsteps either." Her eyes widened with a sudden realization. "There weren't two people running outside. I'm fairly certain of that. And only one car—or pickup—door slammed."

"So that leaves us with the question," Daisy said, "was

it one of the men who stole the cream cheese, or was it
somebody else?"

Brenda drew a raspy breath. "I told you they'd come
back!"

"But why?" Daisy retorted. "Why would one of them
come back? Especially if they're not going to do anything
while they're back. They're just raising their risk of getting caught."

"Maybe they were looking for us?"

"Except they didn't actually look for us. You said the
person didn't even take a peep into the kitchen, and the
kitchen is where they found you the last time."

"Huh." Brenda wrinkled her pug nose. "I don't understand."

"I don't either," Daisy agreed.

"Do you know how many of those geocachers are still
hanging around?" Deputy Johnson asked, seemingly ap-
ropos of nothing.

"Geocachers?" Brenda echoed.

"Not a lot," Daisy answered him. "Most of them left as
soon as the event ended, but a few have stayed on."

"Are you acquainted with any of them personally?"

"Only two—Chris and Laurel Page—although I might
recognize some of the others."

The deputy scribbled a note of the names.

"They're brother and sister," Daisy went on. "They
could probably tell you who else from the group is still in
the area."

He scribbled some more.

"What on earth do the geocachers have to do with
this?" Brenda said with a touch of indignation. "They
bought our scones and dug stuff up. They didn't break our
window or shoot poor Caesar."

"They may very well have done both," Deputy Johnson countered. "The man who died here last Saturday—
the man you stabbed—he was a geocacher."

Daisy was so stunned that her body froze. Brenda's reaction went in the opposite direction. She took a couple of
wobbly steps toward nothing in particular, then her legs
swayed like a hurricane-force wind had suddenly struck
her. Just as she was about to topple over, Daisy shook herself awake and grabbed Brenda's arm for the second time
that morning, only instead of stopping her from making a
wasted trip inside to check on burning biscuits, she kept
her from slamming face-first into the dirt.

"The man . . ." Brenda stammered, still wobbling. "He
was a geocacher?"

"He was," Deputy Johnson confirmed.

"How did you identify him?" Daisy asked. "And when?
I thought you were having trouble figuring out who he
was."

"We were having trouble," the deputy admitted. "And
I wasn't the one who identified him. His parents did. They
showed up yesterday at my office. They drove over from
Richmond, because they were worried that there had
been some sort of an accident when their son quit sending
them updates on the hunt. Apparently they're geocachers
too, but they didn't come along since this event was geared
toward a younger crowd."

"I assume you told them what happened at the bakery?"
Daisy said. "Could they give you any kind of explanation?"

"None at all." He shook his head. "They couldn't believe it. They didn't have a clue why their beloved, angelic
son Jordan—that was his name, Jordan Snyder—would
want to break in to a bakery and steal something. When I

told them that the theft involved ninety pounds' worth of cream cheese, they were completely flabbergasted."

"They aren't the only ones," Daisy muttered.

"After I found out who he was," Deputy Johnson continued, "I checked every database that we have access to. Up until this past weekend, Jordan Snyder from Richmond, Virginia, never had a lick of trouble with the law. He was twenty-six years old, had graduated from his local community college, worked in the family furniture business, owned a pair of golden retrievers, and really liked this geocaching thing."

Daisy threw up her hands in frustration. "And now he's dead for no comprehensible reason!"

"There doesn't have to be a reason," the deputy rejoined. "Some criminals are just late bloomers."

With effort, Daisy restrained herself from rolling her eyes. Based on his curriculum vitae, Jordan Snyder didn't sound like much of a criminal to her—late bloomer or not. Obviously he was a criminal, considering that he and his friends had come in to her bakery and taken her cream cheese, but he certainly wasn't a hardened career criminal. And he had paid an awfully steep price if this was indeed his first lapse in judgment.

"Late bloomers are often the worst types of criminals. They think they can get away with anything, but they can't." Deputy Johnson pointed a stern finger in the air. "Not while I'm here. I'll stop 'em. I stopped Jordan. I can stop the others too."

Daisy was tempted to remind him that Brenda was actually the one who had stopped Jordan, but she didn't want to upset Brenda any more than she already was, so she prudently bit her tongue.

"Even if it was just a dumb prank, there still needs to be consequences." The deputy waved his finger around like he was conducting an orchestra. "We can't let strangers come waltzing into Pittsylvania County believing that there won't be any consequences to their shenanigans."

That remark made Daisy think of Aunt Emily and her reference that morning to hooligans. Maybe she was right. Maybe the broken window at the historical society was simply a product of mischief, and the maps had been taken merely to cause trouble. The same could apply to the broken window in the storage room. Perhaps something had been stolen from Sweetie Pies too, only she and Brenda hadn't discovered it yet. It wasn't anything valuable or important. It was taken just to cause trouble. That would also explain the otherwise inexplicable cream cheese. A childish idea to steal something from the local bakery had gone horribly wrong, and Jordan Snyder had ended up dead as a result.

"I'll need to talk to those people you mentioned—the brother and sister." Deputy Johnson glanced at the notes that he had scribbled earlier. "The Pages. You said they might know which of the geocachers were still in the area?"

"Yes," Daisy began, "they should be able to—"

"Oh heavens, Ducky," Brenda cut her off. "Rick's here."

"He is?" She was surprised. "Where?"

"Around the side near the ambulance. He must have been driving by and seen the commotion."

Daisy turned toward the side of the building.

"Oh heavens, Ducky," Brenda said again, her voice anxious. "We're going to have to tell him about Caesar. Do you think he'll be mad?"

"He won't be mad at you," Daisy assured her, searching the small crowd that was collected around the ambulance. "But he's going to be plenty mad at whoever—" This time she cut herself off.

"Can you tell me where I can find the Pages?" Deputy Johnson inquired.

Daisy didn't respond. She was too busy staring at the spectacle before her, wondering if her eyes could possibly be deceiving her.

"Are they staying at the Tosh Inn?" the deputy pursued.

It took a minute before she finally answered. Her words came out slow and uneven.

"You don't need to go to the Tosh Inn. Laurel Page is right over there."

As she spoke, Daisy gestured toward the corner of the bakery, where a woman was standing in a tight embrace with a man. It was Laurel, wrapped in Rick's arms.

CHAPTER
15

"That sure is a load off my mind," Brenda said with a weighty exhalation.

"What is?" Daisy asked.

"We won't have to be the ones to tell Rick about Caesar. He must have seen him in the ambulance or found out from a deputy."

"How do you know that?"

"Well, look at him. Look at how Laurel is comforting him."

Daisy blinked at the pair. Laurel Page was pressed against Rick Balsam's chest. There wasn't a sliver of daylight between their bodies. She blinked again, hard. The scene didn't change.

"Or maybe Rick is comforting Laurel," Brenda added after a moment. "Maybe it's given her a shock."

The embrace continued—and showed no sign of weakening.

Doubt began to creep into Brenda's voice. "Laurel's marrying Bobby, right?"

"As far as I'm aware," Daisy replied, echoing her misgiving. "Or at least she was the last I heard."

Brenda frowned. "I wonder about that, Ducky. I think there might be trouble."

Trouble was a very fitting word for the Balsam brothers. There were plenty of other words also, but *treacherous* was not one that Daisy would have used, which was why the lingering embrace surprised her so much. Although Rick and Bobby had certainly had their share of spats and disagreements over the years—some more and some less serious—she had never seen them be truly disloyal to each other. And fooling around with a fiancée was most definitely disloyal. Daisy remembered how a couple of days earlier in the bakery she had noticed Rick admiring Laurel. At the time she had thought that the admiration went on a little too long and a little too intently to be appropriate for a future brother-in-law, even an irrepressibly rakish one like Rick. The current level of intimacy between him and Laurel appeared to go well beyond admiration, and it piqued her curiosity.

As though he could sense that she was thinking about him, Rick's gaze suddenly shifted to her. Daisy met his eyes. They were black with wrath. It shook her slightly. She had expected him to be mad about what had happened to Caesar, of course. In her experience, Rick was just as loyal to his friends and associates as he was to his brother. It was, in fact, one of his finer qualities. But there was something more to the darkness in his eyes than plain anger. Brenda really had used the right word. There was trouble.

Rick held Daisy's gaze for a long minute, then his arms finally loosened their grip around Laurel. She looked up at him, and they spoke briefly. Although Daisy couldn't hear what either of them said, she saw Laurel smile and nod. Maybe Brenda was right about that as well. Maybe Caesar's dead body had been too much of a shock for Laurel, and Rick had been trying to comfort her.

Together the pair turned away from the steadily growing crowd at the side of Sweetie Pies and started to walk across the gravel toward Daisy. Watching them, Brenda clucked her tongue.

"Something sure is strange there," she said.

Daisy agreed.

"I can't quite put my finger on what it is, Ducky, but—" Brenda clucked her tongue again. "Well, I suppose it isn't any of my concern." She shrugged. "I got no dog in that hunt."

That brought a smile to Daisy's face. No dog indeed. It wasn't any of her concern either who was marrying, embracing, comforting, or even simply admiring whom, so long as she was told in a timely fashion whether or not she was supposed to make a cake for the occasion.

"Would it be okay if I went inside and got myself cleaned up?" Brenda asked Deputy Johnson.

"Cleaned up?" he responded distractedly. While Daisy and Brenda had been scrutinizing Rick and Laurel, the deputy had been silently scrutinizing the throng that was swelling around the ambulance.

Brenda lifted her stained palms in his direction. The dried blood was peeling away from her skin like rust flakes cracking off an old metal mailbox.

"Oh, yeah." Deputy Johnson waved his hand back at her. "Go ahead."

Picking at the crusty blood, Brenda headed toward the back door of the bakery.

"Try not to touch anything important," the deputy shouted after her. "We don't want you destroying clues."

Daisy raised a dubious eyebrow at that remark. The man was about as capable of finding clues as he was of identifying corpses. Thank goodness poor Jordan Snyder's parents had driven over from Richmond, otherwise their son would probably still be nameless. Too bad they couldn't also provide some sort of explanation for why he and his friends had wanted to steal her cream cheese.

"How is she?" Rick said to Daisy, as Brenda disappeared into the building.

"She wasn't so good at first, but she's holding her own now," Daisy replied.

"Is there anything I can do?" Laurel asked. "For her? For you?"

She spoke with such warmth and evident sympathy that Daisy was genuinely grateful.

"Thank you for the offer, but I'm all right. And I think Brenda will be all right too, after a while. She had a pretty nasty fright this morning."

"I can only imagine." Laurel shuddered. "What a terrible thing to see—a man shot right in front of you."

"Brenda didn't actually see it," Daisy corrected her. "But she did find him. She tried to save his life, only she couldn't."

Laurel gave a deep sigh of commiseration. "It's so sad, but I'm very glad that both of you are safe."

Daisy thanked her again for her kindness, then she looked at Rick. "I'm sorry about Caesar."

He looked back at her with a murky expression.

"You will let them know how to contact his kin, won't you?" she pressed him after a minute.

"Of course," Rick responded flatly.

"I don't understand it," Laurel mused. "How could someone do that to him? Do they have any idea why, or who it was?"

Laurel's questions sounded so much like her own that it reminded Daisy of Deputy Johnson wanting to talk to her and Chris about the other geocachers still in the area. She turned to the deputy, whom she discovered wasn't paying the slightest attention to their discussion.

"This is—" Daisy began in introduction.

"No photographs!" Deputy Johnson hollered.

He gestured furiously at a spectator who was merrily snapping pictures of the body in the ambulance. The man didn't heed the admonition, and the deputy rushed off to put a quick halt to it.

"Another time, I guess," Daisy mumbled after him.

"They'll match the gun," Laurel declared with confidence. "That's how they'll figure out who it was. They'll match the bullet to the gun."

Daisy looked at Rick once more. His jaw twitched, but he didn't speak.

"First they have to find the gun," Daisy told her with decidedly less confidence, "which won't be easy on these long, isolated farm roads. And even if they do find it, it probably won't have any fingerprints on it, or no fingerprints that are in the system."

"But that shouldn't matter," Laurel said. "They can match the gun to the person who registered it."

"That's not possible." Daisy shook her head. "There is no firearm registration in the Commonwealth of Virginia."

"No registration? But then how do they know who has a gun?"

"They don't know. Although they can pretty well assume it, because most everybody around here has a gun, usually somewhere between half a dozen and several dozen guns. And a lot of people carry one with them at all times. There are more concealed weapons permits listed in the local newspaper each week than there are marriages, divorces, births, and deaths combined. Frankly, I'm amazed there's anyone left to issue a permit to. I would think that nearly every citizen in the county—or the state, for that matter—has one by now."

Laurel gaped at her. "Do—do you have a permit?"

"Nope." Daisy shrugged. "When it comes to concealed carry, I'm a peace-loving holdout."

"I keep telling you that's a mistake," Rick said.

"You also keep telling me there's money to be made in hog farming," she rejoined.

"There is money to be made in hog farming."

"So when I take up hog farming, I'll be sure to get a concealed weapons permit."

Rick started to growl at her, but then he seemed to catch himself, and his face abruptly went blank.

Daisy's gaze narrowed. Brenda had been spot-on. Something was strange about Rick—suspiciously strange. "What are you scheming at?" she murmured under her breath.

Laurel reached out and squeezed Daisy's arm. "It's too bad about yesterday."

"Yesterday?" She didn't understand.

"Well—um—Chris said your date had a few bumps along the way."

Rick gave a sharp cough. Daisy glowered at him.

"Maybe you could give it another try?" Laurel suggested, squeezing her arm again. "I know Chris would like to."

Daisy hesitated. There was the whole awkward situation with the nip joint to consider. It hadn't quite been resolved.

"How about tomorrow?" Laurel continued. "I'm still working on collecting the remaining caches from the hunt, and Chris was going to help me with that today. But he's free on Thursday."

This time Rick snorted.

"Or maybe Friday would be better? After what happened this morning, I understand that you might not feel like . . ." Glancing at the ambulance, Laurel paused.

The mention of Friday triggered Daisy's memory.

"I almost forgot," she said. "Aunt Emily wanted me to invite you to a combination bridal shower and bachelorette party Friday afternoon."

Laurel took a step backward in surprise.

"It's not going to be anything big or overblown," Daisy explained. "Just some food and drinks with a few of the girls at the inn."

"I—I don't know what to say," Laurel stammered.

"I hope you'll say that you'll come, because otherwise Aunt Emily is going to throw a fit about how she hasn't been a proper hostess for your wedding. And," Daisy added with greater sincerity, "I think it could be fun."

"Of course!" Laurel exclaimed, gathering herself. "It's so nice of you all to think of me. I didn't expect this."

Rick's sharp cough repeated itself.

Daisy glanced at him quizzically. Was he upset? But why would he be upset about a bridal shower and bachelorette party? It suddenly occurred to her that neither Rick nor Laurel had made a single comment about Bobby that morning. Had something gone wrong in relation to the wedding?

"Is everything still going forward as scheduled on Saturday?" Daisy inquired, reluctantly.

"Of course!" Laurel exclaimed once more.

Daisy glanced at Rick a second time. If he had any reaction—good or bad—to Laurel's confirmation, he didn't show it.

"Oh, wow." Laurel checked her watch. "How did it get so late? I was just hoping to pop in for a croissant and have a quick chat about Chris. Then I saw the ambulance and Rick pulling up in his truck. And now I've left Chris waiting for me for over an hour."

"So can I tell Aunt Emily that you're on board for Friday afternoon?" Daisy asked. "Is four o'clock okay?"

Laurel smiled graciously. "Four o'clock is perfect." She turned to Rick. "Would you mind walking me to my car? I'd like to talk to you about a wedding gift that I was thinking of getting for Bobby."

Rick agreed, good-byes were exchanged, and the pair set off in the direction of the front parking lot. As Daisy watched them depart, she noticed that they were walking awfully close to each other. But how close was too close?

When they turned the corner of the building, Rick paused and took a quick look back at her. His expression was once again murky. Daisy wondered at his strange behavior. She had the distinct impression that he knew something she didn't and that he was up to something— something in all likelihood troublesome—but she had no inkling what. And she couldn't think about it now. She had Brenda, and the bakery, and Deputy Johnson to worry about.

With a weary sigh, Daisy remembered that she still needed to give the deputy the three crates that were sitting

inside her trunk. There didn't seem to be much of a reason for it anymore, now that the man Brenda had stabbed
had been identified. But there was still a small chance of
finding a useful fingerprint on them. Maybe it could be
linked to another geocacher. Except even if Deputy Johnson somehow managed to make such a connection, it would
surely come too late. The last geocacher would be long gone
from Pittsylvania County, and Fuzzy Lake Campground
would be empty and shut tight for the winter.

Unless she succeeded in nosing around the campground first. Perhaps she could discover some clue there
that would help her piece together the enigmatic puzzle of
the cream cheese and the broken window—or broken
windows. Daisy pondered the idea with growing excitement. The timing was good. Laurel had just told her that
she and Chris would be out all day collecting the remaining caches from the hunt, which meant that she didn't
need to be concerned about running into either of them
at the campground. And Sweetie Pies would have to stay
closed until tomorrow, in any event, while the surrounding area was searched for the gun and the storage room
was cleared of glass shards.

Daisy looked at Deputy Johnson. He was busy dealing
with the crowd, the ambulance, and the other deputies—so
busy that he probably wouldn't notice if she left. She could
talk to him about the crates and Caesar and everything
else later. Daisy congratulated herself on not mentioning
to him where Laurel, Chris, and the rest of the geocachers
were staying. He would figure it out eventually, of course.
But he wouldn't get to the campground before she did
and interfere with her investigation.

First she would check on Brenda and apprise her of

the plan. That way Brenda could cover for her temporarily if Deputy Johnson did happen to detect that she had disappeared. As Daisy headed toward the back door of the bakery, she saw that Rick was still stopped at the corner of the building. Although he wasn't actually touching Laurel, he was standing very close to her. Laurel was speaking, and Rick seemed to be listening attentively, but his eyes remained on Daisy.

She smiled at him, shrewdly. Rick could stand as close to Laurel as he wanted, just so long as he kept her away from the campground. He didn't smile back. There was an uneasiness in his gaze, as though he had in that moment realized that she might be up to something too—that she had her own agenda—and he didn't appear to like it in the least.

"Daisy—" Rick started to say, in a tone of warning.

But he was too late. Daisy had already slipped through the door and out of sight.

CHAPTER
16

"Tell me again, what exactly are we looking for here at the campground?"

"You'll know it when you see it."

"Or smell it?" Beulah returned.

Daisy laughed. "After four days out of refrigeration, I would think that cream cheese has got to be pretty ripe."

"So then it'll be more of a stink than a smell—just like Duke's feet."

"Duke's feet!" With one leg out of the car and one leg still in, Daisy looked over at Beulah, who was sitting on the passenger seat next to her, pulling back her red mop and securing it with a pink rubber band. "Should I even ask?"

"Duke and Connor were working at the salon this morning," she explained, "when all of a sudden water started pouring in from out of nowhere. Duke's boots got soaked through, and he pulled 'em off. The stench was so bad, I was sure the flood had carried in a dead raccoon from underneath the stoop. I couldn't imagine it came from anything still alive, but it did. It was Duke's feet."

"Lovely." Daisy wrinkled her nose.

Beulah nodded. "Even after wading around in his socks for a full hour, the smell still didn't get any better."

"Maybe instead of delivering Rick's moonshine," Daisy said, "Duke should try soaking his feet in it."

"They do call it rotgut for a reason. Enough of the stuff will kill just about everything."

"Whether you want it to or not!"

"Too bad a little 'shine can't also make Rick a little less of a weasel," Beulah remarked dryly.

Daisy merely shrugged. Her focus wasn't on Rick. "When did Duke and Connor get to the salon today?" she asked Beulah.

"Around eight, maybe a few minutes after. Why?"

As she climbed out of the car and closed the door behind her, Daisy tried to calculate how long it all took. Could Duke or Connor have broken the storage room window, shot Caesar, and made it to the salon by eight, or a few minutes thereafter?

Beulah finished tucking up her curls, then she climbed out of the car too. "If you're worried about Aunt Emily talking to them, she knows that they're going to have to dig in the yard. She's not happy about it, of course, but she understands that it's got to be done if we ever want to figure out what the problem is."

"I wasn't thinking about Aunt Emily," Daisy replied, somewhat absently. "I was thinking about Duke and Connor. Did you see them when they first arrived? Did they act peculiar in any way?"

"Act peculiar?" Beulah snorted. "It's Duke and Connor. They're always a bit peculiar, and it's never an act. I just told you about Duke's feet."

Daisy frowned. Surely Beulah would have noticed something unusual about the pair if they had been at Sweetie Pies. Neither Duke or Connor was the slick, callous sort of person who could gun down a man one minute, then calmly tinker with the plumbing the next minute. They'd be spooked, and they'd show it.

Suddenly Beulah's hazel eyes widened. "You don't believe they had something to do with what happened at the bakery this morning?"

"No." Daisy shook her head. "The timing doesn't work. They couldn't have driven from one place to the other, not by eight. The distance is too great."

"Forget about timing and distances. Think about Rick! Caesar worked for him, didn't he? Nobody who knows Rick would dream of messing around with someone who works for him. It's suicide! And *killing* Caesar? You might as well flay and barbecue yourself, because Rick won't be so nice when he catches up with you."

Beulah was absolutely right. Rick protected his own, fearlessly. Everybody in Pittsylvania County knew that— Duke and Connor included. Duke himself worked for Rick bootlegging. Daisy remembered how nervous he had gotten at the nip joint, and that was just in relation to a clay marker and a jelly jar. He would never test Rick's wrath by hurting Caesar, not even inadvertently.

"Well, at least that rules two people out," Daisy said. "Last evening when I saw the crates outside the nip joint I was thinking that practically anybody could have stolen the cream cheese. Anybody who knew both about the bakery and the nip joint. Now I know it was a geocacher—or at least one of them was a geocacher—and it makes me think that maybe it was a geocacher at Sweetie Pies today also."

"A geocacher who obviously doesn't know Rick!" Beulah exclaimed.

"None of them do, other than Laurel and Chris."

The hazel eyes circled around the campground. "How many of them are still here?"

"I don't know." Daisy's eyes circled around too. "But I'm hoping we're going to find that out."

Beulah gave a little grunt. "Preferably without ending up like Caesar in the process."

"If we see anybody, we just say we're looking for Laurel. That's perfectly plausible. I am making her wedding cake, after all."

"I'll remind you of that when we're staring down the barrel of a gun."

"Don't be silly," Daisy scoffed. "The gun from this morning is long gone. I told that to both Laurel and Deputy Johnson. There are those ponds along the farm road by the bakery. They're an ideal spot to dump a firearm."

"Maybe." Beulah grunted again. "It's a good plan for someone who's actually thinking. Except I'm not so sure these boys have their heads screwed on straight. They took cream cheese, remember? That's probably what they dumped in the ponds."

"And then hauled the crates to the nip joint?" Daisy retorted. "That doesn't make much sense."

"There's no sense in any of it. Which proves my point. They don't have their heads screwed on straight!"

Leaving the car at the end of the entrance road, Daisy and Beulah began to walk toward the center of the campground, where the cabins were clustered together like fallen pine cones collected around the base of a tree. They were the same faded shade of brown as old pine cones and just as weathered looking. It had been dark the last time that Daisy was there—the night of the geocacher party—so she hadn't noticed it then, but seeing the cabins now in the daylight, she realized how similar they all were, nearly identical, in fact. The design was uniform. Three short steps up to a narrow deck, followed by a small square plywood hut with washed-out, graying stain, hence the resemblance to old pine cones.

"I can understand why Bobby got confused," she mused.

"Confused about what?" Beulah asked.

"Apparently he got lost a couple of days ago trying to find Laurel's cabin. Chris told me that he found him wandering in circles, talking about going into the wrong cabin while being positive that it was the right cabin, only it wasn't."

Beulah chuckled. "That sounds like Bobby. Lucky for him, these cabins aren't the kind where somebody is apt to plink you for trespassing. I hope we have the same luck."

They passed the hewn log bench that Daisy had shared with Chris during the party, where they had admired the night sky and each other. Daisy couldn't help glancing at it with a touch of wistfulness.

"Speaking of Chris," Beulah said, looking at the bench too, "are you going to take Laurel's advice and give him another try?"

"I don't know. Ignoring everything else, there's the issue of geography. Sooner or later he's going to have to go home and back to work, probably right after the wedding."

"He can always visit," Beulah countered. "That's why we have cars and planes and phones. Laurel doesn't seem to think it's a problem."

"But she's naturally biased as his sister. She wants Chris to have an extra reason to come here. Otherwise she might not see him much," Daisy reminded her. "And I have the feeling that she really enjoys being a matchmaker."

"It doesn't mean she's not a good matchmaker."

Daisy didn't respond. They continued onward in silence until they reached the wood-chip path that branched off to the individual cabins.

"How do we do this?" Beulah dropped her voice. "Do we just go up and knock on the nearest door?"

Even with the low tone, her words seemed jarringly loud. There was no movement and no noise at Fuzzy Lake Campground. On the night of the party there had been nearly fifty people gathered around the blazing fire pit. Now there wasn't a single one anywhere in sight. Although the entrance to the campground had been open, it seemed as though the place was already closed for the season. No vehicles were parked on the grass. No backpacks or fishing poles were lined up, waiting for action. There was no sign of human activity whatsoever.

"Maybe we don't need to knock," Beulah answered herself. "Maybe they're all gone."

"But if they're all gone," Daisy said, "who was at the bakery this morning?"

"So maybe they aren't really gone. Maybe they're only away for the day and coming back tonight like Laurel and Chris."

"Then we better move fast, before somebody decides to return early."

With quick steps, Daisy went up the short set of stairs onto the deck of the first cabin. The screen door was tattered. Its handle was tarnished almost to black. She hesitated for an instant, then knocked. There was no answer. She tried the handle and found it locked.

Beulah peered through the window. "It's empty," she reported.

"Well, a lot of the geocachers left as soon as Laurel called off the hunt. This cabin must have belonged to them."

"I guess that means we're going to have to try them all."

Daisy nodded. "How about if I take this side of the path and you take the other? Splitting it up will get it done that much faster."

Agreeing, Beulah headed toward her assigned group.

"Holler if you see anything interesting," Daisy called after her.

"If I find something good, can I keep it?" she called back.

"Sure. But if it's cash or booze, you're going to have to share!"

There were twenty cabins, so Daisy's allotment consisted of the ten on the left half of the wood-chip path. She proceeded to the next in line. It was like the first cabin, only with a slightly more tattered screen door. This one was locked too. Through the deck window she could see four bare mattresses on rusted metal bed frames lining the walls. Next to a tiny kitchenette in the corner, there was an empty table surrounded by four empty chairs. Two blue checkered sofas and a rocking chair with a matching blue cushion took up the center of the room. Aside from a faux fur throw rug, the floor was clear.

The third cabin was no different. Neither was the fourth or the fifth. The number of beds varied—as did the color of the checkered sofas—but none of the cabins was occupied. There wasn't any debate about that. And all of them were clean, so they had been vacant for at least a day already.

By the sixth cabin Daisy no longer bothered with the door. She simply jogged up to the deck, glanced through the window, and jogged back to the path again. But at the eighth cabin she stopped in surprise. The shade on the window was drawn down from the inside. Did that mean this cabin was still in use? Tiptoeing to the door, Daisy gently rapped a knuckle on the frame. There was no response. She knocked again—harder this time—and listened. No voice, no footsteps. Her fingers went to the handle. It turned.

"I've got one!" she shouted across the path in Beulah's general direction.

Feeling a twinge of scruple, Daisy wavered for a moment. Even unlocked, it didn't seem right to walk into the cabin without permission. There were plenty of campers who never bothered to lock up while they were out during the day, mostly because there was so little point to it. They didn't leave anything valuable behind, and it was just too easy to slice open the side of a tent or break into a cheap plywood hut. But somehow that made Daisy feel even worse about entering uninvited. Then she reminded herself why she was doing it, and she pulled open the door.

The ceiling light was switched on, as was the attached fan, which whirled around with a loud, rhythmic ticking that sounded like kernels of corn popping. The cabin was definitely occupied and, just as definitely, by only one person. There was a single bed made up with a pillow and set of sheets. A single water glass stood on the table by the kitchenette. And a single towel hung from the hook next to the bathroom cubicle.

Daisy surveyed the suitcase lying open on the floor with its contents scattered around it, the magazine and hairbrush sitting on the lemon yellow rocking chair cushion, and the clothes tossed on the bed. She recognized two of the shirts and a sweater.

"What is it!" Beulah's shoes pounded up the steps to the deck. "What did you find?"

"Nothing," Daisy answered with a sigh. "It's Laurel's cabin. She wore that striped pullover on the night of the party here."

Glancing around the room, Beulah sighed too. "Boring."

Turning on her heel, Daisy walked out. "That's all I've come up with so far. How about you?"

"Empty, empty, and more empty. I've only got one left."

"I've got two. Meet you at the end?"

With a nod, Beulah sauntered off again. Daisy shut the door behind them with an extra-firm push. She was extremely glad that she knew for certain Laurel was away collecting the remaining caches. It would have been awfully embarrassing to have her suddenly appear and see them standing in the middle of her cabin.

She found the last pair of cabins vacant. Clearly, all the geocachers had departed. But that left the question of who was at the bakery that morning. It occurred to her that it still could have been one of the geocachers, even if they were no longer staying at the campground. They could have easily moved elsewhere—to a motel in the area, a concealed tent on the edge of the woods, or even just to a car for a few days. It was actually the smart thing to do. If you were going to steal cream cheese, break windows, and shoot people, you probably wanted to change your address, quickly and often.

"Daisy!"

Daisy spun toward the wood-chip path.

"Up here!"

Beulah's hand waved from the deck of the last cabin on her side. Daisy promptly trotted over to it.

"Now you can answer all of your questions," Beulah drawled.

Stepping through the open doorway, Daisy looked around eagerly. Clothing, books, a rumpled bed, dirty dishes stacked on the table, a wet towel mounded on the floor. It looked pretty much the same as Laurel's cabin— only considerably messier—and the ceiling fan didn't sound like popcorn.

"What questions am I answering with this?" Daisy said, frowning in disappointment.

"Whether you want to give Chris another chance."

"This is Chris's cabin?"

Beulah held up two heavy tomes that were lying on the red-checkered sofa. "They're about the Confederacy and a thousand pages apiece. You think anybody but a college professor would bring these along for some light reading?"

That made Daisy smile.

Setting down the books, Beulah returned to the duffel bag that she had been rifling through when Daisy first entered. "I haven't been able to find any evidence of a secret girlfriend."

"You shouldn't be going through his stuff," Daisy chastised her.

"I'm not pocketing any of it," Beulah retorted. "I'm just having a wee look-see."

Although Daisy shook her head in further reproof, her smile slipped into a grin. "You are a bad seed, my dear."

Grinning also, Beulah continued rifling. Daisy went back outside and sat in one of the plastic lounge chairs on the deck. After a few minutes, Beulah joined her.

"Boring," she concluded. "Just like his sister."

"After everything that's gone on over the past week," Daisy replied, "boring is mighty welcome to me."

Beulah didn't disagree. "So what now? Do you want to drive around the rest of the place and take a look at the tents?"

"No. What purpose would it serve? We're not going to find the right tent, if there even is one. Whatever geo-cachers were involved, they aren't here anymore, at least not at the campground."

"So what now?" Beulah repeated.

"I don't know. I'm fresh out of ideas and open to suggestions."

"Maybe it doesn't matter," Beulah submitted. "Maybe everybody really is gone—gone from Pittsylvania County, gone for good."

"And this morning?" Daisy rejoined.

"Maybe they came back to the bakery because they thought they had left something behind the last time and they didn't want the law to find it."

"But they didn't take anything."

"Maybe once they were inside they realized that they didn't actually leave behind what they thought they had."

"That's a lot of 'maybes,'" Daisy said dubiously.

Once again, Beulah didn't disagree.

They remained on the deck for some time. Beulah picked at a chipped fingernail and mumbled intermittently about the salon—whether Duke and Connor would ever be able to fix the flooding and whether she would have any clients left by the time that they did. Daisy gazed out at the cabins. All empty but two, and those two were of absolutely no help. What a wasted trip. She would have been better off staying at Sweetie Pies, talking to Deputy Johnson and giving him the crates. And she still needed to get the banana pudding and bring it to the historical society for the fundraiser that evening, after she dropped Beulah at the inn.

Leaning her head against the back of the chair, Daisy closed her eyes. She would rest for a minute first. She was tired, and it was so peaceful on the deck. No shattering glass, no ambulance sirens, no hint of hooligans or sundry late-blooming criminals. A momentary shadow passed across her vision. Then came another. She cracked an eye. Vultures. They were circling in the sky above her. One bird swooped down behind Chris's cabin. A second did the same. More quickly followed.

Something was dead. Daisy's eyes flew open, and her heart thudded in her chest. A dead deer was one thing. A dead person was quite another. She rose abruptly from her chair. Beulah looked at her.

"Are you okay? You're kind of pale."

"Vultures are landing behind the cabin," Daisy informed her.

"And?" Beulah shrugged. "We see vultures all the time. We passed a bunch of them on the highway driving out here."

"And on the highway they were eating roadkill, not geocacher."

It was Beulah's turn to pale. "You're joking, right? Please tell me you're only joking about the geocacher."

Daisy sincerely wished that she were only joking. But vultures didn't circle and land for no reason. Hopefully, her initial guess had been the correct one, and there was nothing more than deer bones behind the cabin.

With some trepidation, she walked down the stairs

from the deck and around the side of the plywood hut. As she turned the corner toward the back, the startled vultures retreated to the neighboring trees.

"That sure is a relief," Beulah exhaled, rounding the corner on Daisy's heels.

There was no carcass—human or otherwise. The vultures had been attracted by two sizable heaps of garbage, both of which included an abundance of food scraps.

"I'll say it again," Beulah sucked on her teeth, "those boys don't have their heads screwed on straight. Doesn't everybody know you don't leave food out when you're camping? That's how you wake up at dawn with a bear eating your face."

"I wonder whether bears like cream cheese," Daisy mused.

"If your cheese isn't in the ponds by the bakery, then it's probably in these piles."

Although it was possible, Daisy thought it unlikely. The heaps were large, but not so large that ninety pounds of cream cheese wouldn't have been visible in some way.

She scanned the trash. Beer cans, potato chip bags, mustard bottles, remnants of hot dog buns. It looked a lot like the leftovers from the party that she and Beulah had attended. There were also beer bottles, and they looked a lot like the pieces of the bottle that she had found on the storage room floor of Sweetie Pies that morning.

For a fleeting second, Daisy got excited. It was another clue. Then she stopped herself. Beer bottles were not exactly an endangered species. Plenty of beer bottles looked like plenty of other beer bottles. On closer inspection, she noted that the ones in the trash piles had all sorts of different labels. She couldn't remember if there had even been a label on the pieces in the bakery. And she had no clue what the beer bottle that had been used to break the window at the historical society looked like.

Wings flapped from a nearby branch, and Daisy glanced over at them. The vultures were eyeing her with annoyance, waiting for her to vacate the premises so that they could return to their scavenging. She was about to oblige them when something in one of the heaps caught her attention.

Some of the garbage had been bagged, but many of the bags had been torn open, no doubt by hungry critters searching for a midnight snack. A sneaker was sticking out of one bag. It seemed very white against the black trash bag. That was what made Daisy notice it. Walking over for a better look, she saw the sneaker's mate lying on the ground next to the bag. It had obviously tumbled out first. She reached down and picked it up.

"Do you really want another pair of sneakers that bad?" Beulah chortled. "Because those are about five sizes too big for you and have probably been chewed on by something with rabies."

The shoe in Daisy's hand hadn't been chewed on. In fact, it appeared almost new. The tread on the bottom was barely worn.

"Why would somebody dump perfectly good sneakers?" Beulah said, leaning over Daisy's shoulder.

Daisy pulled the other shoe from the trash bag and held the two next to each other. Although they were both white, the one that had still been in the bag was whiter somehow. Squinting at it, she realized that the whole shoe wasn't actually so white. It was just the mesh in the front and on the sides. There was something on the mesh—and in the mesh too—that made it look whiter.

"It can't be," Daisy murmured.

"Can't be what?" Beulah asked.

She didn't answer, too focused on her discovery. She rubbed a finger into the mesh. A thin coating of white powder stuck to her skin.

Beulah's brow furrowed. "What the heck is that?"

Still not answering, Daisy put the finger to her lips.

"Have you lost your mind?" Beulah exclaimed. "You can't eat that! It might be rat poison! Do you know how sick you could get?"

Not heeding the warning, her tongue touched the white powder.

"You're insane!" Beulah hollered at her. "What am I going to tell Rick when he wants to know how you ended up half dead in the hospital? The weasel will kill me!"

Daisy stared at the remaining powder on her finger for a long moment, then she raised her gaze to Beulah and calmly replied, "You don't have to tell Rick anything. I'm not going to the hospital. If I get sick, it isn't from this."

Beulah opened her mouth, but no words came out.

"It's not rat poison," Daisy said. "It's flour."

CHAPTER
17

Flour was surely no more of an endangered species than beer bottles, but in this case Daisy was quite confident that the flour on the shoes at Fuzzy Lake Campground matched her flour at the bakery. Which meant that she could now answer Beulah's question. Why would somebody dump perfectly good sneakers? Because they had worn them while stealing cream cheese, and they didn't want to take the proof home.

The proof was a gift from Brenda, albeit a rather inadvertent one. A scoop of flour originally intended for the shortcake dough had been thrown in an attempt to protect her darling Blot from the vicious cat kicker, aka Jordan Snyder. Brenda had said it best to Deputy Johnson—like flour does, it went everywhere. On the kitchen floor. In Jordan's eyes, causing him to slip and fall into the chef's knife. And into the mesh of one of the other men's sneakers.

The man had probably tried to get it out, but flour could be so stubbornly clingy, as Daisy could well attest.

No matter how often and how meticulously she and Brenda scrubbed the kitchen, a layer of flour dust always seemed to remain behind. Washing the shoes would have worked, but either the man didn't want to bother with that or he didn't think of it. Instead he chose the garbage bag, and if he had disposed of the garbage bag a bit more carefully—with less access to hungry critters—Daisy never would have spotted the whiter-than-white sneakers in the trash heaps behind Chris's cabin.

Unfortunately, the sneakers didn't really do her much good. She already knew that geocachers had been involved. The flour on the shoes and the shoes being at the campground merely confirmed it further. They also added weight to Aunt Emily's theory of hooligans, along with Deputy Johnson's theory of dumb pranks and shenanigans. Serious criminals didn't wear nice new sneakers to steal cream cheese and then carelessly discard those sneakers at the place where they had been vacationing for the past two weeks.

Daisy took the sneakers along regardless. Like the crates at the nip joint, they were evidence, and she figured that it was best not to leave them behind. There was always the chance—slim as it might be—that they would prove useful somehow. When she later delivered both the crates and the shoes to Deputy Johnson after dropping Beulah at the inn, it didn't take the deputy long to inspect them and tell her what she had already supposed. There weren't any fingerprints, at least no legible ones. Two of the crates had a couple of smudges, but they could have just as easily come from her as from anybody else.

Although Daisy had expected it, it was still disappointing news. It left her with nothing, nothing but nagging doubts and unresolved questions. She could only hope that Beulah's guess at the campground had been correct. All of the geocachers—Laurel and Chris aside, of course—were now gone from Pittsylvania County, and they were gone for good. While stealing the cream cheese and breaking the storage room window could be considered mischief, Caesar's death certainly could not. And Daisy wasn't eager to stumble over any more bodies at her bakery, even if this time they belonged to Jordan Snyder's partners in crime.

Also as she had expected, Deputy Johnson informed her that the gun which had been used to shoot Caesar couldn't be located in the area immediately surrounding Sweetie Pies. He was convinced that it would ultimately turn up, however. Daisy didn't bother arguing with him. Even if it was found—and not at the bottom of a farm pond, as she strongly suspected—most likely the gun wouldn't have any fingerprints on it either.

The deputy concluded their meeting with a tedious, self-congratulatory speech about how he had been right all along. It had been strangers—strangers who were criminals, who had come waltzing into the neighborhood. Daisy was tempted to ask him whether he also thought they had waltzed back out again, but she restrained herself. Such sarcasm would only prolong the speech, and she had a banana pudding to deliver.

It was late in the afternoon when she finally arrived at the historical society. Thankfully, the lecture wasn't scheduled to begin until seven, so her contribution to the cause wasn't tardy. Weatherwise, it had all the hallmarks of being a pleasant evening: a comfortably warm temperature for the middle of October and just a hint of a breeze, so it wouldn't be too chilly after the sun went down, ideal for sitting outdoors with a light sweater. Apparently, the fundraiser organizers had the same idea, because they were busy carrying out folding chairs from the building and setting up refreshment tables at the far end of the small parking lot.

The Pittsylvania Historical Society was an old, venerable organization, but its current home was a sad beige warehouse that looked like it was in the business of selling spare tractor parts instead of serving as the county visitors' bureau and assisting in important genealogical and historical research. It was immediately adjacent to the aged Chatham Railroad Depot. The depot hadn't been in use for nearly half a century—when passenger service to the area had ceased—but it was in the process of being lovingly restored, albeit slowly, as funds allowed. The beautiful red brick had been cleaned and grouted. The crumbling roof had been replaced with burgundy French tile. And the surrounding ironwork had been stripped and freshly painted in gleaming black.

The long-term goal was to move the society from the shoddy warehouse to the shiny depot, but the interior of the depot still needed considerable work, hence the fundraisers. Even without the move, the historical society was in desperate need of a cash infusion. The electricity and gas had gone unpaid for far too many months, and the parking lot had more potholes than asphalt. If that wasn't enough, now courtesy of a presumed hooligan with a beer bottle, a new window to the back conference room was necessary.

"Hullo, Ducky!"

Daisy glanced around and promptly smiled. "Hey there, Mr. Brent!"

"You need any help with the precious cargo?"

"No, I think I've got it." She lifted the pudding from

the passenger side of her car, where she had strapped it in like a toddler in a booster seat.

"Okey-dokey. You just bring it on over when you're ready. I've got a place of honor waiting for it."

Closing the car door with a shove from her foot, Daisy slowly walked the pudding to the designated spot.

"Set it right here on the wagon, Ducky. Center stage, so to speak."

The wagon was actually a restored railroad baggage cart—four fire-engine-red wheels with a bright yellow handle and trim. It was spiffy, and the perfect height and size to serve as a refreshment table. As promised, the grand banana pudding had a place of honor in the center. An assortment of cookies, crackers, cheese squares, and cut vegetables with dip took up the rest of the cart.

"Well, now. Doesn't that look purdy?"

"Aw, thank you, Mr. Brent." Daisy stepped back to admire her creation. It was a darn fine pudding, even if she said so herself.

"Yes, ma'am. Purdy as a monarch on milkweed."

Her smile grew. It was impossible not to like Henry Brent. At ninety-four, he was one of the oldest citizens of Pittsylvania County still to be puttering around on his own, with all of his faculties in full function. Aunt Emily called him the dapper clacker. He was, in fact, exceedingly dapper. Today he wore a light green seersucker suit with a green and white polka dot clip-on bow tie. Scuffed white buck wingtips completed the outfit. The *clacker* portion of the name referred to his dentures. Not only did they clack when he talked, he also seemed to enjoy clacking them now and again for no particular reason.

"Have you seen my momma?" Daisy asked him, as she surveyed the bustling organizers.

"I don't believe she's coming until later, Ducky—with Edna and May."

"They're the ones doing the lecture tonight, right? It's on appraising antiques?"

Henry Brent nodded. "And they're the perfect pair for the job. If anybody in this area knows about antiques, it's the Fowler sisters. Those two have been running that shop over in Motley for thirty years now. Have you ever been?"

"A few times, though not recently," Daisy answered. "I know that Aunt Emily loves the place. She goes crazy for all the folk art they've got there."

"They've got some pretty good pottery too. And lots of nice furniture, along with a collection of very interesting old maps and documents."

"Speaking of old maps," she said, "my momma told me that someone busted a window here this past weekend, and they took a couple of maps from the back conference room."

The dapper clacker responded with an especially loud clack. "I can't understand why everybody insists on calling it the back conference room. There's not a front conference room. And as long as I've been a member of the society, we've never had a conference, not indoors, at least. There's the spring picnic and banjo festival, but I don't think you can really consider that a conference, do you?"

Daisy shook her head politely, then steered the conversation back to the more important subject. "My momma also told me that the maps which were taken weren't valuable."

"They weren't," Henry Brent confirmed. "I'm the one who gave your momma—and the other members—that information."

"You were?"

He chortled at her evident surprise. "I do know a few things, Ducky. It's why they let me wander about unattended. And I should know a few things about old things, after all. I'm an old thing myself, or haven't you noticed?"

"You look as spry as a grasshopper in June to me, Mr. Brent."

"Aren't you a sweet-talker!" he exclaimed, chortling harder.

Again Daisy brought the conversation back to the more important subject. "So if the maps weren't valuable, why do you think somebody stole them—just to cause trouble?"

"Maybe. It all depends on who it was that stole them. Value is always in the eye of the beholder, Ducky."

She frowned in confusion. "But a minute ago you said they weren't valuable."

"They're not," he reiterated. "They're not valuable to me, or to your momma, or to Emily Tosh, or to the Fowler sisters, or—"

"Then who might they be valuable to?" Daisy interrupted him impatiently.

"Somebody who's searching for treasure."

"Treasure?" Her frown deepened. "What treasure?"

"The great treasure of the Confederate States of America."

Daisy burst out laughing. "Oh, Mr. Brent, everybody knows that's nothing more than a silly old folktale!"

"There are still believers," he retorted.

"Of course." She nodded amiably. "All good Southerners know the stories of the cherished Confederate treasury that was carefully hidden away from the thieving hands of the evil Union until the glorious South could one day rise again. Treasure hunters and historians have been going on about it forever. They've also looked for it forever and everywhere—from the far-western corner of Virginia to the far-eastern corner of Georgia—and they haven't found a lick of anything glittery."

"True." Henry Brent straightened his bow tie. "All very true. The fabled Confederate gold is nothing more than a gleam in the eye on Lee-Jackson Day."

"But you still think somebody might have taken the maps to search for the treasure?"

"I do," he replied. "Only, I don't believe the treasure that they're looking for is the gold. I believe it's the silver."

"Silver?" Daisy's laughter stilled. "I've never heard of any silver."

"Most people haven't, probably because it's not worth anywhere near as much as the gold."

"Or because it doesn't exist either," she returned dryly.

The dapper clacker answered with an extra clack. "It exists. Only, I don't see how the maps are going to help anybody get to it. If I did, I wouldn't have donated them to the society fifty years ago. I would have used them myself."

Daisy didn't doubt that. If a person was in possession of honest-to-goodness Confederate treasure maps, he went out and—as promptly as possible—found Confederate treasure. He didn't hang the maps in the back conference room of the Pittsylvania Historical Society.

"So the maps aren't real?" she said. "They only appear real?"

"No, no," Henry Brent corrected her. "The maps are very much genuine—nineteenth-century originals. They're in excellent condition too," he added proudly. "No damage or repairs, just a tiny bit of foxing around the margins.

I always took good care of them. We don't actually own antiques, you know. We just preserve them for the next generation."

She couldn't help but think that whoever had the maps now most likely didn't share that generous philosophy.

"Five maps were taken," he continued. "They range in date from 1865 to 1870, and they show the county— different views, predominantly of the mountains. Two of the maps are large and more detailed. The others are smaller and not as comprehensive. But in one way, all five are identical. None of them show Danville."

"That makes sense though, doesn't it?" Daisy responded. "Danville isn't in Pittsylvania County. It's adjacent to it."

"And Danville is where the silver is."

"Seriously?" She blinked at him. "You're seriously telling me there's Confederate treasure in Danville?"

"I am indeed. Thirty-nine kegs of Mexican silver dollars." As he spoke, Henry Brent's craggy face was both earnest and excited at the same time. "It was payment to the Confederacy for the sale of cotton to Mexico. The coins were transported to Danville—as the last capital of the Confederacy—by train. It was several thousand pounds of silver, and when further retreat became necessary as a result of the rapidly advancing Yankee forces, that was much too heavy and burdensome to move very far by wagon. The only option was to bury it in the area. So that's what they did."

Daisy went on blinking dubiously. "Thirty-nine kegs of Mexican silver dollars are buried under the city?"

"The kegs themselves would have rotted in the ground by now," he rejoined.

"But kegs or no kegs, nobody's ever found these coins?"

"You can't go digging willy-nilly around city property, Ducky. Or private property, neither."

There was a short pause as Daisy tried to decide how much of the story—if any—she was willing to credit. In her experience, Henry Brent didn't usually have flights of fancy. But the whole thing seemed awfully far-fetched. Confederate silver hidden under Danville? And no one had ever come across it in all these years, even accidentally during some construction project? Then it occurred to her that it didn't really matter one way or the other. The maps were the important point, not the treasure—real or fictitious.

"If the maps don't include Danville," Daisy said, "then why would somebody who's searching for the silver want to steal them?"

The dapper clacker gave a double clack. "Because they don't think the silver is buried under Danville."

"You just said it was buried there."

"It is buried there. Except that doesn't mean every treasure hunter and historian believes it to be so. There are always those who hold out hope. They imagine that they're smarter and cleverer than all the others who preceded them. They're convinced that they'll be the one to finally discover the coins."

"Okay," she shrugged, "but how do the maps help with that? I presume there isn't a giant X to mark the spot of the prize or an arrow pointing out the correct path to it. So do they have some other sort of clues on them? Secret signs and codes?"

Henry Brent and his dentures grinned. "That sure would be fun, wouldn't it, Ducky? It would make for a real treasure hunt! There could be a special decoder ring too, like the kind kids used to find in cereal boxes back in the good ol' days. But sadly," the grin faded, "that isn't the case here. The maps are just plain, ordinary maps. There's nothing secret—or unusual—or even particularly interesting about them, not unless you're fascinated by an in-depth tour of the mountains around Fuzzy Lake."

That instantly caught Daisy's attention. "The mountains around Fuzzy Lake?" she echoed in astonishment. "Does that include the mountain between the lake and Fuzzy Lake Campground?"

"I'm not familiar with the campground, but I would assume so," he told her. "The maps are focused on the mountains surrounding the lake, so if the specific mountain that you're referring to borders Fuzzy Lake, then it would be on the maps."

A thousand thoughts raced through Daisy's brain all at once, and her knees quaked slightly beneath her. Henry Brent put his gnarled hand on her arm.

"Are you feeling all right, Ducky?"

"I—I—" Her mind was whirling so fast that she wasn't capable of a proper reply.

"You look dizzy. If you're dizzy, you shouldn't drive."

She had to drive. She had to go somewhere quiet and think.

The dapper clacker gazed at her with concern. "Maybe you should sit down for a moment."

Daisy took a deep breath in an effort to gather herself. "I'm fine. Thank you. I just really need to leave. Will you tell my momma that I was here?"

"Sure will, Ducky. But—"

Not waiting for him to finish, she hurried toward her car. After a few steps, Daisy stopped and turned back.

"Mr. Brent," she asked, "how did the people who stole the maps know they were at the historical society?"

"I'm afraid that's probably my fault," he confessed. "As I've been working on updating the society's Web site, I've added images from our collection. I started with the book and pamphlet covers, then I moved to the old letters and maps. I haven't gotten through everything, but I've done all the maps on the walls. Or at least," he amended a tad sheepishly, "the maps that used to be on the walls."

"So anyone could have seen them," Daisy said, more to herself than to him. "Anyone could have known they were here."

"I'm afraid that's my fault," he repeated.

"It's not your fault at all," she corrected him. "You can't help it if stupid people get stupid ideas into their heads."

And as Daisy walked away, that was precisely what worried her—stupid people with stupid ideas. They were dangerously unpredictable. That was how other people wound up dead.

CHAPTER
18

Henry Brent wasn't just an aged dapper clacker in seer-sucker who reminisced fondly over cereal box decoder rings. He also knew how to use the Internet, and obviously, so did the geocachers. That was how they had seen the maps. That was how they knew they were hanging on the walls of the Pittsylvania Historical Society. Considering the extreme unreliability of all things satellite and cellular in the area, it seemed most likely that the geocachers had learned where the maps were before ever stepping foot in the county. The maps were probably the reason why they had chosen to attend this particular geocaching event.

Of course, Daisy had no actual proof for any of it. She could only fit the pieces together in the way that seemed to make the best sense to her. There was always the possibility that she was wrong. The geocachers hadn't been involved. Somebody else had stolen the maps from the back conference room. But that wasn't nearly as logical. For starters, there was the timing of the two thefts. The one at the bakery—for which the geocachers had definitely been responsible—took place on Saturday. The theft at the historical society was the very next day, and it had occurred late at night after the geocacher party, during which numerous beer cans and bottles had been emptied.

Then there was the location. The maps dealt with Fuzzy Lake. The geocachers had been staying at the conveniently situated Fuzzy Lake Campground. Finally, there was the general absurdity of it all. Beulah had put it quite aptly—the boys didn't have their heads screwed on straight. Considering how dim-witted Jordan Snyder's partners in crime had been about the cream cheese and the sneakers, it wasn't much of a stretch to assume that they would be just as dim-witted about the maps and the treasure.

And it really was dim-witted. If there was any treasure— which Daisy continued to seriously doubt—from every historical indication according to Henry Brent, it was under Danville. Except the maps that had been stolen didn't show Danville. They showed the mountains around Fuzzy Lake. Assuming for a moment that the geocachers were brighter than they appeared, that they had indeed taken the correct maps and the treasure had actually been hauled from Danville to the mountains around Fuzzy Lake, how exactly did they plan on finding it? By single-handedly digging up those mountains on the remote chance of stumbling across thirty-nine rotted kegs? It was nothing short of ludicrous.

The irony was that even if the geocachers did somehow manage with the assistance of the maps to narrow down the scope of their search to a more specific spot, as of this past Monday the whole area surrounding Fuzzy Lake was closed. All access had been blocked as an emergency measure to protect the bats living in the nearby caves. Daisy knew that from Laurel. It was why the hunt had been called off early. If Laurel needed special permission to enter the area to do nothing more than collect the remaining caches, it seemed highly unlikely that the geocachers would be able to continue digging without being noticed by someone and promptly tossed out on their ears.

In theory, Daisy should have been comforted by the fact that the area was closed, but she wasn't. She had little confidence that the geocachers had truly left Pittsylvania County or that they would so easily give up their search for the treasure. It wasn't because she believed them to be especially wily and determined. On the contrary, her concern was the exact opposite—stupid people with stupid ideas. She had left Henry Brent and the historical society thinking it, and she continued thinking it all that evening and the following day, when she returned to the bakery to reorganize after the chaos of the previous morning and to clean up the shards of glass still lying on the storage room floor.

Sweetie Pies' broken window troubled her the most, for the simple reason that she couldn't come up with a good explanation for it. Beulah had suggested that the geocachers thought they had left something behind the last time and they came back to retrieve it. But Daisy wasn't convinced. It seemed too straightforward in comparison with the convoluted saga of the maps and the treasure. Her instinct told her that there had to be more to it, except she couldn't figure out what else there could possibly be. The bakery had nothing even slightly resembling a map. There were no treasure-hunting tools hidden in between the wire whisks or secret codes taped to the bottom of the refrigerator shelves. There was only flour, sugar, and a new supply of cream cheese—none of which played any role in finding Confederate silver.

The flour, sugar, and cream cheese did, however, combine to make a red velvet cake. As distracted as she was by the disturbing events of the past week, Daisy was resolved to make the best cake that she could for Laurel and Bobby. It was their wedding, after all. There would surely be a few hiccups along the way with such a hastily arranged affair, but she had no intention of letting her cake be among them.

Although she had originally planned on having the bakery open for its full hours both on Thursday and Friday—as well as for a short while early on Saturday before the wedding—Caesar's death changed all of that. Brenda was dearly in need of a rest, and Daisy didn't have nearly enough time or energy to do everything herself. So she decided to keep Sweetie Pies closed until after the weekend to recharge and focus on the cake.

Thursday passed so quietly that it surprised her. She heard from no one—not Laurel or Chris or Bobby or Rick or even Deputy Johnson. It didn't take long for the stillness to start to play on her nerves. Working alone in the kitchen, Daisy found herself unusually jumpy. A semi rumbled down the road a bit louder than normal, and she hurried to make sure that the doors were locked. When a chainsaw wailed in the distance, she immediately double-checked all the windows. Every noise sent her imagination spinning, but the silence also made her uneasy. She told herself repeatedly that there was no cause to be anxious. The geocachers weren't coming back, not again. Whatever they wanted from the bakery, they had already gotten or at least finished looking for. The broken storage room window and poor Caesar in the parking lot were evidence enough of that.

As Daisy waited for the cake to bake on Friday morning, she felt a growing temptation to call Rick. Another guard would be nice—just for a week or so, until everything with the geocachers was conclusively sorted out, or it all went away somehow. And if not a security guard, then a soothing jelly jar. Corn whiskey had a remarkable way of taking the edge off practically anything. But then, she prudently reminded herself that Rick invariably tended to be more trouble than help, and she still didn't know why he had been behaving so strangely the other day.

She just had to be patient until the cake and its decoration were done and the party for Laurel began; then she could relax and have a palliative snort or two. Aunt Emily could most definitely be counted upon to have an even better stocked bar than usual for a combination bridal shower and bachelorette party. And once the cake was safely delivered to the inn, Daisy didn't have to go to the bakery again until Monday. By then her nerves would be back to their customary calm state, Brenda would be better too, and life would hopefully return to a more peaceful routine that didn't involve preposterous thefts of either cream cheese or treasure-hunting maps.

As promised, Aunt Emily had made room in the refrigerator at the inn, and when Daisy slid the finished red velvet cake onto the awaiting shelf just before four in the afternoon, she heaved a great sigh of relief. Everyone was in agreement: the wedding cake, although perhaps a bit untraditional, was beautiful. Laurel would surely be thrilled. Even if all else went miserably wrong on her special day—there was a sudden hailstorm, swarms of angry locusts descended from the sky, a freak tidal wave washed over southwestern Virginia—at least dessert was accounted for.

The group for the party was small—Daisy, her momma, Beulah, Aunt Emily, and a few other assorted friends and neighbors who never failed to take advantage of an opportunity to participate in a glass of something bubbly and a plate of something savory. The mood was excellent. Daisy was happy with the cake and even happier to be together with the little crowd in the parlor of the inn. Lucy was pleased to report that the fund-raiser at the historical society had gone marvelously well and the grand banana pudding, courtesy of her daughter, had been a tremendous hit. After two horrendous days of suffering through the smell of Duke's wet feet, Beulah was thrilled that he and Connor finally seemed to be making progress on solving the flooding at the salon. And Aunt Emily was ecstatic that their solution didn't appear to involve her having to shut off the power to the well. There was only one thing missing from the jubilant celebration—the bride.

"You did remember to invite her, didn't you, Ducky?" Aunt Emily asked, as the clock on the marble mantle chimed the half-hour.

Daisy replied that she had.

"And you told her the correct date and time?"

"Friday afternoon at four," she confirmed. "Laurel even repeated the time back to me and said it was perfect."

Aunt Emily looked at the clock and frowned. "I understand that some misguided folks may be fond of arriving so-called fashionably late, but I do believe that being thirty minutes tardy to a party which is held specifically in your honor is quickly crossing the line into downright rude."

"The girl might have gotten lost," Lucy suggested more temperately. "Has she been to the inn before?"

"She's been to the salon next door," Beulah responded. "That's where Daisy and I first met her."

"Maybe she got held up by something unexpected," Lucy remarked.

Beulah chortled. "Maybe Bobby was the one who got lost, and Laurel had to go find him."

"She was working on collecting those caches," Daisy said. "I thought she had finished with them yesterday—or the day before, even—but maybe it took her longer than she planned. If she was still out doing that this morning, then she had to go back to the campground, get cleaned up, drive over here, and—" She left the sentence unfinished.

"What is it, Ducky?" Aunt Emily prodded.

"Well," Daisy's brow furrowed, "I know I told Laurel that the party was going to be at the inn, but it was Wednesday morning when we talked about it, at the bakery. The ambulance was still there, along with Deputy Johnson. It was all pretty hectic and unpleasant, so it wouldn't be too shocking if she got confused and thought that the party was going to be at Sweetie Pies instead."

The group nodded in sympathetic understanding.

"I'll give her a call," Daisy said, reaching for her phone.

She tried twice, but there was no answer either time. Aunt Emily advised contacting Bobby. Daisy wasn't keen on the idea. Bobby was usually as coherent as a mollusk on the phone. Except that under the circumstances, she couldn't really argue. He was the groom, after all. If anybody knew where the prospective bride was, it should be him. Daisy expected a ceaseless string of rings, followed at long last by a somnolent grunt. To her surprise, Bobby answered immediately.

"Daisy?" He sounded flustered. "Daisy, is that you?"

"Yes, Bobby, it's me. Are you all right?"

"Is Laurel with you? Can I talk to her?"

"That's why I'm calling, actually. We're supposed to be having the party for her now, but she's not here."

"She's not? She should be." His words came out fast and slurred together. "She said she was. She's not there? She should be there. She said she was going. She said she would. She said—she—"

"Wait a minute, Bobby. Slow down. Did Laurel tell you she was coming to the party this afternoon?"

"Uh-huh. She said—she—"

Daisy cut him off before he could start rambling again. "Did she tell you where the party was?"

There was a slight hesitation on Bobby's end. "It's at the inn, isn't it?"

"It is, but do you know if Laurel knows that? I'm afraid she may have gotten the location mixed up."

Another hesitation. "I'm not sure. I can't remember. But where else would she have gone?"

"The bakery. That's my guess, at least."

"The bakery? The bakery isn't far. She wouldn't be gone all day for that."

"Gone all day?" Daisy echoed. "I don't understand what you mean, Bobby. The party was only supposed to be this afternoon, and maybe into the evening, not—"

"Laurel's been gone all day!" he exclaimed.

"Have you tried calling her?"

"She doesn't pick up!"

"When was the last time you saw her?" Daisy asked.

"Yesterday," Bobby said.

"When was the last time you talked to her?"

"Yesterday."

It was Daisy's turn to hesitate. Yesterday certainly wasn't very long ago, but it did seem sort of odd that Laurel hadn't been in contact with Bobby more recently. There could be a dozen explanations for it, though. She was tired from collecting the caches and needed a chance to relax. She was superstitious and refused to see or even speak with her betrothed so close to the wedding. She wanted to spend a little extra time with her brother. She decided to be alone for a few hours to contemplate what it really meant to get married. They were all perfectly legitimate reasons for Laurel to turn off her phone.

"Bobby!" Daisy snapped.

Bobby halted his distressed mutterings.

"I'm at the inn now," she told him, "and I'm going to drive over to the bakery to check if Laurel is there. I'll call you again from Sweetie Pies."

He whimpered like a dejected beagle.

"If you hear from Laurel—or see her—before I call you, you call me."

More whimpering.

Daisy rolled her eyes at the phone. "Don't worry, Bobby. It will all be fine. Laurel is probably sitting outside the bakery at this exact second wondering where the heck everybody has gotten to."

"And if she's not?"

"Then she's sitting somewhere else, like at the campground or with Chris. There's nothing for you to fret about."

The whimpering ceased, so he must have been slightly cheered.

"I'll call you from Sweetie Pies," Daisy repeated, just to make sure that there was no misunderstanding about the plan.

"Okay." Bobby sounded less rattled and more confident. "In the meantime, I'll call Rick. Maybe he knows something."

As he hung up, Daisy's stomach instinctively tightened. Maybe Rick did indeed know something. And knowing Rick, it wouldn't be good.

CHAPTER

19

Up until that point, Daisy hadn't thought of Rick at all in relation to Laurel's absence, but the moment that his name slipped from Bobby's tongue, she felt a strong sense of uneasiness. What if Laurel hadn't gotten confused about the location of the party? What if she wasn't relaxing, or contemplating, or being superstitious, or spending a little extra time with her brother? What if she was spending time with Rick? And considering that Bobby hadn't seen or spoken to her since yesterday, it could very well be a lot of time.

Daisy recalled Rick and Laurel's intimate embrace at the bakery. Could they truly be involved with each other? It would explain Rick's strange behavior, at least partially. But what about Laurel? It seemed entirely out of character for her. Unless Beulah had hit the nail on the head from the outset—Laurel was interested in Rick's money, and that interest took precedence over her bridal shower and bachelorette party.

As Daisy thought about it, it occurred to her that

although Laurel had been polite and gracious about the invitation, she had never actually agreed to attend the party. She had merely remarked on the time and declared how nice it was of them to think of her. Immediately thereafter, she had asked Rick to walk her to her car, ostensibly to discuss a wedding gift that she had in mind for Bobby. They could have easily discussed a rendezvous on Friday instead. The way they had stood so close together certainly didn't refute the idea.

It annoyed Daisy considerably. Rather than enjoying a cheerful glass in the parlor with her family and friends, she now had to drive back to the bakery to look for Laurel, who she increasingly suspected wasn't there. But she astutely kept that suspicion to herself, figuring there was no point in getting Bobby or the group at the inn riled up over something that might in the end turn out to be nothing.

She grumbled all the way to Sweetie Pies. She grumbled even harder when she pulled into the parking lot and didn't see any other vehicles. Unless Laurel had rollerskated, helicoptered, or hitchhiked, she wasn't at the bakery. Daisy climbed out of her car and walked once around the building. There was no sign of Laurel, but thankfully, there were no new broken windows or bodies lying on the gravel either.

With a frustrated sigh, she unlocked the front door, flipped on the lights, and sunk down on one of the vinyl-topped stools at the counter. What was she going to say to Bobby? Although she may not have held him in the highest esteem, Daisy also didn't want to see him crushed, especially not by Rick. If only Laurel would pick up her phone and straighten it out. Aunt Emily would surely be mad that the guest of honor never showed up to the party, but that was infinitely better than a Balsam brother love feud.

Once more she called Laurel, and once more there was no answer. Daisy was staring at the phone—still trying to decide what to tell Bobby—when it suddenly rang in her hand. A warm wave of relief washed over her. Bobby had at last found his bride, or his bride had at last found her way to the inn. All would be well. Then she saw that it wasn't Bobby, or Laurel, or even Aunt Emily calling, and the wave turned cold. It was Rick.

"Please, Rick," Daisy answered grimly, skipping any sort of courteous greeting, "please tell me that you're not in bed with her."

"In bed with her? In bed with who?"

To his credit, he sounded startled. Daisy hoped that meant he was surprised by the idea, not surprised at being caught.

"Laurel, of course," she replied.

Rick laughed.

"Bobby is really worried," Daisy snapped. "He hasn't seen or talked to her since yesterday."

"Good."

"He's going to marry her," she reminded him gruffly. "Tomorrow afternoon at the inn."

"Not if I have anything to say about it."

Her frustrated sigh from earlier repeated itself. "Does it have to be Laurel? Can't you pick somebody else? You can have half the women in southwestern Virginia, for goodness' sake."

"Does that include you, darlin'?"

"Don't be an ass, Rick."

He laughed harder. Daisy bit the inside of her cheek in an effort to maintain some semblance of calm.

"Fine," she growled after a moment. "Sleep with your brother's fiancée. Don't sleep with your brother's fiancée. I don't care either way. Just tell me if you're with her—or know where she is—so I can quit driving around looking for her."

"You're looking for her?" The laughter instantly ceased. "Don't do that, Daisy. Don't—"

The connection got fuzzy.

"I'm starting to lose you, Rick."

"Don't—Laurel—I—campground—"

"I can't understand you. Are you and Laurel together at the campground?"

His words had been replaced by choppy syllables. Rick was apparently somewhere with spotty reception.

"I can't hear you, but if you can hear me," Daisy said, "you better call Bobby and talk to him about it."

There was no response, only silence.

"If you don't," she added unhappily, even though she knew that Rick was no longer listening to her, "I'm going to have to do it."

Daisy set the phone down on the counter and glared at it. In her mind she was glaring at Rick, more than a little peeved that he had put her in such an awkward position. She didn't want to talk to Bobby about his brother and Laurel, and now there was no way of getting around it. She wouldn't go into any details. Mercifully, she didn't know any details. But she couldn't just pretend that Rick hadn't called her or that he hadn't made it amply evident that he was going to do whatever he could to keep Laurel and Bobby from getting married tomorrow.

As she went on glaring, Daisy wondered why Rick had called in the first place. He hadn't actually said much of anything, except that was partly her fault. After her remark about him being in bed with Laurel, the conversation had naturally declined. But he must have had some reason for calling. Rick never picked up the phone for a quick chat about the weather, at least not with her. Just as Daisy was beginning to debate whether he would call back, her phone rang again. This time it was Bobby, and she winced.

Not sure how best to proceed, she hesitated before answering. Then Daisy decided that the wisest course would be to take her cue from him. There was no need to poke a sleeping bear if that bear was contentedly snoring.

"Hey, Bobby—" she started to say.

"Daisy!" he cut her off in a panic.

Daisy winced once more. Apparently the bear was wide awake and hadn't yet found his honey pot.

"Laurel's not at the bakery, is she?" Bobby exclaimed.

"No, I—"

"I think something's happened to her, Daisy!"

The wince changed to a frown. "Something's happened to her? What do you mean?"

"I'm at—I went—I found—"

The connection got fuzzy, the same as it had with Rick.

"You're breaking up, Bobby. Where are you? What did you find?"

"I'm at the campground. You said she might be sitting here. I went—"

The sentence became static.

"Bobby?"

His voice abruptly returned. "Laurel's cabin—"

Louder static.

"Can you hear me, Bobby? I can't—"

"Oh my God, Daisy! Her bed—"

He disappeared again.

"Bobby, are you still there?"

"I don't know if—why would she—then Rick—"

Daisy strained to follow the garbled phrases.

"I can't—he isn't—you need to come here, Daisy! You have to come and help—"

The call ended with a click.

She closed her eyes. This was not good. Bobby was at the campground. Rick was probably at the campground too. And Laurel might or might not be at the campground, but there was definitely something going on with her cabin and her bed.

Although Daisy waited for several long minutes, her phone remained resolutely quiet. Evidently Bobby's reception was just as spotty as Rick's. It didn't necessarily prove that they were in the same place. Most of Pittsylvania County had spotty reception, depending on meteorological conditions, the time of day, and especially the closer you got to the mountains. But both of them had mentioned the campground, and both of them had mentioned it in connection with Laurel.

If only she had called Rick that morning as she had been tempted to do. Then she would have had one of his jelly jars in her hands, and she could have locked the bakery doors from the inside, put up her feet, and merrily sipped her way into oblivion, or at least until tomorrow when the wedding was over. Instead she was supposed to placate Aunt Emily in regard to the party, find the bride— who very possibly wasn't missing or wasn't interested in being found—and keep the Balsam boys from killing each other, if Bobby's reference to Laurel's bed was at all related to what most bed references were related to.

Daisy swiveled on her stool, pondering her options. She didn't have to find the bride. She didn't have to keep the Balsam boys from killing each other. She could simply go back to the inn, shrug her shoulders in apology to Aunt Emily, and let everything else take care of itself. Except Bobby had asked her to come to the campground. He had said that she *needed* to come to the campground. And he was at the campground himself because of what she had said—that Laurel might be sitting there. Daisy hadn't meant it quite so literally, of course, but Bobby had obviously taken it that way. And now he was in all likelihood expecting that she would indeed come and help in some manner.

What was Rick expecting? Had he thought that his brother would go to the campground in search of Laurel? Maybe it wasn't Laurel's cabin that Bobby had gone into. According to Chris, he had had difficulty finding the right cabin previously. But based on what Daisy had seen when she and Beulah were last at the campground, there were only two cabins still occupied. As confused as Bobby could get with directions, not even he could mistake Laurel's cabin and bed with Chris's cabin and bed.

Rick surely wouldn't have any trouble differentiating one bed from the other. He was far too clever—and too fond of women's beds. Wasn't he also too clever to get caught at the campground with Laurel? Daisy would have presumed so. After all, Rick had been the only one smart enough to realize following the cream cheese incident that she needed to improve her security at the bakery. She had argued so adamantly against it, but he had been right, both about getting the new locks and the security guard. And the gun.

Daisy stopped swiveling. She had completely forgotten about the gun. The brown paper bag that Rick had given her. There had been a revolver at the bottom—a snub-nose Smith & Wesson. Although she had tried several times to decline the gift, Rick had insisted on leaving it with her. What had she done with it? She had tucked it under the counter to keep it safely away from customers.

Sliding off her stool, she circled around to the other side of the counter. Daisy felt for the bag with her hand but couldn't find it. Then she bent down and looked. Her eyes traveled the entire length beneath the counter—twice. There was an assortment of odd objects stashed below: a rusted watering can, mismatched knitting needles, and a pair of plastic hummingbird feeders. There was no brown paper sack.

Standing back up, Daisy drew a shaky breath. The bag had vanished, along with its contents. She realized almost instantly where they had gone. That was why the window to the storage room had been broken. That was what had been stolen from Sweetie Pies. The geocachers didn't come back to retrieve something they thought they had left behind the last time. They didn't just climb in the window and walk out the front door. They took a prize along the way. They took Rick's gun, and they probably used it to kill Caesar.

But how did the geocachers—or anybody else, for that matter—know about the sack? It was possible that they simply stumbled across it while looking around inside the bakery. Except the place didn't show any sign of having been rummaged through, which made it much more likely that

the culprits were aware of the bag in advance. Daisy tried
to think of everyone who had known about it. The list
was short. Only Caesar had witnessed Rick giving her
the revolver, and he certainly wasn't talking. Then there
was Bobby and Laurel. They had come in shortly afterward and seen the sack on the counter. They both could
have told somebody else about it, especially Laurel. She
knew all the geocachers. She could have easily mentioned the bag or the gun to one of them, without ever
guessing what that person would then do with the information.

So where was the revolver now? At the bottom of a
pond—under a pile of hiking boots and sweatshirts in a
geocacher's trunk—in the pocket of one of Jordan Snyder's partners in crime as they searched for thirty-nine
lost kegs of silver? They couldn't be doing very much
searching, not with the area around Fuzzy Lake closed.
They could be waiting for it to reopen, however. Too bad
they didn't discuss their plans with Chris. He would have
set them straight. Any history professor worth his salt who
had studied the Confederacy could have told them that
there was no treasure hidden in the mountains of southwestern Virginia.

What if they were still looking regardless? What if they
didn't care that the area was closed or what Chris said?
What if they had returned to the campground to finish
their search, and Laurel and Chris had somehow gotten
in their way? They had already shot Caesar. Would they
really hesitate to shoot again? Bobby had sounded awfully
panicked on the phone. Daisy knew that he would never
call the sheriff's office. Neither would Rick. No matter the
circumstances, even the most dire—the Balsam brothers

always steered clear of the law. But both Rick and Bobby had called her, and Bobby had asked for her help.

With another shaky breath, Daisy hurried to the door. She had to get to the campground. Ironically enough, she suddenly found herself hoping that the only thing she would see there was Rick in bed with Laurel.

CHAPTER
20

Daisy almost returned to the inn first. Her Colt was there, and it would have provided a certain degree of security. As the old saying went, you didn't bring a knife to a gun-fight, or worse yet in Daisy's case, no weapon at all. But the inn was in the complete opposite direction of the campground. It would have required doubling back and losing a good deal of time. If someone truly needed her help, she had to get to them sooner rather than later. She also wasn't eager to go through a lengthy explanation with the group at the inn. And even without her own gun, there would still be firearms in her favor. Bobby could typically be counted on to have a rifle or two. Rick always carried his Ruger.

She drove hard and fast. Along the way she tried call-ing Laurel, and Chris, and Bobby, and Rick, but none of them answered. Daisy told herself that it didn't necessarily mean something bad had happened. If they were all at the campground, then it only made sense that they all had similarly poor reception. She wished that she knew a bit more, though. She hated going in blind. It was like reaching into the center of a thick berry bush: you could come out with a handful of something tasty or a very nasty snakebite.

As it had been earlier that week when she had been there with Beulah, the entrance to the campground was open. The entrance road was just as quiet too. Daisy slowed as she approached the end of the road. There were no vehicles parked along the side, and she had no intention of parking there either—not all alone, with who-knows-who running around in possession of the revolver that had been stolen from the bakery. Pulling her car onto the grass, she crept toward the center of the campground.

The cabins looked dingy and forlorn. There was a gloominess about them that gave the isolation and stillness of the campground an eerie quality. It was the light, at least that was how Daisy explained it to herself. The October sun was weak, and the slinking shadows of the advancing afternoon were more gray than golden. She was grateful that Aunt Emily hadn't scheduled Laurel's party for later that evening. Now she could still see the wood-chip path and the plywood huts. In another hour it would be dusk. And in another hour after that, there would be darkness. Although Daisy's sense of direction was far better than Bobby's, she still wasn't keen on driving—or wandering—around the countryside in the pitch black.

Heading down the line of cabins, she stopped as close as she could to Laurel's. Daisy peered at the little building through her windshield. The deck was empty. The screen door was closed. If something had indeed happened to Laurel as Bobby had suggested on the phone—whether in relation to him, or Rick, or the geocachers—there was no sign of it. Oddly enough, there was no sign of anything. Neither Bobby nor Rick's pickup. Not a jacket tossed over the back of a lounge chair or a pair of muddy boots kicked off next to the doorway. It seemed strange to her, and unsettling.

With increasing regret at her decision not to pick up the Colt from the inn, Daisy climbed out of the car, shutting the door noiselessly behind her. She walked on soft feet toward the cabin and up the short set of stairs to the deck. The shade on the window was drawn down from the inside, just as it had been on her first trip to Laurel's cabin. Except this time she didn't knock and wait for a response or hesitate to enter out of scruple. If there was bad news to be found, then she wanted to get it over with. The handle turned beneath her fingers. The door opened. Half squinting in case there was something going on in the direction of the bed that she really didn't want to see, Daisy took a step forward. She immediately halted in surprise.

The ceiling light was switched on, the same as before. The attached fan was still whirling around with its rhythmic ticking that sounded like kernels of corn popping. But that was where the similarity between the two visits ended. Laurel's cabin was in complete disarray. The sheets had been torn from the bed and the pillow ripped nearly in half. The towels from the bathroom cubicle were strewn on the floor, along with every article of clothing in the room. The lemon yellow cushions had been pulled from the rocking chair and sofas and slashed open. It was as though a tornado had blown through, only instead of shredding the cabin and its contents, it had searched the cabin and its contents.

The fact that the place had been searched instead of

merely vandalized was most apparent to Daisy from the dishes that were stacked next to the sink in the kitchenette. Not a single one had been broken. If your primary goal was to cause damage, the first thing that you did was smash dishes. But even the water glass on the table was still standing upright, partially filled. Except that raised the question of why anybody would want to search the cabin. What could Laurel possibly have—or what did someone think that she had—which was worth such an effort?

Her suitcase was spread open on the floor in the middle of the room, so she hadn't departed, at least not formally. That would make Bobby happy. There was also no evidence of any injury or a fight. That made Daisy happy. It was a fleeting happiness, however. The longer that she stared at the chaos, the more she began to worry that Bobby was right. Something had happened to Laurel. She understood now what he had been referring to on the phone. Bobby had gone to Laurel's cabin, discovered it in its present state, and panicked. He had also mentioned Rick before the connection went dead. But Rick was nowhere to be found. And where on earth was Bobby? Surely he wouldn't have left the campground before she arrived, not after asking her to come and help. Unless something had happened to him too.

Confused and troubled, Daisy walked back out onto the deck. She surveyed the cabins and the surrounding area. There had to be a clue somewhere. Bobby must have dropped a bread crumb, even inadvertently. Only there wasn't one, not that she could see. What perplexed her the most was the lack of vehicles. In addition to Bobby and Rick's pickups, there should also have been Chris's and Laurel's cars. Had everybody driven away, and all sepa-

rately? Could they be parked in some spot that wasn't visible? It was an Appalachian campground. There weren't
any underground garages.

Finally she turned to Chris's cabin. Although Daisy
didn't have much hope of finding anything more interesting there than she and Beulah had previously, it was the
only possibility left to her. Crossing the wood-chip path,
she headed to the last cabin in the row. She no longer
bothered hushing her steps. There didn't seem to be much
of a need for it, considering that she had yet to encounter
any creature larger than an industrious squirrel collecting
acorns for the winter. But that changed the moment her
foot came down on the first stair leading up to the deck. It
creaked, and it was promptly matched by a creak from
inside the cabin.

Daisy's heart skipped a beat, and she instantly stopped
moving. There was another creak. She listened. Someone
had stood up, or at least that was what it sounded like.
Either way it was enough to change her mind. She wasn't
going to the deck anymore. She was going to wait for the
person—or persons—to identify themselves before she
got any closer.

As lightly as she could, Daisy lifted her foot off the
stair, hoping that it wouldn't creak again. But it did, and it
was followed by footsteps inside the cabin. They were
coming toward the door. Hurrying to the side of the building to hide, Daisy cursed herself for not having the Colt.
What was the point of owning the gun if she didn't have it
in a situation like this?

Hearing the screen door swing open, she peeked around
the corner. Part of a leg came into view on the deck, then
an arm and a hand. The hand was holding an extremely

thick book. Daisy let out a relieved sigh. She had seen that book before. Beulah had pointed it out to her, along with its equally hefty companion. They were Chris's history tomes.

"Oh, Chris," she exhaled, reemerging into the open. "I'm so glad that it's you. I was starting to get jumpy."

She was greeted by a sigh twice as weighty as her own. "Lordy, Daisy. I didn't think you would ever get here."

Daisy blinked in surprise. Instead of Chris standing on the deck of his cabin, she saw—and heard—Bobby.

"Sorry, Bobby. I thought you were Chris." She chuckled to herself at the mix-up, then gestured toward the book in his hand. "Brushing up on your Confederate trivia?"

"My Confederate what?" He raised the book to look at it.

Her breath caught in her throat as the sunlight glanced off the cover. "Is that blood!" she exclaimed.

Bobby didn't answer, but his expression showed no astonishment at the sight of the ruddy streaks on the tan spine.

A thousand possibilities flooded into Daisy's brain, and they were all bad. "Good God, Bobby! What did you do?"

"I didn't—" He shook his head frantically. "It wasn't—"

When it became clear that he couldn't piece together anything coherent, she cut him off. "Whose blood is that?"

Gurgling, he pointed at the cabin door.

"It's Chris's?" Daisy dashed up the stairs to the deck. "What happened? Is he all right?"

Before Bobby could respond, she flung open the door. Just as she had at Laurel's cabin, Daisy took one step inside and immediately halted.

Unlike his sister's place, Chris's cabin hadn't been hit by a tornado. It was messy, but the bed hadn't been torn apart and most of his clothing was politely heaped together next to his duffel bag. The rocking chair and sofas were still in one piece too. Except that wasn't what startled Daisy. It wasn't the condition of the room. It was the occupant. Chris wasn't sitting on the red-checkered cushions, as she had expected. Rick was. And the blood dripping onto the fabric from his face blended right in.

He didn't look at her. He didn't look at anything. Rick's eyes were closed, and his shoulders were slumped forward. He was more reclining against the side of the sofa than sitting on it. Although he was obviously alive and breathing, he didn't seem fully conscious. He wasn't making any effort to stop the dripping blood.

"You couldn't pick up a shirt and clean his face?" Daisy rebuked Bobby, after recovering from her initial shock.

Instead of a shirt, she grabbed what appeared to be a relatively clean towel from a hook in the kitchenette. Leaning over the arm of the sofa, she inspected Rick's injury. There was a substantial cut on his right temple, combined with a nicely swelling bruise. She wiped the blood from his cheek and jaw as well as she could, then she pressed the towel against the lacerated skin. Rick moaned and shifted. The wound was evidently tender. Daisy lightened her touch but tried to maintain enough pressure to stop the bleeding.

"You hit him?" She frowned at Bobby, who was standing in the doorway. "What were you thinking? He could have killed you."

Without any doubt, Rick was tougher, stronger, and a much better fighter than Bobby. Throwing a few brotherly punches was one thing. Whacking Rick upside the head with a giant history tome was quite another. It led to pistol-whipping, and pistol-whipping most frequently led to shooting. Ninety-nine times out of a hundred, Bobby was going to be on the losing end of that fight.

His eyes widened in dismay. "I didn't hit him."

"Then why are you holding a bloody book, Bobby?"

"It was on the floor."

"And?" she retorted.

"And I picked it up when I heard somebody on the steps. I thought I might need it. I didn't know it was you out there, Daisy."

She said a silent word of thanks that she had heard the creaks coming from inside the cabin and had promptly scurried away from the deck. Otherwise she might also be lying semiconscious with a cut and welt on the side of her head.

"I was looking for Laurel," Bobby explained, shuffling into the room. "I went to her cabin first, but she wasn't there. So I came over here. You told me she might be sitting with Chris."

Daisy made a mental note that she needed to be more careful in her conversations with Bobby in the future. Apparently he liked to do exactly what she said, no matter how offhand her remarks were.

"Except Laurel wasn't here neither. But Rick was. He was over there." Bobby motioned in the direction of the bed. "On the ground next to it."

As serious as the present situation was, Daisy couldn't help but think how good it was for everybody involved that Rick had been found next to the bed—rather than in it—and Laurel was nowhere in the vicinity.

"The book was next to him too," Bobby continued. "I knew it was how he'd been hurt. I could tell from the way he was lying. Somebody had come up behind him and smacked him."

Keeping the towel pressed against the wound, Daisy reached her other hand around Rick's back. The Ruger was there, tucked into its holster.

"He must have been surprised," she said. "He didn't pull out his gun."

Bobby's brow furrowed. "I didn't think of that. I could have used it instead of this stupid thing." He dropped the book. It landed with a loud thump on the floor, making a sizable dent in the wood.

She looked at the resulting hollow. "I guess in one way Rick was lucky. He could have gotten a hole like that in his head."

"He'll be okay," Bobby returned anxiously. "He'll be okay, won't he, Daisy?"

"He'll be fine," she told him. "Probably a doozy of a headache for a day or two. The cut itself won't cause any permanent damage. It just needs to be disinfected and maybe get a few stitches." Her gaze went to the spot where Rick had been lying on the ground. "It doesn't look like he lost too much blood."

"I moved him to the sofa," Bobby said. "I thought that would be good. Then he could sleep it off."

Daisy restrained a smile. Bobby equated the remedy for a possible concussion with that of a likker binge. But she didn't bother correcting him. It would only make him more anxious, and she needed him to stay at least semi-focused.

"How come you don't have a gun with you, Bobby?" she asked.

"Laurel doesn't like 'em."

She knew that to be true. Laurel had been uncomfortable both about the revolver in the bag at the bakery and during the discussion with Rick regarding concealed weapons permits.

"When I see her," Bobby went on, "I always leave my Winchester in the truck."

"Where is your truck?"

"At the trailhead."

"What trailhead?"

"The one for the trail that goes up the mountain and then down to Fuzzy Lake. It's the trail Laurel, Chris, and the rest of 'em were using for their so-called hunt."

That grabbed Daisy's attention. Was it an old trail? Old enough to be on the maps that had been stolen from the historical society? Would the geocachers try to use it to search for the treasure?

"The first thing I do whenever I come to the campground," Bobby told her, "is go to the trailhead. It's where Laurel parks. That's how I can be sure if she's here or not. Her phone is pretty iffy by the cabins, and it's even worse when she's out on the trail."

"Is the trail part of the area that's closed?" Daisy asked.

"I think so." He shrugged. "I think Laurel said it was all closed."

"It probably doesn't matter either way," she replied, more to herself than to Bobby. "If they want to keep searching, they'll keep searching—closed or not."

"Who's searching? Huh?"

Daisy responded with a question of her own. "Was Laurel's car at the trailhead when you got here today?"

Bobby nodded. "Chris's car too. And Rick's truck."

"But you haven't seen Chris?"

"Naw."

"Have you ever gone on the trail, Bobby? Do you know what it's like?"

"I ain't been up it myself, but it looks the same as any

other trail in the mountains, at least from the beginning."

She was thoughtful for a moment. Her eyes went to Rick. Although he still wasn't fully sentient, his condition didn't appear to be worsening any. The bleeding had slowed, and there was a healthy tint to his cheeks.

"I think you better take me to the trailhead," Daisy said at last to Bobby. "Can you find it okay from here?"

"Yup." His eyes also went to Rick. "Are you sure we can leave him?"

"We won't be gone long." Under her breath, she added, "Hopefully."

As carefully and gently as she could, Daisy leaned Rick's head—together with the towel—against the sofa cushion. Then she took a step back. He looked comfortable, and it seemed to be a safe position. He couldn't topple over. He couldn't choke or suffocate. The wound was elevated and protected. Rick would be all right alone until they returned.

Bobby started toward the deck. Daisy began to follow him, but she stopped abruptly in the doorway. Spinning around, she walked back to Rick and bent over him. He murmured at her. His breath was warm against her neck. Daisy leaned closer. Her hand went to his shoulder. Her fingers glided down his arm. Then she pulled the Ruger from his back.

CHAPTER
21

The gun was too big for her little hand—and Daisy had no doubt that it had one heck of a recoil—but considering the circumstances, having the Ruger was much better than not having the Ruger. Rick certainly wouldn't be using it in his current condition.

When she caught up with Bobby, he was already down the deck stairs and marching toward the side of Chris's cabin. He was so preoccupied with his concerns about Laurel, he didn't even notice that Daisy had taken his brother's gun.

"Do you think Laurel will be at the trailhead?" he asked her. "She wasn't there before. Do you think she could be sitting there now?"

"Maybe." Daisy was pretty confident that Laurel wouldn't be sitting at the trailhead, but she didn't want to alarm Bobby any more than he already was.

"I don't get it." He scratched his arm. "If she's not there, where could she be? She's not at the inn. She's not at the bakery. She's not at her cabin . . ."

They turned the corner to the back of Chris's cabin. This time no vultures retreated to the trees. The two heaps of garbage behind the plywood hut looked the same as they had earlier that week, sans the flour-dusted sneakers, which Daisy had removed and given to Deputy Johnson. Bobby circled around the trash. She followed him. On the far side was a footpath of trampled grass through weedy scrub.

Daisy stopped and frowned at the path. "You're sure this is the right way, Bobby?"

He nodded.

"Because it's going to get dark soon, and I don't want to go roaming into the wilderness if you're not absolutely positive this is the way to your truck and the trailhead."

"It's the way," he answered without hesitation. "I've used it at least half a dozen times before, and I've never gotten lost on it."

Her frown remained. Even though that was as convincing as Bobby could be when it came to his lousy sense of direction, Daisy still had some trepidation. He must have gone to Laurel's cabin at least half a dozen times before too, and he had still managed to become confused about which cabin was the right one. But she figured that in this instance, he couldn't get them seriously lost, as long as they stayed on the path and didn't branch off to any side shoots.

"Fine." She motioned forward. "After you."

Bobby took the lead, which was what Daisy wanted. If he was in front of her, then he couldn't accidentally wander away without her noticing. When she later had to go back to Rick to check on his wound and return the Ruger, she didn't want to have to explain to him how she had let his brother go missing while trekking to his truck.

They walked in silence for several minutes. It was an

easy path—flat, relatively straight, and no rocks or brambles.

"About Laurel's cabin," Daisy said after a while, hoping that Bobby might have some insight on the subject. "Do you have any idea why somebody would rip the place apart?"

He shook his head. "I don't get that neither. Who did it? There isn't anyone here. There isn't anyone anywhere around here. Who even knows that she's here?"

Daisy's mind went immediately to the geocachers. They fit two of those categories. They weren't at the campground, but they could very easily be around the campground. And they definitely knew that both Laurel and Chris were there.

"I thought at first maybe somebody was mad at her." Bobby began scratching his arm again. "But why would they be mad at her? It wasn't her fault the so-called hunt had to be canceled."

"I don't think they're mad," Daisy responded. "I think they might have been looking for something. Didn't it seem to you from the way the bed had been torn apart and the sofa cushions were slashed open that they might have been looking for something?"

"Looking for something? Looking for what?"

That was an excellent question. She knew of only two things that were missing—the revolver from the bakery and the maps from the historical society. Except Laurel didn't have either one. It was nonsensical, really. If the geocachers had stolen the maps and the revolver, they wouldn't then be searching for them in Laurel's cabin. So it had to be something else. But what? Money, jewelry, excess prescription drugs? Those were all equally nonsensical. When she and Beulah were previously at the cabin, Laurel had left the door unlocked. People with money, jewelry, and excess prescription drugs didn't leave the door unlocked.

"I'm worried, Daisy." Bobby scratched his arm harder.

"I know, but try not to be." She made an effort to sound more optimistic than she actually was. "We don't know anything for sure, so there's no need to worry yet. I could be completely wrong about them looking for something."

"You could also be right," he said. "Only what if instead of looking for something, they were looking for someone? What if they were looking for Laurel?"

Looking for Laurel? It was an idea that Daisy had never considered before. At the bakery, she had feared that the geocachers had returned to the campground to finish their search for the treasure and Laurel had somehow gotten in their way. But if that was the case, they wouldn't be looking for her. On the contrary, they would do whatever was necessary to get her out of their way, just like they presumably had with Rick.

"That would explain why the cabin was torn up," Bobby continued, following his own line of reasoning. "They were looking for her, they found her, and they tried to take her."

Tried to take her? Why in the world would they try to take Laurel? You only took someone if you believed they might be useful to you. How would Laurel be useful to the geocachers? They already knew the trail, so they didn't need her as a guide. And she only had permission to enter the closed area to collect the remaining caches—not to dig up treasure—so she couldn't give them any special help with that. What could she help them with? Daisy's thoughts returned once more to the maps. Maybe Laurel knew the trail or the closed area so well that she could better read or interpret the maps?

"They tried to take her, and she fought them." Bobby's voice rose. "She fought them, but she lost. And now they've got her!"

"But it didn't look as though there had been a fight," Daisy replied, trying to stay rational and keep Bobby calm. "There wasn't any sign of a struggle in her cabin. It wasn't like Rick and the book in Chris's cabin—"

She didn't finish the sentence. The instant that she said Chris's name, it occurred to her that maybe it wasn't Laurel who would be useful to the geocachers. Maybe it was her brother. Chris was the history professor, after all. He was the one who had done his graduate work on the war and carried around Confederate history tomes. Maybe he could better read or interpret the maps.

"What if they've hurt her!" Bobby exclaimed. "They gunned down Caesar in your parking lot. What if they've shot her too?"

He was scratching his arm with such ferocity that he was ripping open his skin. Daisy reached out and grabbed his wrist to stop him.

"Quit it, Bobby! If you don't, I'm going to have to take you to the doctor with Rick. You being all bloody and injured isn't going to help Laurel—or Chris—a lick."

Turning around, he blinked at her. "You think Laurel is with Chris?"

"Don't you?" Daisy said. "It seems logical, doesn't it? Neither of them is at the campground or anywhere else that we know of. Which must mean they're together. If we find one, then there's a mighty good chance we'll find the other."

Bobby went on blinking.

"Maybe there was a fight," she told him. "Maybe Laurel was taken, or maybe Chris was taken. Maybe by taking one, they got the other. I don't know, and I honestly don't think the details matter at this point. Right now we have to get to the trailhead and see what we find there."

To her relief, he didn't argue or ask any questions. Bobby just turned back around and started walking on the path again. Daisy was grateful. She couldn't explain to him what she didn't understand herself. Had Laurel or Chris truly been taken? Perhaps by taking Laurel, the geocachers were forcing Chris's compliance. Perhaps he really could decipher something on the maps that they couldn't.

As they proceeded, Daisy noted that Bobby wasn't picking at his arm anymore, nor was he whimpering about Laurel. His pace had quickened, and he appeared to be gaining courage with every step. She was pleased. Although he could be exasperatingly absentminded and a bit too whiny on occasion for her taste, Bobby had some tough country roots. Now was the time for him to show them. If there was going to be any trouble at the trailhead—or farther on down the line—she needed him to be ready for it.

The path ended abruptly. It opened into a small clearing, consisting of a few old knotty tree stumps and patchy dirt. If this was the site of the trailhead, Daisy realized immediately that there would be no trouble. It was for one very simple reason: there were no people in sight. There were, however, six vehicles—three trucks and three cars. Two of the cars belonged to Laurel and Chris. Two of the trucks belonged to Bobby and Rick. The third car and truck she didn't recognize.

Bobby hurried over to Laurel's car. The doors were locked. He peered through the windows.

"Nothing, Daisy. It looks like it always does."

Although she hadn't expected anything different, she

still felt a slight stab of disappointment. How nice it would
have been to discover a friendly little note tucked under
one of the windshield wipers—*Gone with Chris to collect
caches/prepare for wedding. Will return shortly.*

Bobby went to Chris's car next. Its doors were locked
too. Daisy almost smiled at the irony. Their cabins had
been left wide open, but their cars were sealed tight. The
unidentified vehicles were the same way. All of the windows were closed, and all of the doors were locked. Even
the truck bed was covered. Following Bobby's example,
Daisy peered through the windows, but there wasn't much
for her to see. The interiors were too shadowy. There appeared to be some papers on the seat of the car and a few
soda cans on the floor of the truck. Both vehicles could
have belonged to the geocachers. They also could have belonged to somebody else.

"Anything?" she called to Bobby, who was still in-
specting Chris's car.

"Naw."

She walked toward Rick's truck. His doors were un-
locked. Unfortunately, the inside wasn't at all helpful.
There wasn't one item that had any connection to Laurel,
Chris, or the geocachers.

"Bobby," Daisy said, "do you know why Rick was here?"

"I guess he was looking for me. He knows this is where
I park."

"I assume that he also knows this is where Laurel and
Chris park?"

Bobby answered with a shrug.

Daisy sighed. There wasn't a single clue to go on.
Nothing that told her whether Rick had come there for
Laurel, either romantically or because he had somehow

figured out that things were in the process of taking a bad turn. And also nothing in relation to the geocachers. No maps. No inkling of treasure. Only the Confederate history tome in Chris's cabin that had been whacked against Rick's head. It may have proved that they wanted him out of the way, but it didn't offer a hint in locating Laurel or Chris. The one bit of good news from Daisy's perspective was that she hadn't encountered any evidence of the stolen revolver. Better not to find the gun at all, than to find that it had been used a second time.

Shutting the door to Rick's pickup, she looked around the clearing. It was roughly circular and was bordered by the same weedy scrub that lined the path leading to it.

"Where do you drive in?" Daisy asked Bobby.

"See that scrawny rhododendron?" He gestured toward a spot opposite from where she was standing. "Next to it is the road."

Referring to it as a road was a gross exaggeration. It was really just another path of trampled grass that had grown wide enough to accommodate vehicles. The incline was so steep, it made the path difficult to see from the clearing itself. There was no marking for it or for the smaller path that Daisy and Bobby had used from the campground.

Daisy looked around the clearing again, slowly and more carefully this time. Finally she saw it—a narrow, barely visible break in the scrub not far from the unidentified truck.

"Is that the trailhead, Bobby?"

"Yup."

She approached it. It wasn't marked either, except that didn't surprise her. This wasn't groomed park land. Rarely were the trails leading into the mountains marked. There were too many of them—too many that went nowhere and whose original purpose had long ago been forgotten, too many that snaked around in seemingly endless loops or that vanished suddenly halfway up a ridge.

Pushing back an even scrawnier rhododendron, Daisy stepped from the clearing onto the trail. She had assumed that it would be as narrow as its opening, covered with the usual layer of pine needles and dried leaves that blanketed the mountains of southwestern Virginia in October, but she was wrong. The ground was bare red clay that had been ripped raw by all-terrain vehicle tracks.

"Bobby!" she called.

"What?"

"Did Laurel ever mention to you that they were using ATVs out here?"

"ATVs?" He jogged over to her.

"Take a look." Daisy pointed at the unmistakable tracks.

"That's weird." Bobby's brow furrowed. "They weren't there before."

"When before?"

"Last week. I told you I ain't been up the trail myself, but I'd seen the beginning of it. I came with Laurel. We'd been foolin' around and—"

"Thank you, Bobby," Daisy interjected, rolling her eyes. "I'm not interested in all the lovely specifics."

His cheeks reddened, and he grinned like a wily barn cat.

"But Laurel wasn't using an ATV on the trail?" she pressed him.

He shook his head. "She always hiked. Chris too. As far as I know, they all hiked."

"Of course," Daisy replied, more to herself than to Bobby. "They hike, because they like geocaching and it wouldn't be the same with off-road vehicles. The hunt would be a whole lot easier, nowhere near as competitive. It's like Laurel said about the GPS. That's why they picked this place for the event. With so many experienced participants, the fickle GPS around here made it tougher for them. They had to rely on their actual skills more. They wouldn't have needed to do that nearly as much if they had used ATVs."

Bobby went on shaking his head, understanding her words but clearly not their relevance.

"So the ATVs came later," she continued, working it out aloud. "They came this week after the area was closed off and the event was canceled. The ATVs would be ten times faster than hiking boots. With them, they could explore more of the trail quicker, and they could go back and forth between the cabins and the trail before you and I could even get to the campground this afternoon."

"The cabins? This afternoon?" Bobby echoed. "Wait a minute, you don't think—"

Daisy didn't bother to let him finish. "That's exactly what I think. Whoever is driving those ATVs whacked Rick in the head with the book, is responsible for the condition of Laurel's cabin, and in all likelihood knows precisely where she and Chris are."

Bobby stared at her for a long moment—processing what she had said—then spun around and raced to his truck. Pulling his Winchester from the gun rack behind the seat, he slung it over his back.

"Hold up!" Daisy hollered, following him. "You're not going to—"

This time Bobby didn't bother to let *her* finish. "I'm gonna go after 'em. That's what I'm gonna do, Daisy."

"Out on the trail? At this hour?"

He responded by grabbing a handful of cartridges from an open box on the floor of the pickup and stuffing them into the pocket of his jeans.

"You don't know how far the trail goes," Daisy cautioned him pragmatically. "It could run for twenty miles. They could have turned off onto another trail somewhere along the way or be hunkered down for the night on the side of the mountain. You don't know how many of them there are, what kind of weapons they've got . . ."

Grabbing a second handful of cartridges, Bobby stuffed them into his other pocket.

"Be smart about this, Bobby," she said. "It's already almost dusk. How are you going to follow a trail in the dark?"

"ATV tracks are easy to follow," he rejoined simply.

She couldn't dispute him on that. ATV tracks on bare red clay were certainly much easier to follow than footprints in dried leaves—day or night.

"I'll bring a light," he added, digging a flashlight out of his toolbox.

Daisy hesitated, debating how hard to argue with him.

"I've only got one, but Rick's probably got another." Bobby began walking toward his brother's truck. "He's always got everything."

Rick was an exceedingly clever moonshiner living on the edge of Appalachia. Of course he was going to have a flashlight in his truck, along with a plethora of other rural essentials. Regrettably—based on her earlier inspection of the pickup—Daisy knew that in this instance the essentials did not include a supply of likker. Otherwise she might have been able to convince Bobby to sit down with her for a nip or two and further discuss the situation, instead of watching him gallop heedlessly onto an unmarked mountain trail at sundown with every probability of him inadvertently drifting off that trail a quarter of a mile in.

"Maybe you should wait," she suggested, even without having a jelly jar as a prop. "Maybe we should talk to Deputy Johnson about all of this first."

As she said it, Daisy winced slightly, anticipating Bobby's unhappy reaction. She wasn't mistaken. His head snapped toward her with a look of undisguised horror, as though she had just proposed putting down his favorite bluetick.

"I know. I know." Daisy raised her hands in apology. "You and Rick don't do well with the law. You don't trust 'em, and I understand why. But it would only be the sheriff's office, not anybody federal. Don't you think Laurel would want us to call Deputy Johnson and ask him for his help?"

"We don't need his help," Bobby retorted stiffly. "We can take care of ourselves."

"Yes, but—"

"We can't call him from here anyway," he cut her off with vigor. "There's no reception. And even if we could reach him, he wouldn't come until tomorrow. What good is tomorrow gonna do Laurel? She needs me now!"

Daisy found herself almost impressed. That was as assertive and self-possessed as she had seen Bobby in ages. Had she been there, Laurel would have no doubt been flattered. Bobby obviously cared for her dearly. Even though Daisy was still of the opinion that they should contact Deputy Johnson for assistance—or at least to apprise him of the state of affairs—she decided that she wasn't going to argue with Bobby any more on the subject. If he wanted to go after Laurel, then that was what he should do. She was his fiancée, after all.

"She's been gone for a day already," he said, surveying the contents of Rick's pickup. "Can you imagine what might happen to her overnight? Even if they don't hurt her, she could freeze to death!"

"She won't freeze to death," Daisy assured him. "We're not even getting frost around here yet. Temperature-wise, Laurel will be just fine. Maybe a little chilly, depending on what she's wearing." She stood on her toes next to him and looked into the bed of the truck. "Why don't you take that sweatshirt with you, Bobby? You might get cold too."

"You should take it," he countered. "You'll need it."

Her eyebrows lifted in surprise.

Bobby turned to her. "You're coming with me, aren't you?"

The eyebrows went higher.

"That's why I wanted the second light," he explained, picking up Rick's wide-beam flashlight and holding it out to her. "So we could both have one."

Daisy didn't touch it.

"Oh please, Daisy. You've got to come. What if Laurel's really hurt? What if Chris needs help too? What if I—" Bobby's voice dropped to a mumble. "What if I get lost out there?"

They were all legitimate concerns, and that was the problem. Laurel could be hurt. Chris also. And Daisy was fairly sure that Bobby would indeed get lost out there. Given enough time, he could even end up meandering into North Carolina. Who would help Laurel and Chris then? And who was going to explain it to Rick?

"All right," she muttered, taking the flashlight from

him with a grim expression. "But you're staying on the trail! Do you hear me, Bobby? No marching off in whatever direction you feel like just because you suddenly think you might have caught the rustle of some poor pheasant hiding in the underbrush."

He nodded in agreement and let out a cheery whistle.

"And no whistling either!" Daisy warned him. "We don't want everybody between here and Fuzzy Lake to know that we're coming."

"Okey-dokey, Daisy."

"You take Rick's sweatshirt. I'll take his jacket."

She was dressed for a combination bridal shower and bachelorette party at the inn, not a search-and-rescue mission through the backwoods of Pittsylvania County. At least thanks to Rick, she now had a jacket for the occasion: a warm, comfortable, albeit considerably oversize jacket with a pair of deep and sturdy pockets located conveniently on the outside. Perfect for holding Rick's other temporary gift to her—the Ruger.

Daisy pulled on the jacket. It was made of rugged waxed cotton, and it smelled like its owner: old tobacco barn and the slightly sweet aroma of aged corn whiskey. She raised the Ruger. In the orange blaze of sunset, Daisy looked down at the cylinder and slowly rotated it with her thumb. Six chambers, all loaded. Her lips curled into a smile. Rick could always be counted on to have his gun at the ready. And she intended on having it at the ready too. You never could quite predict what you might stumble across in the backwoods of Pittsylvania County.

CHAPTER
22

With Rick's Ruger in her pocket and his flashlight in her fingers, Daisy set off on the trail with Bobby. Courtesy of the damage caused by the ATVs, it was wide enough for them to walk abreast, which allowed their flashlights to work in conjunction. That was good. She could tell within the first mile that they were going to have problems as it got darker. Although the tracks themselves were easy to follow, the trail was rough.

For starters, the ascent was steep. Some slope was to be expected, of course, considering that they were heading up the side of a mountain. But the grade was particularly sharp, and the continual switchbacks only made it worse. In theory, the switchbacks should have helped by rendering the route less precipitously vertical, and they surely did help more casual hikers, as well as the ATVs. For Daisy and Bobby, however, the switchbacks made the trail significantly longer. The relentless zigzagging also forced them to look at the interminable climb ahead—how far, how high, how strenuous it was going to be.

Under different circumstances, while still physically demanding, it would have been a beautiful late-day ramble. The fireworks of color shooting up from the sinking sun were glorious. Ginger and ruby rockets joined with the glittering gold reflection from the early evening stars. The farther Daisy and Bobby climbed, the better they could see the spectacle. The orange blaze in the horizon set the vast expanse of land beneath them aflame in dazzling hues. The already painted maples became a carpet of shimmering copper, and the oaks turned into a blanket of gleaming bronze. But they couldn't really enjoy it, not when they didn't know where they were going or what they might find when they got there.

Gradually, the orange blaze faded to a russet glow. The waning puffs of clouds grew pink, then periwinkle. And the only remaining metallic luminescence came from the previously sedate pines that glimmered silver against the violet sky. It would be a clear night, which meant two things: it was going to be considerably colder, and the lingering light would last longer, especially when combined with the round, rising moon.

As dusk fell, the trail got rougher. The rocks jutting out of the clay became harder to see. The protruding roots were more easily stumbled over. And the creeping vines and broken branches became increasingly difficult to push out of the way. The hairpin turns got tougher too. They were tight, so much so that Daisy and Bobby had to slow down and tread with extra care. There were no guardrails or protective natural barriers. If the crumbling dirt suddenly decided to slide away beneath their feet, then they would slide down the face of the mountain with it.

The first time that Daisy felt the ground shift under

her, she realized that even though she and Bobby needed to be more cautious on the turns, they were actually an advantage. The heavy and less nimble ATVs couldn't manage them in the dark. So wherever they had stopped at sunset, they had to stay until dawn. That provided her a certain level of comfort. Until daybreak, she and Bobby were safe both from being run off the trail and from being run over on it, at least by a motorized vehicle.

She also realized why the trail was such an excellent choice for true geocaching. The terrain was challenging. The scenery was fantastic. And most important of all, there were countless recesses and crevices in which to conceal the caches, with varying degrees of difficulty to accommodate everybody from the novice to the expert. Daisy understood now why it had taken Laurel so long to collect the remaining caches. Climbing the trail was hard enough all by itself, but then she had to head off into the woods in a dozen different directions to locate each specific hiding spot. That took time and energy.

They stepped onto a stone outcropping and a sudden gust of wind blew past them. Startled, Bobby tripped over the remnants of a dead dogwood.

"Ow!" he complained, grabbing Daisy's shoulder to keep from falling. "Where the heck did that blast come from?"

"I don't know. We're getting pretty high, so I guess—" As she steadied him, there was a second gust. Daisy lifted her head toward it and was too surprised by what she saw to finish her sentence.

It wasn't wind. It was an enormous rush of bats—hundreds, maybe even thousands of them. The exact number was impossible to calculate. They were a swirling tornado. A thick vortex of fluttering creatures spiraling upward into the sky. The sound of their wing beats was like falling rain, except their bodies were lighter than the dusk surrounding them, so they looked more like flurrying snow. It was an immense blizzard of bats, circling tightly counterclockwise and then spreading out as a long ribbon unwinding from a spool. In a great noisy mass, they disappeared around the edge of the mountain.

"Dang." Bobby exhaled in admiration. "Where do you think they're going?"

"Fuzzy Lake," Daisy said. "There are millions of moths and mosquitos down by the water. For a bat, that's about the perfect place for a drink and dinner."

He nodded. "But where did they come from?"

She squinted at the opposite side of the ridge. There were numerous black spots speckled in between the trees. The usual mountain grottos and hollows, no doubt. They varied in size. Most were quiet, but a few had movement in front of them—flapping stragglers racing out after their brethren.

"Over there." Daisy pointed toward two of the dark areas that had the most movement. "Those must be the entrances to their roosting caves."

With a grumble of pain, Bobby switched from nodding his head to rubbing his knee.

"Are you okay?" she asked him.

"Stupid stump," he muttered.

"You should sit down. Give it a rest."

"But, Laurel—"

"Wherever Laurel is," Daisy interjected, "I'm sure that she can wait one extra minute for you. You're going to have to walk a lot more tonight, so you better take it easy while you can. I'm not carrying you down the mountain, Bobby."

Still rubbing the knee, he didn't protest further.

This time Daisy squinted around their immediate environs. There was a fallen birch a few feet off the trail into the undergrowth.

"That trunk will work," she said, reaching for Bobby's arm. "How much help do you need?"

With her assistance, Bobby hobbled over to the provisional birch chair. Daisy seated herself next to him. Although her knees felt fine, she didn't mind the break. They had been trekking hard and fast for a while now. A short breather would be nice, both for them and the batteries in their flashlights. Clicking off the lights, they sat together in silence amid the inky gloom.

The noises of the night enveloped them. The final shriek of a jay before it settled down to sleep. The first shriek of an owl about to strike out on a hunt. Something was burrowing through the dried leaves on the ground not far behind them. A possum digging for slugs, perhaps. Something else was rustling off in the distance. The respite and relative peacefulness gave Daisy an opportunity to think about the bats and their caves. The swarm that she and Bobby had seen obviously belonged to the colonies living around Fuzzy Lake, which meant that they were sitting smack in the middle of the area that had been closed off in an effort to halt the spread of the deadly white-nose syndrome. The bats—and the fungus killing them—were in all likelihood immaterial to anyone searching for lost treasure. But what about the caves?

She had never considered the caves before. Caves by their very nature made outstanding hidey-holes, and although she hadn't examined them up close, Daisy had little doubt that these particular caves were old enough to hold Confederate treasure. As far as she was aware, there had been no modern-day mining in the vicinity of Fuzzy Lake, so no new caverns or shafts had been created. It was the same with the trail. The unending switchbacks and its dogged route over the mountain resembled an old wagon trail much more than a new recreational hiking or bike path. That brought her back to the maps which had been stolen from the historical society. If the trail could be on them, then maybe so were the caves.

The problem with the whole idea, however, was that if the caves were the key, the geocachers couldn't go searching in them, not when the area was specifically closed because of the bats. While the ATVs could help the geocachers explore more of the trail quicker, they couldn't help them get into the actual caves. The only possibility that Daisy could think of was they were somehow sneaking in at night, when the entrances were less visible and less protected. There didn't appear to be any sort of guards around or even admonitory postings. Nobody had stopped or questioned her and Bobby at the trailhead. Perhaps that was one of the reasons why the geocachers had wanted Laurel after all. Since she had permission to enter the area, she offered them a bit of cover in case they did at some point get stopped or questioned about their activities.

Bobby touched Daisy's elbow. "Did you hear that?"

"No." She had been too busy with her musings to hear much of anything.

"Listen," he said.

Daisy focused on the sounds around her. The presumed possum was still digging for slugs in the leaves behind them. A whippoorwill issued its haunting refrain. More leaves rustled in the distance.

"There it is!" Bobby exclaimed in a low tone.

"You mean the rustling? That's been going on ever since we sat down."

"I know, but it's moving."

"That's what animals do, Bobby," she replied dryly. "They move. Especially when they're nocturnal and looking for food."

"There it is again! It's getting closer."

He wasn't mistaken. The rustling did indeed seem to be getting closer. Something was moving through the leaves in their direction.

"It's probably a raccoon," Daisy said.

"That ain't no raccoon," Bobby retorted. "I know my critters, and that critter is a lot bigger than a raccoon."

She didn't argue with him. His ability to distinguish between animals in the dark was far superior to hers. For better or worse, Bobby had been a hunter in rural southwestern Virginia from the day that he had learned to walk and hold a weapon. So if he decided that it wasn't a raccoon, it wasn't a raccoon.

"Okay, then what is it?" she asked him.

"I think it's a person." He paused. "I think it might be two people."

Sitting up straighter, Daisy listened once more. The rustling continued. Was it footsteps? She couldn't really tell. Suddenly the rustling stopped.

"Where did it go?" she whispered. "What happened to it?"

Bobby put a finger to his lips. He was concentrating. She watched him and waited.

"They're on the trail now," he reported softly after a minute.

Although she concentrated too, Daisy couldn't hear whatever it was that he heard.

"They're coming down," he added after another minute, "not going up."

It was an impressive skill. Bobby may have had trouble on occasion locating his fiancée's cabin, but he had absolutely no difficulty determining what direction unidentified people on a mountain trail were heading.

Daisy was about to ask him how positive he was that there were two of them, but she answered the question herself a moment later when she finally caught the sound of boots scuffing against clay. They were definitely walking on the trail, and there was definitely more than one set. A voice followed.

"Damn, it's hard to see out here at night. I sure will be glad when we get back to the truck."

"I told you we should have left earlier," a second voice said.

They were two men. That was clear enough. Daisy didn't recognize either of their voices, but that didn't surprise her. Aside from Laurel and Chris, she wouldn't have recognized any of the geocachers' voices.

"Yeah," the first man responded, "it would have been nice to go earlier, but we didn't have much of a choice."

Lights flickered in between the trees like fireflies. The men were moving down the trail toward them. Bobby started to pull the rifle from his back. Daisy slid her hand into the pocket containing the Ruger.

"We couldn't just leave the equipment up there," the man went on. "And I sure didn't want to come back for it tomorrow morning. Did you?"

"No! I've got plans to—"

The second man's voice dropped away and the flickering lights vanished as they turned on a switchback. Daisy could only catch intermittent words. The first man's reference to equipment interested her greatly. Her initial thought was that they were using the equipment to dig for the treasure, but upon further reflection, that didn't seem entirely logical to her. With the area closed, the geocachers would almost certainly be digging at night, not during the day. Now was the time when they would be beginning their work rather than finishing it. They wouldn't take away their equipment at this hour or discuss coming back for it in the bright light of morning.

"—I'll tell you one thing, I won't miss this place."

"It was the worst assignment I've ever gotten."

Daisy frowned. Assignment? The geocachers wouldn't get assignments, would they?

"Maybe not the worst assignment, but definitely the weirdest."

"You aren't kidding there."

The men shared a chuckle.

It was becoming increasingly evident to her that these men weren't geocachers. But then, who were they? Who got assignments, used equipment, and climbed around a mountain at night? Suddenly remembering what Laurel had told her earlier that week at the bakery, Daisy withdrew her hand from the pocket and the Ruger.

"Bobby," she shifted nearer to his ear, not wanting to take any chance that the men might hear her, "I don't think these guys have Laurel."

He kept a firm grip on his rifle.

"My guess is that they're biologists, or something similar," Daisy explained. "Laurel said that she spoke to a state biologist when the area was first closed and the hunt had to be called off. They're here about the bats."

After several long seconds of tense stillness, Bobby relaxed his hold on the Winchester, apparently agreeing with her theory. "What do you want to do?" he asked her.

She hesitated.

"We could just stay where we are," he proposed. "Let 'em walk right past us."

That was a mighty tempting suggestion. It was nice and safe sitting on the fallen birch in the black undergrowth off the trail, especially considering that Daisy had no concrete proof the men were in fact biologists. There was still a risk that they could be geocachers.

"They might start asking questions," Bobby continued, "wanting to know what we're doing out here."

And she didn't have very good answers. She and Bobby weren't supposed to be on the trail. But then again, how much trouble could they really get in? Was there such a thing as bat encroachment? They weren't in any way hurting the bats or disturbing them during hibernation, which was usually an automatic death sentence to the poor things. They weren't even near the bats, most of which were presumably sucking down copious quantities of gnats at Fuzzy Lake at this moment.

Daisy looked into the trees. The flickering lights had returned. The men had rounded the opposite end of the switchback and were getting close. They weren't speaking much anymore, probably because they had to concentrate too hard on not crashing down the side of the mountain.

After deliberating a short while longer, she said to Bobby, "I think one of us should get up and meet them.

They probably won't know anything specific, but they might be able to give us a clue about Laurel and Chris."

Slinging the Winchester over his back, Bobby immediately began to rise. Daisy put her hand on his arm to stop him.

"No. I'll do it, Bobby. When they see you with that rifle, they're going to pull out their own guns, or they're going to think you're hunting. Don't forget that it's out of season, and if they are state biologists, they'll know it. Then you'll have to spend the next hour arguing with them about licenses and permits and tags."

This time Bobby hesitated. "I don't know, Daisy. You're right about the hunting, but I'm not so sure you should be meeting 'em alone."

She wasn't so sure either. A dark trail in the middle of the backwoods. Two men who might or might not be the geocachers who killed Caesar. It was not an exciting new friendship opportunity.

"Rick wouldn't like it," Bobby added.

"Well, Rick's not here," Daisy stood up, more than a little irritated at that remark, "so it doesn't much matter what he likes."

Not willing to debate the subject further now that it included Rick, she walked away from Bobby and the fallen birch in the direction of the trail. She moved with soft, slow steps, trying not to make any noise, or at least no more noise than was absolutely necessary. Hopefully the men wouldn't pay attention to the gentle crack of a twig breaking against her ankle or the quiet crunch of leaves under her feet.

"Be careful, Daisy," Bobby whispered after her. "And don't worry, I've got you covered."

Daisy heard him pull the rifle from his back once more, and it did reassure her somewhat. Without question, Bobby knew how to handle his firearms. And he hadn't been drinking. That meant he could be a darn fine sniper.

The lights from the men were growing bigger, and the sound of their boots treading on the clay was getting louder. As she climbed out of the undergrowth and returned to the trail, Daisy slid her hand back toward the pocket containing the Ruger. Although she wasn't exactly a fast draw, she figured that there could be no harm in being prepared. She strained her eyes in the direction of the stone outcropping that she and Bobby had been standing on when the tornado of bats had swirled into the sky. The men would have to walk down it just like she and Bobby had started to walk up it.

They were coming. They were almost on the other side of the outcropping. Daisy could hear their limbs moving, and she could feel the ground shift ever so slightly from their collective weight. She clicked on her flashlight. She knew that she was going to startle them in any event, but she didn't want to appear so abruptly out of the blackness that they took her for a ghostly wraith and got a heart attack in the process—or worse yet, that they shot her first and asked for an explanation from Bobby afterward.

One of their flashlights turned the corner. It was followed by an arm, a body, and then a face.

"What the hell are you doing out here!" it hollered as it spotted her.

CHAPTER
23

For an instant, Daisy stopped breathing. Then with the aid of her flashlight, she saw the man's clothing and took a big gulp of refreshingly cold air. He wasn't a geocacher, not unless he had stolen both a jacket and a hat with badges on them that depicted the Commonwealth of Virginia and were inscribed with the delightful words *Department of Game and Inland Fisheries*. It didn't matter to her in the least if he was an actual biologist. All she cared about was that he obviously wasn't searching for Confederate treasure.

The second man also wore a jacket and a hat with badges, but his were different from his colleague's. They featured an illustration of a bat in flight—*Bat Conservation International*. Daisy almost smiled when she read the name of the organization. It was very welcome double proof that she wasn't standing in front of the geocachers who had taken the revolver from her bakery and shot Caesar in the parking lot.

Both men stared at her for nearly a minute, trying to catch their own breath and recover from the shock of her suddenly materializing before them like an otherworldly apparition. Daisy used the interval to think of an excuse. Of course they would want to know why she was there. She needed a plausible reason for being out on the trail when the area was closed. She had never been a remotely good liar, so if she had any hope of being at all convincing, it had to be something at least bordering the truth.

Her mind promptly went to Laurel. She was the perfect pretext, especially because she wasn't really a pretext. Daisy could tell the men that her friend had gone missing and she was looking for her. They might even know who Laurel was—having perhaps seen or talked to her on the trail during the last week—and that way they might also be more inclined to share any current information they had about her or Chris.

"I'm terribly sorry if I startled you," Daisy drawled, adding an extra bit of sweetness to her tone.

"I was just so surprised to see you," the possible biologist replied.

The bat conservationist agreed. "We weren't expecting to see anybody at this time of night."

"I know I shouldn't be out here," Daisy confessed, "but before you read me the Riot Act—"

"Read you the Riot Act?" the biologist cut her off. "Why would we do that?"

She blinked at him.

"It's not any of our business when—or where—you hike," the conservationist said.

Daisy blinked again. It wasn't the response that she had anticipated.

"I do feel obligated to point out, though," he went on, "that it's never a smart idea to hike alone, particularly in the dark. If you fall and sprain an ankle or break your leg, no one might find you until tomorrow, or maybe even for a couple of days. You can't rely on your phone around these parts. The reception is pretty much nonexistent."

Her brow furrowed. "So you don't mind if I'm on the trail?"

"No." The biologist's brow furrowed back at her. "Why would we mind if you're on the trail? It's public land."

"But it's closed," she returned, thoroughly confused.

"Oh, that's what you mean." His brow relaxed, and he nodded. "Only it's not closed."

"Then what about the event?" Daisy countered, partly to him and partly to herself. "The geocaching event that was going on up here a week ago. It had to be called off early because the area was closed."

"You're right," the conservationist said. "All access to the area was blocked. It's since been unblocked."

"When?" she asked.

"Yesterday. First thing yesterday morning, if you want me to be precise. That's when we got the test results back."

"What test results?"

He sighed. "How much do you know about bats?"

"I know the area had to be closed—" Daisy stopped and corrected herself. "At least I thought the area had to be closed after white-nose syndrome was discovered in some of the caves around the lake."

"You're right again." The man was visibly impressed. "Except it was only discovered in one cave. We were afraid that it would spread to the others."

"And you're not afraid anymore? I realize I'm not any sort of an expert on the subject and you are," she gestured toward the badges on his clothing, "but didn't you just find the fungus in the cave a few days ago? Is that really long enough to be sure it won't spread?"

"Ordinarily it wouldn't be long enough." The conservationist smiled grimly. "Ordinarily I would have said the fungus will definitely spread. In other caves and other states there has been no way to keep it from spreading. But this is not an ordinary case."

Daisy waited for him to explain.

"A couple of those geocachers were the ones who first reported it," he told her. "That was plenty ordinary. It's usually either spelunkers or Forest Service folks who discover the fungus in a new location. They're poking around the inside of a cave, and they see the telltale powdery white residue on the muzzle and wings of the bats that are inhabiting it. White-nose syndrome looks pretty much like it sounds, although the wings actually bear the brunt of the attack. When the fungus infects them, they tear and crumple the same as tissue paper."

"Don't forget the hibernation part," the biologist interjected.

The conservationist gave a little snort. "Of course not. It should have been the first clue that something was wrong."

"The hibernation part?" Daisy echoed with a frown. "But the bats aren't hibernating. Just about an hour ago, we—I—" she amended quickly, "saw a whole swarm come around the side of the mountain and fly off toward Fuzzy Lake."

"That's exactly it," the conservationist replied. "The bats aren't hibernating yet, and white-nose syndrome doesn't appear unless they are hibernating. The fungus can only grow in cold conditions. That's why humans aren't at risk. We're too warm. But during hibernation the bats' body temperature drops significantly. Combined with the cool cave in winter, it's the ideal recipe for infection."

"So what does that mean?" Daisy asked him. "The fungus has adapted to warmer temperatures? It can attack bats in fall after the heat of summer is over but before they settle down for hibernation?"

"I was worried about that," he said. "I was worried that it might even be a new variety of the fungus. When we looked at the bats roosting in the cave from a distance, there were white spots on their wings and muzzles, but on closer examination it seemed to be a more solid substance than the typical powdery residue."

"That should have been the second clue," the biologist muttered.

With a nod of agreement at him, the conservationist continued, "It was strange, but we followed the standard procedure—the same as we have at dozens of other sites where white-nose syndrome has appeared and been confirmed. As an emergency measure to keep anybody from inadvertently carrying the fungus to the other caves on their shoes or their gear, we immediately blocked all access to the area. Then we took samples and sent them away to be tested. The results came back yesterday morning."

"And?" She gazed at him expectantly.

"And it's not white-nose syndrome," the two men responded in unison.

"Then what is it? Some other nasty fungus?"

The men looked at each other and laughed.

"Nope," the biologist chortled. "Not a nasty fungus."

The conservationist chortled too. "It's cream cheese."

Cream cheese. The blood drained from Daisy's face, and the lustrous stars above her head spun like a golden carousel.

"All things considered," the conservationist said more earnestly, "we were very lucky. I've seen far too many instances where people have vandalized and even torched caves. There's never any reason for it—other than ignorant cruelty—and tens of thousands of bats have died as a result. Thankfully in this case, whatever idiots decided to spray something on them, at least they didn't use paint. That would have killed the bats for sure. But cream cheese is a natural product. As far as we've been able to tell, it hasn't injured them."

"The really funny thing," the biologist added, still chortling, "is that it hasn't gone bad. Based on when we received the report of the discovery from the geocachers, the cheese must have been sprayed on the bats this past weekend, but it hasn't spoiled. The cave worked just like a refrigerator, and the cheese is fine. You could eat it today the same as you could have a week ago."

"If you don't mind a bit of bat fur on your bagel," the conservationist remarked dryly.

"And you would have to be able to catch one of them to scoop some of the cheese off," the biologist returned.

They started laughing again.

Daisy didn't laugh with them. She heard their words, and she understood them, but she was too dumbfounded to make a sound. The cream cheese that had been stolen from her bakery wasn't rotting at the bottom of a farm pond. Nor was it sitting in a great melted, mushy, stinking pile on the edge of a field by Rick's nip joint or with the rest of the trash behind Chris's cabin at the campground. It wasn't stinking or rotting at all. It was apparently in good condition inside a cave and flying around Fuzzy Lake. Ninety pounds of cream cheese on the muzzles and wings of hundreds—or thousands—of bats.

She could only think about how wrong she had been—completely and utterly wrong. Beulah and Aunt Emily and Deputy Johnson had been wrong too. So had everybody who believed that the theft of the cream cheese was nothing more than a simple act of mischief. A silly, childish prank that had gone horribly awry when Brenda stabbed Jordan Snyder. Except it turned out that Jordan and his partners in crime didn't take the cheese merely to cause trouble. They weren't dim-witted hooligans as everyone had been so quick to assume. They had purposely chosen the cream cheese because they had an actual purpose for it.

The conservationist was right: it wasn't an ordinary case. He had been referring to the cheese, of course, but the real reason that it wasn't ordinary was it had nothing to do with vandalism or ignorant cruelty. At its heart, it didn't even have anything to do with the bats. They were just a convenient tool, and the white-nose syndrome was no more than a cunning deception. It was all about the cave and getting into the cave, to the exclusion of everybody else. Daisy could see that now. She could see it as clearly as her fingers could feel the rosewood grip of the Ruger in her jacket pocket.

It was a brilliant plan, and the timing had been executed perfectly. Take the cheese from the bakery on Saturday morning. Spray it on the bats in the cave on Saturday afternoon or Sunday. Report the supposed discovery of white-nose syndrome to the appropriate officials on Monday, and the area was promptly closed. That was precisely what Jordan Snyder—before his untimely death—and his partners in crime had wanted to happen. They were there entirely because of the area.

Daisy had already begun to guess it in regard to the maps that had been stolen from the historical society. She had wondered if they were the reason why Jordan and his partners chose to attend this particular geocaching event. Although she still didn't know how exactly the maps helped them, she was certain that the hunt allowed them to make a meticulous examination of the mountain. No one paid any attention to where they climbed or dug or poked around, because they were expected to climb and dig and poke around, along with the rest of the geocachers. And when they thought they had at last found the right spot, they wanted to protect it.

The fake fungus worked beautifully. The other geocachers were forced to leave, so there was no risk that any of them would stumble across the correct cave, or the correct chamber inside the cave, before they did. Then when the officials learned that the bats were safe and there was no white-nose syndrome affecting them, the area was reopened. Even that had been superbly calculated. As the conservationist had said, paint would have killed the bats for sure, and the area might have been closed indefinitely for a full-blown investigation. But the cream cheese didn't cause any permanent damage, which meant that everyone just shrugged, chuckled, and walked away. The rogue geocachers were able to go about their business without a lick of interference. They were all alone, just them and the maps, which were perhaps necessary for the ultimate step—finding the treasure.

For so long Daisy hadn't been able to figure it out. She couldn't get the pieces to match in any sort of rational manner. But finally they fit together for her. The cheese had started the puzzle, and it had also solved it. The only question left was whether the lost Confederate silver truly existed. How right—or how wrong—was Henry Brent on the subject? Were there thirty-nine kegs of Mexican silver dollars buried somewhere in southwestern Virginia? And were they under Danville, or were they in the mountains around Fuzzy Lake? Could the maps offer a clue as to their location?

As she stood on the dark trail listening to the men grouse about their wasted work over the past week, Daisy felt a growing sense of impatience. Precious minutes were rapidly ticking by. Now that she knew how intelligent the geocachers were and to what lengths they would go to ensure that no one reached the treasure before they did, she worried more than ever about Laurel and Chris.

Laurel was supposed to be getting married tomorrow. She wouldn't be gone both yesterday and today unless something bad had happened. And Daisy was increasingly beginning to fear that it was something really bad. No doubt Bobby was getting anxious too. He was probably twitching on the fallen birch like a jumping spider. From his standpoint, she had been talking to the men for a very long time, especially if he couldn't hear them or didn't fully understand what they were saying. She had to find a way to get the men to continue down the mountain, so that she and Bobby could continue up it.

"I sure do appreciate you telling me the area is open again," Daisy interjected the moment there was a break in the discussion. "I'm also sure you want to get on home. I won't keep you any longer."

Nodding appreciatively, the conservationist adjusted the pack on his back. "I won't lie. This thing is getting heavy."

"Mine too," the biologist griped, adjusting his pack as

well. "We wouldn't have to carry all the equipment if somebody hadn't stolen our ATVs."

"Someone stole your ATVs?" Daisy said.

She wasn't overly surprised at the news. In comparison with the cream cheese, the revolver, and the maps, the ATVs had probably been the easiest for the geocachers to steal. No windows needed to be broken, and nobody was shot or stabbed in the process.

"Thieving bastards," the biologist spat. "I hope they ride right off a cliff."

"You wouldn't happen to know what direction they were headed?" Daisy asked.

The conservationist shook his head. "We thought we heard them driving on the trail this afternoon, but we never saw them. Everything around here echoes, so we couldn't tell if they were actually on the trail or just near it. For what it's worth, it did sound like they were going up and down the mountain. Joyriding, I presume."

There was a distinct rustling in the undergrowth behind her. She knew it was Bobby. He must have heard the remark. It wasn't joyriding. On the contrary, it was exactly what they had discussed earlier at the trailhead. The ATVs were how the geocachers had gone between the trail and the campground so quickly. If she and Bobby could find the vehicles, then they would in all likelihood find the geocachers—and hopefully also Laurel and Chris.

"Well, thanks again." Daisy tried to sound casual and not suspiciously eager to have them move along. "Hope you have a nice weekend."

"It will be if we ever get out of here," the biologist grumbled.

Shifting his light toward his feet, he started walking

down the trail. The conservationist followed suit. Daisy pretended to head in the opposite direction, hoping that Bobby would be smart enough to wait until the two men were a good distance away before appearing.

After only a few steps, the conservationist suddenly spun around. "Wait!" he exclaimed.

Reluctantly, Daisy turned back.

He shone his light on her face. "You never told us why you were up here."

"Stargazing." She gestured toward the bulky pocket in which her hand was still holding the Ruger. "I have my binoculars. Now I just need to find the perfect spot."

And as she said it, Daisy moved swiftly out of the light, before the man could see how badly she was fibbing.

CHAPTER
24

After a long moment of hesitation, the conservationist finally turned back around and continued with his colleague down the mountain. Daisy listened to their departing footsteps with a mixture of relief and regret. She was happy not to have to answer any of their questions, but at the same time, there was some security in their company. She didn't know how many geocachers there were—two at a minimum and maybe more. The conservationist and biologist were numbers in her favor. With the generally poor reception in the area, it was unlikely that she would be able to use her phone if she needed to get help. At least she didn't have to worry about the ATVs driving around in the dark.

Bobby wisely waited until the lights from the two men were once again no more than flickering fireflies off in the distance, then he emerged from the undergrowth.

"How's the knee?" Daisy asked him.

"It's okay." He bent his leg to test it. "A little stiff, but nothing serious."

"That's good." She paused, not quite sure where to begin.

"Did you understand them?" Bobby said, taking the initiative. "All that stuff about the bats and the fungus and the cream cheese?"

"I did," she answered truthfully.

"It's your cream cheese, isn't it, Daisy? The cheese that was stolen from Sweetie Pies last Saturday?"

"It must be, especially considering the timing."

Bobby nodded. "Do you think it was some of the geo-cachers?"

She nodded back at him, pleased that he was able to make the connection without her having to give a lengthy explanation.

"If it was them," his voice quivered, "then Laurel's in real trouble, isn't she?"

"I'm afraid so, Bobby."

"But what do they want from her? And what do they want with the caves?"

Daisy chewed on the inside of her cheek, debating what to tell him. It couldn't hurt if he knew. It might even prove useful somehow.

"I think they're looking for treasure," she responded. "I think they're looking for lost Confederate silver."

He frowned at her. "You mean those thirty-nine kegs from Danville?"

Her lips parted in astonishment.

"I know the stories," Bobby said. "We all know the stories. But I can tell you from personal experience, those kegs don't exist. Or if they do, they're not anywhere around here. Rick and I and most every other boy we knew used to go digging for treasure in these mountains when we were kids. You must have heard us talking about it. We'd head over the minute school let out in summer, and we'd always see a zillion old geezers roaming around with their charts and notebooks and metal detectors. They were looking for lost gold, lost silver, lost Confederate anything. And do you know what they found? The same as the rest of us. Nothing worth a bean. Rusted soda bottle tops and shell casings."

"Did you go into the caves?" Daisy asked him.

"Naw. We crawled through occasionally, but most of 'em aren't really big enough for people."

"Not enough to get in, or not big enough to move around once you're inside?"

Bobby shrugged. "The openings are only a foot or two, maybe three for the largest."

"The bats don't need more than that as an entrance," Daisy replied. "But the chambers further in the cave could be huge."

He squinted at her.

"What if I told you the geocachers stole some old maps—"

"Old maps?" he echoed.

"From the historical society," she said. "My guess is that they show this trail and the caves and something else which could be used to narrow down the location of the silver. The geocachers—"

Not waiting for her to finish, Bobby turned on the heel of his boot and immediately started marching up the trail.

"Bobby—"

"We've got to hurry, Daisy! We've got to get to those caves."

"Yes, but—"

"That must be why they took Laurel. She's little

enough to get in. She could crawl through one of the smaller openings when they couldn't."

"Maybe, but—"

"And now she might be stuck. She could be trapped in a cave and scared out of her mind!"

Daisy couldn't argue with him on that point. Being trapped inside a pitch black cave with threatening men and at least one revolver blocking your exit as countless bats swooshed continually over your head did not sound enjoyable. She wasn't convinced, however, that Laurel's size was the reason why the geocachers had wanted her. Now that she knew for certain their interest in Laurel didn't have any relation to them gaining access to the area while it was closed, Daisy was more inclined to believe that it had some connection to Chris. It seemed to be too much of a coincidence to her that the geocachers were searching for Confederate treasure and the Confederacy was Chris's area of historical expertise.

"She might have been trapped since yesterday!" Bobby went on. "She's probably cold and hungry and tired and thirsty—"

He had darted ahead of her so quickly that Daisy had to rush to catch up. The trail seemed somehow easier to follow than it did before. Maybe it was because her eyes had fully adjusted to the darkness, or because the moon was particularly bright that evening.

When she finally reached him, she touched his arm. "Hush, Bobby. Laurel's not a hothouse rose. She won't wilt from one bad day."

The litany of his fiancée's potential ailments halted.

"The important thing is getting to her—and Chris," Daisy added. "But we need to do it quietly. We don't want the geocachers to hear us if we can avoid it. It's bad enough that they can see our lights."

Bobby promptly lowered both his voice and his flashlight. "Can you find the cave?" he asked her.

"Which cave? That's the question."

Although he kept walking at a rapid pace, Bobby hesitated before answering. "The one the bats came out of?"

"I can try," Daisy said. "Or at least I can get us near it."

She chastised herself for not asking the conservationist and biologist if the cave that she had seen the bats emerge from at dusk was the one with the cream cheese. She assumed that they were the same, but she didn't really know. If the two were different, she could only hope that they were close to each other.

They continued hiking briskly up the mountain. As they rounded another switchback, Daisy peered toward the opposite side of the ridge. It was much closer than it had been previously. The black spots that speckled in between the trees were significantly larger and more distinct. She could tell now that some were merely depressions and patches of bare rock, but others were definitely caves. They were all still. None appeared to have any movement in front of them—bat or human.

Daisy touched Bobby's arm again, and this time she stopped him. "Do you see those dark areas over there?" She tried to guide his gaze toward the caves without using her flashlight. "Three of them in a row to the right of that big cluster of boulders and just above the pointy outcropping?"

He followed her directions. "Are those them? The roosting caves?"

"I think so. It looked like there were only two before,

except we were a lot further away then. If you want my opinion, that's where we should go."

Bobby agreed without the slightest deliberation. "We'll cut over from the trail after the next switchback. We're going to have to go across the boulders, because we can't come up from under the outcropping. But that's good. We won't be as visible or make as much noise on the rocks as we would in the woods."

It was an excellent approach, and it gave Daisy an increased sense of confidence. If they were lucky, the geocachers might not see their lights after all, at least not until they were actually at the caves. Although he needed her to show him their destination, Bobby had a remarkable forte for figuring out the best—and most concealed— way to get there. It was the hunter in him. Only instead of an eight-point buck, he was tracking his fiancée.

Keeping their flashlights down and speaking as little as possible, they finished their trek on the trail. As soon as they hit the switchback, Bobby slowed his stride and studied the undergrowth for the right place to turn toward the caves.

"Maps," he mumbled under his breath.

"What was that?" Daisy asked.

"You said old maps."

Her brow furrowed, not understanding the relevance.

"Ha!" Bobby exclaimed suddenly in a low tone. "I knew I'd find 'em. Look!"

Straining her eyes in the darkness, Daisy followed his outstretched finger. He was pointing at something just off the trail in between the trees. It was a thick pile of branches. They appeared to have been cut and stacked. Then she saw what was under them. The branches had been cut and stacked to cover a pair of ATVs.

She squeezed his elbow in excitement. "You may get lost a lot, Bobby, but you've also got some awesome backwoods skills. If Rick were here, he would be mighty proud of you."

"Aw, shucks. Thanks, Daisy."

The man practically beamed with gratitude and pride.

"Well, let's go then," she said with a smile. "We don't want to keep Laurel waiting any longer than she already has."

Bobby headed into the trees first, which Daisy didn't mind. Just as with the path from the campground to the trailhead, if he was in front of her, then he couldn't wander away without her noticing. But unlike the path from the campground to the trailhead, there was no clear route for them to follow. All they had was a general direction— through the woods, across the boulders, to the caves. At least there was no longer any question about them being the correct caves. The secreted ATVs were proof enough of that. And because of them, Daisy found her confidence waning a bit. As happy as she was that they had found the ATVs, so they knew for certain they were on the right track, it also meant that the geocachers were close. Very close.

Twigs snapped against their legs, and dried leaves crackled beneath their feet. Both Daisy and Bobby moved as lightly as they could, trying to keep the noise to a minimum. If the geocachers were inside the caves, they probably wouldn't hear them. If they were outside, they most likely would. Bobby paused occasionally to listen. No twigs snapped or leaves crackled in reply. It was growing late. The night seemed to have fewer sounds now. Except Daisy knew that it was just an illusion. She was listening so hard for some sign of the geocachers that she heard nothing else.

Finally they reached the boulders. Upon closer in-spection, it turned out to be one massive sheet of rock rather than a collection of individual stones. Daisy reached out and touched it. The face of the rock was smooth—too smooth to make it an easy climb. But thankfully, it was solid stone, not the typical Pittsylvania County clay, which tended to first compact and then crumble when subjected to any substantial amount of weight.

"How's the knee?" she asked Bobby for the second time that evening.

"It's fine," he answered without quailing. "It's going to have to be."

Nodding at him encouragingly, Daisy reached out and touched the rock again. She felt around for the craggiest part. It was where she would start. When she found a suit-ably rough and uneven spot, she freed her other hand by tucking her flashlight into the placket of her jacket. That way she would have at least a little light to guide her. Daisy wished that she had a headlamp instead, and she could already guess that she was going to wish it even more when they got to the caves.

"Good luck," she said to Bobby, as she stepped from the relatively safe and level dirt onto the sloping stone.

It wasn't a fun climb, primarily because Daisy couldn't really see where she was going. She had to move by a com-bination of touch and pressure. Her fingers first tried to find a place to grip, then her feet tried to find a place that would hold her. She slipped repeatedly, and on one occa-sion, she slid nearly a full body length before managing to grab a jagged piece of rock to stop herself. Based on the muffled mutterings and cursing not far from her ear, Daisy knew that Bobby wasn't having a good time, either.

She ended up half crawling like an unsteady toddler and half slithering like a slightly tipsy snake until her legs at last landed on the blissfully flat and horizontal outcropping on the other side of the sheet of stone. The trio of caves lay above her. Below her and the pointy outcropping was open air. If she accidentally stumbled off its edge, then she tumbled down the mountain. As Daisy waited for Bobby to join her, she couldn't help but think that if there actually was silver hidden in the vicinity, this would be a particularly well-chosen hidey-hole for it: accessible but definitely not too accessible. The old geezers with their charts and notebooks and metal detectors weren't climbing around here.

"How the heck did they do that while carrying all the cream cheese?" Bobby wondered, skidding over the final section of rock and coming to a wobbly halt next to her.

"Very carefully," Daisy replied, gesturing toward the precipitous drop-off beneath them. "And probably during daylight hours."

He grunted and looked up. She looked up too. There was a ledge in between them and the caves. It was neither thick nor high. They would have no trouble scrambling over it, but it blocked their view completely. If there was anything—or anyone—at the entrance to the caves, they wouldn't know it until they were directly in front of it.

"I hate going up blind," Bobby grumbled.

"There's no light shining out," Daisy said.

"They might have turned it off to lull us."

A noise echoed from the caves. It sounded like a cough.

Bobby clucked his tongue. "Somebody sure is in there." He adjusted the rifle on his back. "I'll go first. At least that way they can't get both of us at once. If it's clear, I'll give you a signal."

Putting his hands on the ledge, he gave a little jump and pulled himself up. Daisy winced in anticipation as his body disappeared. Mercifully, nothing happened. No shouts, no shooting, not even another cough. After a minute, Bobby clucked his tongue again. It was safe. He reached an arm down to help lift her over the ledge. Daisy clambered up next to him, and together they gazed at the caves.

There were three openings. None was tall enough for an average-size adult to walk through upright. One was too small for even a coyote to squeeze inside. But the other two were usable. A man could hunch down and enter both of them. And although Daisy could only guess at the size of a Confederate keg filled with Mexican silver dollars, she thought that the two entrances were probably also wide enough for a keg to be rolled through.

Dropping to his knees for a better look, Bobby reported in a whisper, "This one's got some light. It's way back in there, but it's definitely light."

Daisy gulped.

He inspected the other openings. "There's light in this one too. And in the little one."

"All three?" She frowned. "How can that be?"

"Maybe it's like you said earlier. The entrances aren't big, but there's a much bigger chamber further in the cave. They could all lead to it."

"Or there are an awful lot of geocachers with lights," Daisy countered.

It was Bobby's turn to frown. "There's a smell. It's strange."

She bent down next to him. There was indeed an odd odor emanating from the caves. It was faint, and she couldn't identify it.

"So which one do we try?" he asked her.

"I don't know. Flip a coin?"

"Rick always says go with your shootin' hand." Bobby checked his right fist. It was turned slightly to the left. "Left," he determined with all earnestness, and immediately headed toward the opening on the left.

For a moment, Daisy stared after him. They were picking a cave based on the direction of Bobby's shooting hand? Then she shrugged. If all the entrances did in fact lead to one big chamber, it didn't really matter which they chose.

The cave was cold and damp—the kind of cold and damp that sunk deep into your bones, making them feel rigid and brittle. With the unidentified light shining dimly from the back, the surrounding walls looked more inky violet than black. Both Daisy and Bobby had to stoop over too much to have their guns at the ready, but Bobby kept one hand vigilantly on the strap of his Winchester, and Daisy slid her palm back into the pocket containing the Ruger. After a dozen feet, they heard the same noise echo as before. It was almost certainly a cough.

"Could you tell if that was Laurel?" Daisy whispered.

Bobby shook his head.

They continued another dozen feet, and the cave gradually began to expand. It grew both in height and in width, until they could eventually straighten up and stand next to each other. Bobby stopped and circled his flashlight around. Everything was wet from condensation— the floor, the ceiling, and the walls. There were no bats in sight, but there were numerous side passages. Some were too tiny to hold anything more than spiders and newts. Others could have housed a slumbering bear.

"This place is like a maze," Bobby mused.

"That could be why they needed those maps," Daisy responded, more to herself than to him.

The cough repeated itself—twice.

She turned her light from the side passages to the main cave. "It's coming from up ahead, isn't it?"

He nodded.

As they proceeded forward, the previously faint smell intensified. It was acrid and pungent, but Daisy still couldn't identify it.

"Maps," Bobby mumbled once more.

"What about the maps?" Daisy asked.

"You keep talking about old maps, and I keep thinking I saw some old maps."

"You couldn't have seen these, Bobby," she told him. "They were stolen just this past weekend, and if they really are that valuable in regard to finding the treasure, the geocachers wouldn't let them out of their sight."

"But I did see them," he insisted. "Only I didn't realize then they were old."

With every step, the mysterious smell became stronger. It was bitterly sharp, almost like ammonia. As hard as she tried, Daisy couldn't figure out what it was. She couldn't think of anything in a cave that would cause such a harsh, almost overpowering scent—at least not that occurred there naturally. Maybe the geocachers were using some sort of industrial chemical to aid in their search.

"I did see them," Bobby said again. "I know I did."

"Okay," Daisy replied with a touch of annoyance, wishing that he would focus on finding the origin of the cough instead of fruitlessly sputtering on about the maps. "So where did you see them?"

He didn't immediately answer.

She listened. There was some heavy breathing. It seemed labored. Then the cough joined it.

"Over there!" she cried in a low tone. "In that corner!"

Daisy hurried toward the noise. Her fingers curled around the grip of the Ruger as she reached the spot. Two passages came together with the main cave to form a small nook.

"Where did I see them?" Bobby repeated over and over, trailing after her. "Where did I see them?"

Her light traveled slowly around the nook. Water dripped from the walls. It hit the ground in great splashy drops. It also hit a bulky shadow. Daisy moved her flashlight toward it. She saw the outline of arms and legs and a torso. The shadow was a person—a person sitting on the floor of the cave. Shifting the light to the person's face, she gasped.

"I saw the maps," Bobby declared emphatically, all doubt at last removed. He pointed at the figure. "I saw the maps with *him*."

CHAPTER
25

As Daisy stared at Chris, her heart twisted with pain. It wasn't a lovesick sort of pain. It was the pain of embarrassment, of feeling horribly duped. Bobby had seen Chris with the maps, which meant that Chris was one of Jordan Snyder's partners in crime. The truth was bad enough, but it became even more painful to Daisy when she realized that Rick had guessed it all along. To his credit, he had tried to warn her. At the nip joint he had told her flat out that Chris could be involved, that he might be one of the men who had broken in to her bakery. But instead of wisely listening to him, she had dismissed it. She had gone so far as to call it ridiculous. Only, it turned out not to be ridiculous in the least.

It seemed so patently obvious to her now. Chris had been to Sweetie Pies. He had been to the nip joint where the crates were dumped. He was a geocacher who could have easily befriended Jordan weeks, months, or even years earlier in order to make all the necessary arrangements. Chris was also one of the organizers of the event, so he had a hand in choosing its location. And he chose the ideal place that would allow him to both steal the maps from the historical society and then use them to search for lost treasure—Confederate treasure, no doubt well researched by a Confederate history professor.

Everything that had confused Daisy before was suddenly explained with perfect clarity. Of course Chris objected to Laurel marrying Bobby, but it wasn't for the purported reason that Bobby didn't have a steady profession and spent his days in a broken-down trailer playing with his dogs and cleaning his guns. It was because Chris intended on wreaking havoc in Pittsylvania County, and he didn't want his sister to remain behind when he had finished.

Why had Chris been so sweet to her, getting cozy with her during the barbecue at the campground and while driving around the neighborhood viewing historical markers? It was all a distraction, nothing more. By flirting and taking her out on a date, he was gambling that Daisy wouldn't suspect him. And she hadn't. Nobody had, except, evidently, Rick. Chris's behavior at the nip joint should have been the ultimate warning to her. If he was willing to cheat at cards for a little bit of cash, then it wasn't too much of a stretch to believe that he was also willing to lie, steal, and kill for a lot of cash in the form of thirty-nine kegs of Mexican silver dollars.

Bobby pulled the rifle from his back and leveled it at Chris. "Where's Laurel?" he demanded.

Chris didn't respond. His head was slumped forward, his knees were curled up to his chest, and his shoulders trembled. He was a darn fine actor, but Daisy wasn't fooled. She had already seen him play the kind and polite gentleman. That was before he shot Caesar in her parking lot.

"Be careful, Bobby," Daisy said, thinking of the missing revolver. "He's got a gun. I don't see it, but I know he has it. He took a revolver that Rick left at the bakery."

"You try to draw it," Bobby spit venomously at Chris, "and I'll blast you. This Winchester will make a hole in you like a grenade hittin' an ant."

To Daisy's surprise, Chris still didn't respond. She squinted at him. Although he was strangely huddled, he didn't appear to be injured.

"Where's Laurel?" Bobby demanded again, pushing the muzzle of his rifle toward Chris's chest.

Chris answered with a cough. The noise was nearly as odd as his hunched position. It sounded like a strangled gasp of breath, almost as though he were choking.

Daisy found herself gasping slightly for breath as well. The longer that she spent inside the closed walls of the cave, the more concentrated and caustic the smell became. It stung her nostrils and made her throat thick.

"What is that gosh-awful smell?" she asked Chris. "Is it some chemical you've been using?"

"No. It—it's not—" He broke off, wheezing heavily.

"Don't play stupid," Bobby snarled at him.

Chris lifted his wobbly head in Daisy's direction. It seemed to require a good deal of effort. "It—it's not a chemical," he said, also apparently with a good deal of effort. "It's from the bats."

"From the bats?" She frowned, not following him.

"The bats," he confirmed. "It's only an inch or two out here, but it's a couple of feet deep back there." He gestured toward the interior of the cave.

"An inch or two?" Still not following, Daisy moved her flashlight from Chris to the ground directly in front of her. When she looked down, she finally realized what he was talking about.

She wasn't standing on the floor of the cave. She was standing in a layer of waste. Bat guano, to be precise. Daisy understood now why the smell was so similar to ammonia and why it was so terribly potent. Thousands of bats flying out every evening at dusk and returning every morning at dawn: that was a lot of excrement. And it obviously accumulated over time. The cave must have been used as a roost for many, many years, if Chris was telling the truth and the guano was a foot or more deep farther inside.

"Don't play stupid," Bobby snarled at him again. "Don't tell us about bats! Tell us about Laurel! Where is she? What did you make her do?"

Daisy's gaze returned to Chris.

"Is she trapped somewhere?" Bobby pressed him. "Is she in one of these passages? Is she in this cave?"

"Bobby—" Daisy started to interject.

He didn't listen to her. "Do all the caves connect in the back? Is that where Laurel is? Do I need the maps to get to her?"

"Stop a second, Bobby." As she said it, Daisy took a cautious but curious step toward Chris. Even in the shadowy light, she could see that his eyes were glassy and distended. "He's not right."

"He's plenty all right," Bobby countered. "Don't let him trick you, Daisy. I know he had those maps. I saw them in his cabin when . . ."

The sentence trailed away unfinished, but Daisy didn't pay any attention to it. She was too busy looking at Chris.

In contrast with the dark cave, his face was as gray and pale as if it had been coated with ash.

"The cabin," Bobby murmured behind her.

"I didn't— It wasn't—" Chris faltered, seemingly unable to continue.

"The cabin," Bobby repeated. "It was the wrong cabin. I thought it was the right one, but it wasn't."

Chris's jaw contorted.

"The fan was ticking," Bobby went on. "It was ticking just like popcorn."

"Popcorn?" Daisy's head snapped around. "Did you just say the fan was ticking like popcorn?"

He nodded. "That's why I thought it was the right cabin. The ceiling fan always sounds like popcorn."

Daisy remembered a ceiling fan that sounded like popcorn too.

"I opened the door," Bobby explained. "The fan was ticking, and the maps were there. They were spread out on the bed."

She blinked at him. It wasn't Chris's bed. It wasn't Chris's cabin. Chris's cabin didn't have a ceiling fan that ticked.

"I couldn't figure out why they were there. Nobody was using maps for the so-called hunt. They were all using GPS, or at least they were trying to. That's why I thought it was the wrong cabin. And he agreed." Bobby motioned toward Chris. "He told me it was wrong, and I thought I had gotten lost."

"But you didn't," Daisy whispered in reply. Instead of thick, her throat felt suddenly raw. It had been ripped raw by the ghastly realization. "You didn't get lost, Bobby. You were in the right cabin all along."

A guttural groan came out of Chris. She looked at him. His previously trembling shoulders began to shake hard, almost to the point of convulsions. He wasn't coughing, as Daisy had originally assumed. He was retching. Chris had been in the cave too long. It was making him seriously ill.

"The right cabin?" Bobby responded slowly. He was so focused on what she had said that he didn't notice how Chris's condition was deteriorating. "But if it was the right cabin, then he wasn't the one who had the maps. It was—it was—" As he reached the same appalling conclusion that Daisy had come to only a minute earlier, Bobby's voice rose to a rumble that echoed through the cave like the roar of a lion. "Where the hell is Laurel!"

"Here I am, sweetheart."

The purring words were promptly followed by a sharp crack. Bobby's body twisted, and he crumpled to the ground. The Winchester dropped from his grasp as he landed heavily on his stomach.

"Bobby!" Daisy exclaimed, dashing over to him.

"Oh, aren't you just so sweet . . ." Laurel cooed.

"Laurel—" Chris spluttered.

She ignored her brother. "Don't even think about touching that rifle, Daisy. You may be sweet, but that doesn't mean you also have to be stupid."

Daisy had absolutely no intention of touching Bobby's rifle. In that moment, she was far too worried about him. He had been shot in the back. She couldn't tell where exactly. There wasn't enough light for her to see the wound clearly. It was low—close to his waist and more toward his right side than his spine. That was good, or at least Daisy hoped that it was good. The blood was coming fast, soaking through Rick's sweatshirt in a dark circle.

"Laurel—" Chris spluttered again.

"Shut up," his sister snapped at him. "If you weren't such a gutless fool, we wouldn't be in this mess."

Bobby moaned.

"You'll be okay." Daisy put her hand gently on his head in an effort to comfort him. "I'm going to get help, and you'll be okay."

"Get help?" Laurel chortled. "Who on earth are you going to get help from? Rick? He's certainly not helping anybody any time soon. I got him good in that cabin. He didn't even see me coming. He's probably still out cold on the floor."

Daisy's mouth opened, but not a syllable emerged. It hadn't been some enigmatic geocacher. It had been Laurel. Laurel had whacked Rick with the book.

"I would have shot him, except this gun's only got so many bullets." Laurel waved the revolver that she was holding.

It was Rick's revolver. Daisy recognized it instantly. The snub-nose Smith & Wesson from the brown paper bag.

"I already used one on that annoying security guard at your bakery," Laurel told her. "I didn't want to waste another on Rick. I wasn't sure how many I might need. And now I'm glad I kept what I had. They're obviously going to be necessary."

Daisy still didn't speak. She couldn't. Her mind was desperately trying to process what was happening. However good Chris was as an actor, Laurel was a thousand times better. She had pretended to dislike firearms, and then she had taken the revolver from under the counter at Sweetie Pies. She had viciously killed Caesar, and then she had been so warm and sympathetic in the parking lot.

It was no wonder that Laurel had appeared on the scene so quickly that morning. She was already there. And she didn't dispose of the gun afterward by dumping it into a farm pond or burying it under a heap of trash. She used it to shoot her fiancé—the man who she supposedly adored and dearly wanted to marry. Daisy recalled Laurel talking to Rick about giving Bobby a wedding present. Well, putting a bullet in his back sure was one heck of a gift.

"I do wish you wouldn't have come here," she said to Daisy. "It makes it all so much more complicated. Why couldn't you have just stayed at that silly bridal shower? I thought there could be problems when you told me about it. I knew that I might not be done here in time and someone would start wondering where I was. It took me so long to figure out those maps. They were nearly impossible to decipher—which mountain and which caves and how the chambers connected inside. It was like trying to untangle a spiderweb. The plan was for my darling brother to help me with the maps, but he wouldn't do it. He didn't want any part of it. Idiot!" Laurel kicked Chris hard in the leg.

He let out a muffled cry, and Daisy winced. It was partly because of his evident pain and partly because of how quick she had been to blame him. One remark from Bobby about seeing Chris with the maps, and she had immediately assumed that he was responsible for everything. Except clearly he wasn't.

"I knew about the maps from him," Laurel continued. "I knew about everything from him. Chris has so much information stored in that big brain of his. It's from all those years of reading all those fat old books. But he doesn't do a damn thing with it, just gives boring lectures and writes boring papers. Idiot!" She kicked him again.

Daisy closed her eyes. She tried to breathe, and she tried to think. Bobby was hurt. Chris was sick. Rick was at best semiconscious and nowhere nearby. She was on her own. She was going to have to help herself.

"At least I could talk the boys into working with me. They're not smart like Chris," Laurel remarked, "but they're smart enough for the jobs I gave them. Unlike my idiotic brother, they understand the value of money."

"The boys?" Daisy asked, struggling to regain her voice.

"Jordan, Mike, and Roger. All geocachers, of course. They've been good partners. Well, Mike and Roger have been." Laurel crinkled her nose. "You know what happened to Jordan. That was bad luck, for him anyway. For me, it wasn't really an issue. Mike and Roger could handle the cheese and the bats just fine. And it meant that there was one less person to cut in on the treasure."

Bobby's body twitched. Daisy looked at him. The entire bottom half of Rick's sweatshirt was saturated with blood. She had to think harder and faster. Even if Laurel didn't shoot him again, he wasn't going to make it indefinitely with that much blood loss. Daisy tried to slow the flow by putting pressure on the wound with her palm. Bobby whimpered.

"I know it hurts," she said as soothingly as she could. "I know it hurts real bad, Bobby. But hang in there with me. It'll be all right. I promise."

"You promise?" Laurel snickered at her. "Didn't your mother teach you not to make promises that you can't keep?"

"My momma also taught me not to pretend to love a man and agree to marry him as some sort of cruel ruse," Daisy retorted.

Laurel grinned. "But it was such a good ruse. When I first came here, I could only guess how long it would take me to get the maps, find the right cave, and come up with a way to get rid of the other geocachers. I needed an excuse to stay in the neighborhood if it all dragged on. I was a stranger in the hills of Appalachia. I couldn't afford to attract that much attention. And then I met Bobby." She turned her grin on him. "I realized in an instant that he was the one. He was such an easy mark, so dim and gullible. A few kisses and caresses, and he was mine. An engagement was the perfect ploy. I wasn't a stranger anymore. Of course, I was never actually going to saunter down the aisle with the sniveling chump! The relationship—such as it was—expired the minute I no longer needed it."

Daisy looked at Bobby again. She dearly hoped that he wasn't listening, that either he couldn't hear Laurel's words or he was too muddled to understand them fully. She needed him to be strong, to want to survive, not to be crushed by Laurel's coldhearted callousness.

"My only concern," Laurel went on, "was his brother. Rick is obviously clever. You can see it in his eyes. I figured that it was just a matter of time before he got suspicious of me. I could tell he knew something was off when we were in the parking lot of your bakery that morning. He was so friendly, except he didn't want to sleep with me. A man who's that friendly but doesn't want to sleep with you is always one to be wary of. It means that he doesn't trust you and you can't bribe him with sex."

"Maybe Rick didn't trust you," Daisy replied sharply, remembering her and Beulah's initial suspicions, "because he thought you wanted to marry Bobby to get closer to all of his money."

"All of his money?" Laurel burst out laughing. "I don't want Rick's money. I want my own damn money! That's why I'm here. That's the reason I've got two boys digging through a hundred and fifty years of putrid filth back there." She glanced toward the interior of the cave.

Although Laurel's gaze was only averted for a couple of seconds, it was long enough for Daisy to switch hands. Her left palm went onto Bobby's back, while her right palm went into the jacket pocket.

"Laurel—" Chris croaked.

Daisy froze. He must have seen what she had done, and it occurred to him that it could have some detrimental purpose. He was going to warn his sister.

"What is it?" Laurel answered crabbily. "You've already caused me enough trouble, Chris. If you cause me any more, I might just decide to leave you here. Then you can die with your new friends. It'll only make it that much easier for me."

Forcing herself not to panic at the sheer ruthlessness of Laurel's tone, Daisy's eyes went to Chris. He looked back at her with such grief and regret that she realized he wasn't going to warn his sister. He was trying to distract her instead. He was giving Daisy a chance to fight back. Her palm slid farther into the pocket.

"You should—" Chris rasped at Laurel. "You should show them to Daisy."

The suggestion evidently pleased his sister, because the scowl on her face faded. Laurel took several steps forward, and as she got closer, Daisy could see that neither she nor Chris had been exaggerating about the amount of guano farther inside the cave. Laurel's clothing and boots were covered with it. The pungent odor didn't seem to bother her, however, or she was better able to ignore it for the sake of the treasure.

With the revolver still in one hand, Laurel held out her other hand in Daisy's direction. She uncurled her fist to reveal half a dozen black nuggets. They looked like small hunks of dirt, only they plainly weren't. They were too round, and there was a telltale glimmer to them. It was very faint, because they were extremely tarnished, but it was enough for Daisy to identify them. They were silver coins.

"We're going to find more," Laurel informed her confidently. "We're going to find all of them—thirty-nine kegs' worth. The kegs are long gone, of course. It's far too wet in here for them. The wood must have decayed a century ago."

Looking at the coins, Daisy thought of Henry Brent. He was right, both about the treasure and the kegs rotting. Except he wasn't right about the location. The silver wasn't buried beneath Danville. It was hidden in the mountains of Pittsylvania County, in roosting caves under piles of bat guano.

"Now you've seen them." Laurel's fist curled closed again, jealously protecting its plunder. "Now you know why I've done all of this."

Daisy's hand touched the Ruger.

"And I've done it well, if I do say so myself," Laurel declared with unrestrained pride. "I haven't missed a single trick yet."

Trying hard not to make any visible movement, Daisy wrapped her fingers around the rosewood grip.

"My one regret," Laurel lifted the revolver and gazed at it almost wistfully, "is that I'm going to have to kill you now, Daisy. I think perhaps in another life you and I could have been friends."

"Friends?" Daisy cocked the hammer with her thumb. "Friends don't usually shoot each other."

"That's true." Laurel nodded in acknowledgment.

Daisy searched desperately for something else to say. She needed Laurel to be diverted for just one moment— long enough for her to pull out the Ruger and put both hands on it. It was a big gun. She was going to have to hold it tight to aim right and account for the recoil.

As though it could somehow sense her frantic thoughts, a bat suddenly raced through the cave. It darted past Laurel's ear, and she jumped in surprise. Daisy didn't hesitate. Swiftly drawing the weapon, she clasped it as firmly as she could and squeezed the trigger.

The force of the bullet knocked Laurel backward. Dropping the revolver and the coins, she clutched her shoulder. It wasn't exactly Daisy's target, but it had the desired effect. Laurel sank to the ground, staring at her with wide, startled eyes.

"I thought—" she stammered. "I thought you were a peace lover."

"I am."

CHAPTER
26

"That sounds great! I'm looking forward to it. Thanks for calling."

Daisy hung up the phone with a smile.

"What sounds great? What are you looking forward to?"

She glanced over her shoulder and found Rick standing in the open doorway leading onto the wraparound back porch of the inn. Although she was surprised to see him, her attention went immediately to his temple. The cut from Laurel and the giant history tome had been taped. The accompanying bruise was a vivid shade of purple.

"Does it hurt much?" Daisy asked.

"That's what this is for, darlin'." Rick held up a jar filled with amber liquid.

Her smile grew, and she gestured toward the line of white-pine rocking chairs. "Take a seat, if you like. There are glasses on the potting stand over in the corner, next to those brandy bottles."

He gave an amused snort. "Just in case Aunt Emily gets thirsty while starting next year's tomatoes?"

"It has nothing to do with thirst," Daisy retorted jocularly. "It's Grade A medicine to her. You should know that by now."

With another snort, Rick grabbed a pair of glasses from the stand and settled himself on the rocking chair next to hers. "So you didn't answer my question."

"What question was that?"

"Who were you talking to a minute ago, and what are you looking forward to?"

"Oh, that was Drew. He's the bat conservationist I met going up to the caves. He invited me out to dinner next weekend."

Rick arched an eyebrow. "You're going on a date with a man who digs around in bat sh— poop for a living?"

Daisy couldn't help but laugh. It did sound funny when he put it that way. "Drew studies the bats and their hibernation habits, not their guano," she corrected him. "And you really shouldn't pick on the man, Rick. You should be thanking him instead. If he hadn't been so concerned about me hiking alone in the dark, and he hadn't come back up the mountain to look for me to make sure that I hadn't accidentally tumbled down a ravine, it would have taken a lot longer to get Bobby to the hospital."

He responded with a desultory nod.

"How is Bobby?" she said.

"Okay," the nod repeated itself, "everything considered. They're letting him out of the hospital tomorrow. He wanted to go today, but he climbed out of bed too fast this morning and fell over, busting a bunch of the stitches in his back. So the doctor told him that he had to spend another night."

"And he's handling the situation with Laurel all right?"

"Sort of." Rick sighed. "He's got his good moments and his bad, except there's a lot more of the bad."

"Well, that's to be expected." Daisy echoed the sigh. "He really did like her. But it'll get easier for him with time—and distance."

They were quiet. Rick pulled over a little patio table that sat next to one of the other rocking chairs. He set the two glasses on it, unscrewed the jar, and poured a generous serving into both.

"You want one?" He pushed a glass in Daisy's direction.

She hesitated but only briefly. "Why not? It's Sunday afternoon, and I've got no big plans. It's either this, or slice up the red velvet cake that was supposed to be eaten yesterday at the wedding and put it in the freezer."

Tapping the rim of his glass with hers, Rick took a drink. Daisy followed suit. The amber liquid was warm and smooth. It had a faint hint of vanilla.

"This place sure doesn't have a very good track record when it comes to weddings," she murmured, thinking also of her own failed marriage.

"Nothing in this life is ever certain," Rick replied in a low tone.

For several long minutes, they sat together sipping and not speaking. Finally Rick broke the silence.

"Chris asked about you," he said.

Daisy looked at him with mild astonishment. "You talked to Chris?"

"I did. He's still in the hospital, just down the hall from Bobby. Apparently he's suffering from a severe allergic reaction to all the—" Rick's lips curled into a smile. "Guano. According to his doctor, who's some kind of specialist, it's not that uncommon. One of the other boys, Mike,

evidently went into anaphylactic shock shortly after he
was arrested. The doctor told me that he had been breathing in the stuff for way longer than his body could handle." The smile became a grin. "You really should warn
your new bat pal about it, Daisy. After all, you don't want
the guano to ruin your date."

She ignored the remark. "Did you see Laurel?"

Rick grunted. "She's on drugs. Super-powered pain-
killers. She wouldn't be if I had my way. It's far too good
for her." His eyes blackened. "After what she did to Caesar—to Bobby—what she almost did to you, she deserves
a hell of a lot more misery than she's getting. She better
pray that she never sees me again, because if she does, her
shoulder won't be the only part of her that's mangled.
Nice job on that, by the way."

Although he obviously meant it as a compliment,
Daisy didn't respond. It didn't seem right to her to gloat
about shooting Laurel, no matter how justified and necessary it had been under the circumstances.

"That reminds me," she said. "I still have your Ruger. I
assume it's the reason you're here—to get it back."

"I'm glad you had it when you needed it," Rick answered simply.

"I don't know about the revolver Laurel took from the
bakery," Daisy went on. "The Smith and Wesson. It'll probably be held as evidence in relation to Caesar's death. You
might not get it back, at least not for a while."

"Sometimes people lose things." Rick shrugged and
took another drink. "For me, it's the revolver. For you, all
that cream cheese. For the historical society, those maps."

"But the historical society is going to be compensated
for their loss," she informed him.

"They are?"

Daisy nodded. "Quite handsomely, from what I heard. Because the society was the legal owner of the maps which were used to find the treasure, they're guaranteed, apparently, to get a nice percentage of the proceeds. Based on even the most pessimistic of calculations, it should be enough to keep the doors open, pay all the bills, and finish the restoration work on the railroad depot so they can move there permanently. No more fund-raisers required." She added to herself, "Or banana puddings."

"How much treasure actually is there?" Rick asked her.

"That's the big question," Daisy returned. "No one is entirely sure. And evidently everybody—aside from the historical society—is already arguing about how large their share should be. State versus federal. City versus county. Public versus private. I think it's going to take them a long time to sort it all out. According to Drew, it's also going to take a long time to get the rest of the treasure out of the cave. He told me it'll be a very slow process, because they'll have to dig so carefully. They don't want to injure or disturb the bats, especially once they begin hibernating."

"And your pal Drew? Is he going to be part of the digging?"

"He is," she confirmed, restraining a smile. "He's been asked to stay in the area to monitor the health and welfare of the bats, at least initially."

Rick's jaw twitched, but he didn't say a word. He refilled his glass from the jar and turned his gaze toward the group of people gathered on the side lawn. They were what Daisy had been looking at when he first appeared on the porch.

"It's Beulah and Aunt Emily," she started to explain. "Along with Connor Woodley and Duke—" Feeling an irrepressible burst of mischievousness, Daisy interrupted herself. "You know Duke, of course. He is one of your trusty bootleggers, after all."

The jaw twitched again.

"Beulah's salon has been flooding for the past week," she continued quickly, before Rick could offer any snide rejoinder. "Duke and Connor have been trying to fix it, but they can't seem to figure out what the problem is. At first they thought it was the line from the well, then they weren't so sure, and now they think it might be the well itself. The salon and the inn share the same well, which means that Aunt Emily is in an absolute tizzy about the whole thing. She's afraid they'll have to—"

There was a muffled rumble from the direction of the side lawn, like the echo of thunder from an impending storm off in the distance. Except there was no storm. The October sky was a clear cerulean blue.

"Did you hear that?" Daisy asked.

"I did—" Rick began.

The rumble repeated itself, louder this time.

He frowned. "That doesn't sound good."

Daisy frowned too, and the rumble abruptly became a hiss. It had the shrillness of a factory whistle, as though somebody was supposed to turn down the knob on a pressure valve—and fast. Up until that point, the group on the lawn had been arguing and debating vociferously. They suddenly grew still.

Rick straightened up in his chair. "Where exactly is the well?"

"I think it's about where they're standing," Daisy said. "Maybe a bit closer to the salon—"

The lawn started to quiver. All at once, the group spun around and began to run toward the inn. A second later, there was a deep groan from inside the earth. It was followed by a harsh metallic clank, and then a column of water exploded up out of the ground. Shrieks and shouts ensued. After a moment, the group stopped running. It was no use. Like oysters at high tide, they were thoroughly— and inescapably—drenched.

"Lordy," Daisy exhaled, frozen in her seat, staring at the geyser.

She could only watch as the resultant tidal wave hit. In less than a minute, the salon had a river running through it. The side parking lot was no longer visible. And half of the inn's wraparound front porch had broken off.

"I guess there's your answer," Rick responded slowly, also staring. "The problem is with the well."

"Oh, poor Aunt Emily."

"You don't have to worry about her," he replied. "Aside from being wet and probably a tad cold, she's fine. They're all fine."

"But the inn," Daisy said. "The inn is everything to Aunt Emily. Look at the damage, Rick! If that gusher doesn't stop soon, the rest of the porch is going to wash away and the entire first floor will be under water."

"At least she's still got her brandy." With a chortle, he gestured toward the potting stand, which was as safe and dry in the corner of the back porch as they were.

"Medicine or not, it won't be much comfort to her when the furniture from the parlor starts floating down the road," Daisy remarked tartly.

Rick turned to her. His eyes were laughing, but his tone was earnest. "Forget about the porch and the parlor, Daisy. Have you considered what this means for you—and your momma? Because if Aunt Emily is out of a home, then so are you."

Daisy blinked at him as her stomach sunk and her throat tightened. It hadn't occurred to her in the shock of the moment, but the truth of his words was undeniable.

His dark eyes gazed at her for a few seconds longer, then Rick cocked his head and drawled, "I told you before, darlin'. Nothing in this life is ever certain."

There was an instant when she felt slightly panicked and more than a little queasy, but like the force of the water spouting from the well, it faded. Cocking her head back at him, Daisy raised her glass. "Nothing except 'shine."

12-14)